LYNN M

I'm a former TV news writer who took the plunge and finally wrote a novel. I know, right? Insanity. Prior to jumping into novel writing, I spent the majority of my career working in radio and television as a promotions director, writer and associate producer. I love any job that is challenging and creative. I grew up in a small town in Rhode Island before spreading my wings to discover this great, big world. Traveling, like writing, has become a necessary part of my life. My favorite place is and always will be London. It's my home away from home. For now, I'm a displaced New Englander hanging my hat in Northern California. If you can see me through the fog, wave hello.

Catch My Breath

LYNN MONTAGANO

Harper*Impulse* an imprint of
HarperCollins*Publishers Ltd*
77–85 Fulham Palace Road
Hammersmith, London W6 8JB

www.harpercollins.co.uk

A Paperback Original 2014

First published in Great Britain in ebook format by HarperImpulse 2014

Copyright © Lynn Montagano 2014

Cover Images © Shutterstock.com

Lynn Montagano asserts the moral right to
be identified as the author of this work

A catalogue record for this book
is available from the British Library

ISBN: 9780007591749

This novel is entirely a work of fiction.
The names, characters and incidents portrayed in it are
the work of the author's imagination. Any resemblance to
actual persons, living or dead, events or localities is
entirely coincidental.

Automatically produced by Atomik ePublisher from Easypress

All rights reserved. No part of this publication may be
reproduced, stored in a retrieval system, or transmitted,
in any form or by any means, electronic, mechanical,
photocopying, recording or otherwise, without the prior
permission of the publishers.

To my family and friends, for always being my biggest supporters and loudest cheerleaders.

And to my passport (yes, my passport), for opening up the world and introducing me to my favorite place on Earth.

CHAPTER ONE

"Amelia Grace Meyers. Naptime is over. Let's *go*. We're getting picked up at seven for the benefit. I don't want to be late."

The blankets were unceremoniously ripped from my body, destroying the warm cocoon I'd wrapped around myself. I sat up with a start, blinded by the bright light spilling from the bedside lamp. Grabbing the blankets, I flopped back onto the mattress.

"You're mean," I whined into the pillow, trying to figure out what the hell my best friend was talking about. And more importantly, where I was. I opened a sleepy eye and saw Stephanie Tempe, all perfumed and primped, standing at the foot of the bed. *Oh right. Scotland.*

"What time is it?" I yawned.

"Quarter past six. Get up."

I crawled out of bed, shooting a half-hearted glare in her direction. Why I agreed to go to this event with her tonight was beyond me. I stumbled toward the bathroom, deftly avoiding the suitcases that were scattered in a schizophrenic maze on the floor. I'd been in Glasgow for twelve hours and still hadn't technically seen the outside of this room. Who knew jet lag could be so vicious?

Twenty minutes – and a furious effort on my part to look presentable – later, our heels clicked in unison on the marble floor in the hotel lobby.

"You totally set a new record for getting ready," Stephanie remarked as we waited for our ride. I nodded, yawning. When the black Land Rover arrived, I curled up on the seat, watching the streets of Glasgow streak by in a blob of color.

My brain finally sprang to life as I stepped onto the sidewalk, marveling at the hectic, excited energy surrounding me. I didn't get dazzled easily, but this was shaping up to be a fun night. The stunning Victorian building glowed under the bright lights as scores of men and women dressed in their finest suits and gowns chatted amongst themselves. I stood in place, smitten with the old world charm of the city.

I knew I was smiling a bit too much, giving away my status as a tourist, but I couldn't help it. The way the old buildings mingled with eye-popping steel and glass structures reminded me of New York. Only this version had a Scottish accent.

Taking a few steps to my right, I nearly stumbled off the curb. I steadied myself on the backend of a gray Mercedes SUV. *Wake. Up.* I tried to see if anyone was inside to witness my less than suave move, but couldn't make out anything through the dark tint.

"Come on, Lia. Darren's waiting for us inside." Stephanie waved, immersing herself in the twinkling aura of elegance and waltzing toward the main doors. I snapped out of my daze and followed her.

We passed through a grand entrance hall with small domed ceilings covered in tiled mosaics. I was struck by the two massive staircases flanking either side. One was made out of white Carrara marble, while the other was a deep red. Multi colored and gold veins swirled around the staircase, giving it a darker, more alluring feel.

As I walked up the white marble stairs, I felt a twinge of disappointment that the other one led to a different part of the building. All that rich color seemed much more exciting.

We navigated our way through the crowd and found Darren MacCourty leaning against the bar. He looked rather dashing in a black suit and tie.

"Steph! Lia! You made it." He engulfed Stephanie in a giant bear hug and swung her around a couple of times. After he put her down, he gave me a quick peck on each cheek.

"You ladies look gorgeous. Can I offer you something to drink? There's champagne, wine and something called a Kilted Knight." A Glaswegian accent danced around his words, much to my delight. He was our one-man welcoming committee for our extended Scottish vacation.

Stephanie opted for champagne while I chose the Kilted Knight. A delectable combination of peach, melon and mint yumminess floated over my taste buds.

"How's the holiday going?" he asked as we walked to our table.

"Eh, it's going. Lia's been asleep since we got here," Stephanie teased.

"Have a few more drinks." Darren grinned at me. "You'll feel brand new. Never mind the sleep."

"If you say so," I said, smiling back. "Thanks for inviting us to this, by the way."

"Ah, no worries. Probably not as exciting as the events you go to in Orlando, but it's a good excuse for me to look sharp on the arms of two lovely lasses like yourselves."

He winked, draping his arms around our shoulders. I laughed at his easy, boyish charm. I'd met him through Stephanie a few years ago, but he made me feel as though I'd known him forever.

"Looking for someone?" I followed his gaze through the room.

"Yeah. I wanted to introduce you both to one of my mates. He was supposed to meet us here. Probably buggered off to a dark corner to avoid the guests."

"Is he single?" Stephanie grinned.

"That's nice. Ask about the availability of others right in front of me," Darren teased. "You can ask him tomorrow at the football match. Excuse me, soccer game."

I got a kick out of watching them tease each other. There weren't any romantic feelings, just an honest tight friendship that continued to get stronger no matter how far Glasgow and Orlando were from one another.

The three of us meandered around the room, chatting with some of Darren's co-workers. They were intrigued by the "colonials," as one of them put it. Stephanie ate up the attention. I was still so tired; taking a back seat to people watch seemed more appealing.

By the time we sat down for dinner, I was borderline comatose. Several people gave speeches and thanked everyone for their generous donations. Before the silent auction started, I excused myself to use the ladies' room. One other woman was in there fixing her hair.

"I love your dress," she said. "Where did you get it?"

"Neiman Marcus."

"Are you Canadian?"

I shook my head, stifling a yawn. "American. I'm here on vacation."

"Watch out for the local fellas. They're rather sweet on American girls. Something about your accents."

Bright white teeth appeared from behind her over-glossed lips. I wanted to believe she was being nice and welcoming, but I'd had enough experience engaging in high society bathroom small talk to know the difference.

"Thanks for the tip."

After she left, I gave myself a once-over in the mirror, then made a pass at the bar for another drink.

My heel snagged on the carpet, sending me flying. I landed nose-first in a charcoal gray tailored Armani suit. Momentarily stunned, I clutched onto the toned arms that were wrapped around me. As I looked up my heart nearly stopped.

Wide emerald eyes fringed with long lashes gazed down at me with guarded curiosity. His sculpted mouth twisted into a cautious smile, softening his jawline.

"Are you alright?" he asked as he loosened his grip on me. His voice was rich and smooth, like a full-bodied wine. The English accent he had could charm the pants off a nun. It made me want to fall into his arms again.

I stepped back, smoothing down my dress. He didn't look much older than thirty, but his worn eyes betrayed his youth.

"I'm fine. I'm not usually that clumsy. Sorry."

His brows furrowed. "I kept telling them someone was going to stumble over that patch of carpet. You're sure you're okay?"

"Aside from my bruised ego and general lack of grace, I think I'll be alright." I smiled up at him in an effort to thwart the growing blush from creeping up my neck. I wasn't the type who embarrassed easily and needed to regain some sort of composure. No luck.

His expression altered subtly as his stare intensified. Something shifted in the air between us. It was as though he'd tethered me with some freakishly strong invisible rope. My pulse quickened. I was caught smack dab in the middle of his magnetic pull without any means of escape.

Not that I wanted to get away. His tall frame filled out the suit with powerful elegance. The quiet control with which he held himself mirrored royalty. A tousled mass of thick, dark red hair framed chiseled features that would inspire Michelangelo. But it was those eyes that got me.

They were so astute, yet veiled. I wanted to know what was behind them.

"Would you like a drink?"

How he made such an innocent question sound so seductive was beyond me. His dark stare was unflinching. If I said no, he'd probably take it as a personal insult. And I did want another one of those fruity-minty drinks; I just couldn't articulate the words.

"I hear the signature drink is rather good. Would you like that?"

"Yes, please," I finally managed to say.

Forget my cheeks, my whole body flushed as I watched him move toward the bar. A silver cufflink glinted off his crisply pressed gray and white pinstriped shirt. I noticed he paired it with a solid gray tie before he caught me looking. A smile ghosted across his lips as his languid gaze traced my curves. I made a big deal out of inspecting the carpet for more hidden traps that my shoes could fall victim to.

He handed me the drink, my fingers brushing his when I clasped the glass. Against my better judgment I fell captive to his stare once more. Luckily, I remembered my manners and thanked him.

"My pleasure. Have you been enjoying yourself?"

"Yeah. Well, aside from making an ass of myself just now."

A flash of white appeared revealing a dazzling smile. It was extremely sexy and charming. *And dangerous.* I felt myself falling deeper and deeper under his spell.

"Trust me, stumbling on a carpet is not the worst thing I've seen at these events."

"No?"

"Stick around long enough and you just might see some of these well-dressed ladies toss off their shoes and throw some shapes when the band starts playing." He grinned.

"Throw some what?"

"Dance." His eyes flared with humor.

"You Brits and your crazy sayings," I laughed.

"We like to keep you Americans on your toes."

I took a long sip of my cocktail to prevent a stupid grin from spreading across my face.

"Don't have too many of those. They're rather potent."

"But they're so *good*. Don't piss on my fireworks." I smiled broadly.

A deep, throaty laugh filled the space between us.

"'Throwing shapes' baffled you, but you know 'piss on my fireworks?'"

"My sister only taught me the fun slang," I laughed.

"Does she live here?"

"Not in Glasgow, no. She lives in London."

"Well then, you'll have to thank her for me," he said, smoothing down his tie.

"Thank her for what?"

"Pretty Americans who know British slang are rare in these parts."

"Interesting." I looked up at him through my lashes.

"What?"

"Someone just warned me that you guys have a thing for American girls."

His eyebrows arched. "And what did they say?"

"It has something to do with our accents."

"You have an accent?" He angled toward me. "I hadn't noticed."

The way that he was looking at me caused me to completely forget my exhaustion. His dark eyes and sexy grin woke me up in more ways than one, pushing several of my hot buttons.

"Be careful," he said, clasping the glass in my hand. "You don't want to spill it all over your dress."

Way to go. "You must think I'm a hot mess. First I take a nosedive into your suit and now I'm dropping drinks."

"Like I said, I've seen worse."

The longer I held his gaze, the faster my heart raced. There was something…forbidden in the way he looked at me.

"I should probably get back to my friends."

"Do you have to?"

A suffocating aura of want enveloped me. He was closer, dominating the space between us. Our quick, breezy exchange was light years away from the hazy, thick fog of desire that hung in the air. *Get it together, Lia. Walk away.*

"You're rather deep in thought."

I blinked. "Sorry."

"Don't apologize. I thought maybe I was boring you."

A shrill ring sounded from his pocket. He fished out a cell phone, frowning at the screen.

"I have to take this."

And just like that, I was pulled out of his engaging aura and plopped back into reality.

I plastered on a polite smile. "It's okay. Thanks again for the drink."

He nodded at me and answered the call before slipping off to a quiet corner. My head was so cloudy from the jet lag, the drinks and now that guy. I turned on my heel and trotted off to find Darren and Stephanie.

"There you are." Stephanie stood up as I approached the table. "We were about to send out a search party."

"Sorry. I got a little sidetracked."

"You okay?"

"Yep. Why?"

"You have that deer-in-headlights look." She stared at me intently. "You're shaking. I thought we agreed there was to be no worrying about that loser while we're on vacation?"

I attempted to steady my hands as I smoothed down the fitted silk bodice of my dress. "It's not that, Steph. I'm just tired."

"Really?"

"Really."

"Excuse me, ladies? May I take your photograph for the foundation's website?"

A young man with a camera bigger than his head stood in front of us, poised and ready. Not ones to turn down a picture, we posed for him. He thanked us and walked off to find some more willing subjects.

"I wish you had let me do your hair tonight. All that gorgeousness pulled into a ponytail makes me sad," Stephanie pouted.

I frowned, playing with a few chestnut strands. "It's fine. I was going for a simple look anyway since we were running late."

"I would have done a nice French twist or something for you in the car."

I couldn't help but laugh at Stephanie's distress over my hair. In her slinky, full-length ice blue gown, she was the epitome of effortless glamor. The dress matched her eye color perfectly and contrasted with her short, jet-black hair. She was one of those girls who would look fabulous in a trash bag. At twenty-nine, she was a couple years older than me.

"You're doing everyone's hair next week for the wedding. I can go one night without a fancy up-do."

"Fine," she relented.

"Is it fun seeing Darren again? It's been, what, two years or something since you've seen him, right? I'm surprised he remembered what you looked like." I grinned.

"Smart ass. I've known him since I was sixteen. He could pick me out of one of those Where's Waldo things. Blindfolded."

"I could pick you out of one of those things blindfolded. You'd never be caught wearing horizontal stripes."

We linked arms and went to check out the silent auction. Darren was already scrutinizing one of the tables when we found him. We spent a good chunk of the evening ogling all the luxurious items that were up for auction; a weekend for two in Paris, wine tasting in Tuscany, spa getaways and a number of other items that were extremely tempting.

"A group of us are thinking of going to The Living Room. This event is a bit boring. Do you two want to come?"

I was vaguely aware of Darren's question. My thoughts were still tangled around my encounter at the bar.

"Hello. Earth to Lia," Stephanie sang out. "Do you want to come out with us? Or would you rather go back to the suite and catch up on your beauty sleep?"

"Where are you guys going?"

"The Living Room. It's a trendy lounge and nightclub. Right up your alley. Fancy cocktails and all that," Darren said.

"Um, sure. Why not. I have to kick this exhaustion at some point, right?" I kept scanning the room for the nameless, stumble-rescuing, aesthetically pleasing Knight In Shining Armani. He seemed to have disappeared. To say I was sad was beyond an understatement.

Darren escorted us out to our waiting Land Rover. It was still parked behind the gray Mercedes SUV I almost fell onto earlier. The blonde girl from the bathroom was standing next to it. She looked annoyed but brightened when she saw Darren.

"Hi, Mac. I was hoping to bump into you tonight."

"Hey, Sarah. Lovely to see you," he addressed her politely, and then turned to us. "Stephanie, Lia, this is Sarah Everett. She's the vice president at my agency."

"Pleasure to meet you," she smiled. "Lia, you're the girl I met earlier, right? Nice to see you again."

She fixed her gaze on Darren.

"Where are you all off to?"

"Out for a quick bevvie. We're trying to help Lia overcome jet lag by keeping her out as late as possible." Darren slung his arm around my shoulders and grinned. "Waiting for someone?"

"Aren't I always? Have you—"

"Good evening, Miss Everett." A well-dressed man walked over to us from the Mercedes. I assumed he was the driver but his imposing frame made me think he could easily pass for a bodyguard. He smiled at me before continuing to address Sarah. "Sorry you've been waiting for so long, but he's still tied up with some clients. He says to call him at the office on Monday if you'd like to discuss the marketing plan regarding the new acquisitions."

Sarah's face fell. "Oh. Alright. Thank you, Paxton." She glanced at us, waved and walked off.

"Good to see you, Mr. MacCourty." He shook hands with Darren.

"Ah, stop with the formalities, Pax. My dad is Mr. MacCourty."

"Fair enough," he laughed. "Have a good night."

As he retreated back to his car, Darren opened the rear passenger door of the Land Rover for us to climb in. I yawned for the zillionth time.

"You sure you're up for this Lia? We can go back to the hotel."

Stephanie half looked at me while fixing her hair in the rear view mirror.

"I'll be alright. Another hour or so and..."

Noticing the tall toned figure of a man, I shut up abruptly. Walking at a fast clip, he slipped through the crowd on the sidewalk like a ghost and climbed into the Mercedes. It was my handsome mystery guy.

CHAPTER TWO

Kanye West kept trying to convince me that what doesn't kill me, would make me stronger as I jogged along the streets of Glasgow on Saturday morning. It was by no stretch of the imagination a warm April day. A chill hung in the air, wrapping its frozen fingers around the city. It reminded me of the brisk spring mornings in Connecticut, where I grew up. I inhaled the frosty air, daring it to freeze out my lungs as I ran. It was a good way to keep myself honest, seeing as I'd been living in the sweltering heat of Florida for five years. One could get very used to the luxury of warm weather all the time.

Our hotel had a gym, but I preferred the outdoors. I loved to run. It was something I picked up in college as a stress reliever during midterms. Other kids drank; I ran. I often wished I could run right out of my skin sometimes. The escape was wonderful.

Some of my favorite moments were spent running along Cocoa Beach early on a summer morning. But that was with *him*. Thinking about those days brought back a flood of memories that I tried not to dwell upon. When things were good, they were great. Then it all went down in flames. I swallowed hard against the sandpapery lump that fought its way up my throat. I packaged the memories and shoved them to the back of my mind.

I jogged for a little more than a half mile before I came upon a clearing. A huge manicured field stretched out to my left. About seven or eight young boys were playing soccer on one end. A flurry of activity at the far end caught my attention, so I slowed my pace to a brisk walk.

A group of guys was playing rugby. I'd never actually seen the game played in person before, so I walked to the edge of the field. But it was just my luck that the match had ended. The guys all clapped one another on the back and chatted amongst themselves as they grabbed their gym bags. As I got closer, one of them looked right at me. The force of his stare stopped me in my tracks.

He walked over in long, graceful strides. Sunlight glinted off his dark red hair, accentuating the chocolate flecks. *Oh wow, it's him*. I lowered the music and hastily wiped sweat from my cheeks.

"Well, hello." His rich, velvety voice swirled around me.

I swallowed hard. "Hi."

"I thought you looked familiar. Had any more encounters with wayward carpets since last night?"

"No. I walk exclusively on hardwood now."

"Wise choice."

Without the benefit of my high heels, he towered over me. He was hot even with mud caked on his clothes. And wow, did he smell good. Traces of cologne still lingered on him mixed with his post-game sweat and pheromones. It was so intoxicating I had to look away. When I focused on him again, he was studying me with the same guarded curiosity as last night. Part of me wished I wasn't a hot, sweaty mess.

"I'm afraid I didn't catch your name," he said with a small grin.

"Oh. I'm Amelia Meyers. But please, call me Lia."

"Pleasure to meet you, Amelia." My name rolled off his tongue readily, like he'd been born to say it for all eternity. "What brings you to Glasgow?"

"A wedding."

He slung a gym bag over his shoulder, grasping the strap. The small movement caused his muscles to flex.

"Yours?"

"What? Oh God no. My sister's."

"The one in London?"

"Yep."

"Why isn't she getting married there?"

This guy was awfully nosey.

"They thought it would be romantic to have a wedding at a Scottish castle. Her fiancé is from Newcastle, so it was either London, Newcastle or Scotland." I shrugged, stealing a glance at him.

"How long will you be in Glasgow?"

"We leave—"

"We?"

"Yeah. My best friend and I. She's—"

"She," he said quietly. Bright emerald irises slid over my face as he traced one of his slender fingers along his mouth. I wanted to snap at him for all the interrupting, but a flurry of nerves ran through my stomach. *It's not physically possible for someone to become more attractive overnight, is it?* I blinked myself out of this hypnotic state.

"Oi! We're off to eat, mate. Come on," an impatient, stocky man yelled.

Tall, Dark and Sexy clearly didn't enjoy being at the receiving end of that. His expression hardened as he turned around. I could only imagine the look he gave the other guy. It must have been scathing because the poor soul abruptly left.

When he faced me again his eyes were blazing hot.

"Finished with your run? I can drive you back to—"

"No," I blurted out. "I mean, I'm not done yet, but thank you."

The thought of sitting in an enclosed space with him was too much to handle. Standing this close to him in an open field was challenging enough.

"You're sure? You look a bit out of breath."

"Doubting my stamina?" I put my hands on my hips, narrowing

my eyes.

The corner of his mouth ticked up into a small grin. "Not at all. I'm quite sure you can go for a while, but jogging can be taxing on the body. A slow and steady climb is best to achieve maximum results."

I wasn't entirely sure we were talking about exercise anymore. I couldn't form a sentence, so I stared at him.

"Don't let me keep you."

He gestured to the field. That little mischievous grin rankled me to the core. *He's teasing me. He's got me flustered and now he's teasing me.* In an instant he managed to turn me on and turn me off simultaneously.

I still couldn't form a complete sentence, which pissed me off.

"Okay then. Nice to see you again." He kept grinning and sauntered off toward the parking lot leaving me in a funk. Annoyed by my pre-teen giddiness, I turned up my iPod and ran like hell.

Stephanie was awake and all bright eyed and bushy tailed when I got back. She buzzed around the suite in a huge fluffy robe, laying clothes on the couch.

"Hey. How was your run?"

"Eventful." I tossed my iPod on the end table and plopped onto the chair.

"Oh really?" She stopped fussing with the clothes. "How so?"

Since we hadn't had a chance to chat about what happened at the benefit, I quickly relayed the story, and then told her what happened at the field. She blinked at me like I had fifty heads.

"Did you get his phone number?"

"No."

"What? Why not?"

"It really didn't cross my mind."

"Didn't cross your mind? Honestly Lia," she huffed. "It's like you forgot how to flirt. You run into the same hot guy twice and act like it's no big deal. And *why* didn't you ask his name?"

"I don't know. I wasn't expecting to see him on my morning jog."

"Well, we'll have to stalk every tall, super toned, hot guy with red hair in Glasgow while we're here then, won't we?"

"Don't be ridiculous."

"Oh please. The old Lia would not only have asked his name and gotten a number, she'd be out having drinks with him right now."

I fought back a smile. "I hate it when you're right."

"Maybe he'll be at the soccer game," she teased. "Darren did say he was bringing a friend."

"Yeah, right," I snorted. "You watch too many sappy chick flicks."

"So jaded," she sighed.

All talk of the mystery man took a backseat as we prepared for our day out with Darren. He'd bought us tickets to see his team and already announced his intention to convert us into loyal followers. I didn't understand soccer at all, but the players were nice to look at.

I showered and threw on my favorite pair of faded jeans, a light sweater and sneakers. Seeing as we'd be outside all day, I figured casual was best.

"Braids and a baseball hat?" Stephanie giggled.

"It's comfortable. Besides, if the weather goes sour and it starts to rain I'll be covered."

"Always so prepared," Stephanie remarked as she slid on her vintage sunglasses. "Alright, Sporty Barbie, ready to go?"

"Let's do this."

Groups of young men and women clad in various team apparel lined the street leading up to the pub. The air was thick with cigarette smoke and excited chatter. The sun was shining and many people were taking advantage of the rare, nice weather.

"This is insanity. Look at all these people. Figures that Darren would pick the most popular area to meet." Stephanie craned her neck to get a better view through the throng of sports fans. She had a good three inches on me so I just watched all the people nearby.

I became very engrossed in a trio of young men to my right. They debated the merits of one player over another on a particular team. I hadn't the foggiest idea what they were talking about, but enjoyed listening to their accents.

An elbow suddenly greeted me in the side.

"Ow! What the hell?"

"Sorry, sorry. I see Darren. Let's go."

We navigated our way through several groups of people standing on the sidewalk. Once we reached a clearing, I spotted Darren. His spiky blond hair was immobile in the breeze as he chatted to someone next to him. My view of the other person was obstructed by a rather tall, lanky guy. As soon as he walked away, I sucked in a breath.

"Holy shit." I stopped short.

"What? What's wrong?"

"That's him," I barely squeaked out. Stephanie paused and followed my gaze. I drank in every inch of him. Faded black jeans molded to his toned legs perfectly. His lean upper body was showcased in a tight, long sleeved gray cotton shirt. *Snap out of it, Meyers.*

"Shut the front door, no it's not."

I didn't have a chance to answer her. Darren saw us and waved us over. I married my eyes to the pavement and took a deep breath.

"Hey, you two. I ordered up some nice, Florida sunshine for today. What do you think?"

"Not bad," Stephanie laughed.

Glancing up at Darren from under the rim of my hat, I could feel the other guy staring at me.

"Lia, Stephanie. This is Alastair Holden. He's coming to the match with us. Don't let his ginger hair frighten you."

Even his name dripped with elegance. I squared my shoulders and boldly fixed my stare on him. So help me God, he was incredible.

"Get your eyes checked, MacCourty," he said dryly. "It's nice to see you again, Amelia."

Darren's eyebrows shot up in surprise. He looked from Alastair to me. "You two know each other?"

"We met last night by the bar," Alastair answered, "she was having some trouble negotiating the carpet."

"Well then. We should get walking toward the stadium," Darren said. "It's about a twenty-five minute walk from here and the match starts in forty-five."

Stephanie linked arms with him as they started up the street. "We'll lead the way. You guys try to keep up."

I fell into step with Alastair. A nervous, twitchy energy radiated from every cell in my body. We walked silently side by side for several minutes.

"So, this rugby thing I saw you playing earlier. When did you start?"

"This rugby thing…" He mimicked me. "You have quite a way with words."

"Are you going to tease me or answer my question?" I raised an eyebrow, looking at him incredulously.

"University."

"Do you play anything else? Or is rugby it?"

"That's pretty much it for organized sport. Work doesn't allow me much free time, so I only get to join in on the weekends every so often."

"Is this one of those free weekends?"

"It seems to be."

His arm bumped into mine and I noticed a little smile cross his lips.

"What would you normally be doing if Darren hadn't asked you to the game?"

"Working, probably."

"That sounds *amazing*," I snickered. "Do you ever have any fun?"

"You are quite the curious kitten, aren't you? Questions, questions, questions."

"They're instrumental in getting answers." I replied with a grin.

"Fair enough."

As charming as he was, I could tell he was also extremely guarded. He steered the conversation away from himself so it focused more on me. I was just as guarded though. For the time being, I planned to keep him at arm's length.

We all huddled at the street corner waiting for the crosswalk signal to change. As we stood in silence, I noticed several women staring at Alastair. They casually sized me up before whispering amongst themselves. He flicked his gaze from me to them. When we got the go-ahead, Alastair placed his hand at the small of my back. It was a light touch, but I was aware of the warmth bleeding through my sweater.

The stadium loomed large in the distance. I could hear singing and chanting the closer we got to it. Darren passed a ticket to each of us.

"Now, this is very important," he said solemnly, looking at Stephanie and me. "You must only cheer for my side."

Stephanie burst out laughing at Darren's seriousness. "It's just a game, D."

"It's so much more than that, Steph," he exclaimed, turning to walk through the gate. Alastair and I followed close behind. Once we got past the turnstiles, we walked through a tunnel into the stadium. Our seats weren't too shabby; along midfield, tenth row. Darren attempted to explain the finer aspects of the game to Stephanie. She shot me a pleading look of help and surrendered to his lessons.

"Is this your first proper Scottish football match then?" Alastair asked.

"Yep."

"If you have any questions I'll do my best to answer them."

"Thanks, I think."

He smiled slightly as we settled back into our seats to watch the start of the match. It was an uneventful game up until the final two minutes.

Tens of thousands of people erupted into a massive throaty

cheer as the soccer ball scooted past the keeper and hit the net with a low swoosh. Darren and Stephanie leapt to their feet and joined the celebration. The home team had just taken the lead away from the visiting rivals.

A sea of green and white scarves waved from side to side in a show of solidarity for the home team. The crowd noise didn't let up as the last seconds of the match ticked away. When the final whistle blew, everyone roared.

"Now *that* was a goal." Darren pumped his fist in the air. "First good win in a while. A celebratory pint is in order."

Cool, drizzling rain fell as we walked toward the main road. I stifled an *I-told-you-so* while watching Stephanie cower away from the droplets.

Oodles of iconic black cabs zipped through the streets. Alastair hailed one effortlessly. Stephanie bolted inside as soon as it stopped. Darren joined her, leaving me alone with Alastair for several seconds. When I made my move, he wrapped his fingers around the doorframe, blocking my ability to get in.

"I have to admit, I'm not much of a football fan. I almost told Darren 'no' today."

"What changed your mind?"

A sly grin curled his lips. "He said he wanted to introduce me to his American friends, Stephanie and Lia. Since I learned your name this morning, I figured you would be one of them."

He came to see me? My knees almost gave out. A crazy, voracious tremor of desire raced through me. I brushed past him and climbed in. Stephanie gave me a funny look as I settled into the little jump seat facing the three of them. The cab was severely lacking in the visual stimulation department. I struggled to find a place to rest my eyes that wasn't tall, lean, sinewy and hot. Alastair looked far too amused at the expense of my discomfort.

Thankfully, the cab ride back to our hotel in the West End was quick. Darren suggested we all go to a restaurant nearby for some sandwiches and drinks. I dove into my burger the minute it hit the table. My stomach snarled angrily at the unintentional neglect it had received over the past few days.

"They don't feed you in the states?" Alastair asked in mock disbelief. "I would assume you could get a good hamburger there on any street corner."

"Lia has spent most of the past day sleeping," Stephanie teased.

"I said it last night, I'll say it again. Have more pints. Never mind the sleep," Darren waved his hand in the air to ward off the notion.

Stephanie flashed a smile before leaning back against the booth to chat with Darren. I became abundantly aware of Alastair's presence to my left. His arm brushed mine as he turned to face me.

"Is this your first time abroad then?"

"No," I paused. "Where in England are you from?"

"Ascot. It's to the west of London."

"Ascot? Like the races?" Visions of big hats and suits with tails popped into my head.

"Yes, like the races." He smirked.

I rolled my eyes and took another bite of the burger. He ran a hand through his hair. It looked so soft and silky. I clenched my fist to stop myself from reaching out and touching it.

"What do you think so far?" he asked, rubbing the stubble on his jaw. "Of Scotland, I mean."

The hamburger lodged in my throat. Trying to eat next to this beautiful creature was not for amateurs. Every move he made was calculated and seductive.

Draping his arm across the back of the booth, his fingers brushed against the curve of my shoulder. I noticed Stephanie sneak a glance in my direction and grin. I sat up straighter, giving her a look.

"I haven't really seen much of it, but so far so good," I answered.

His fingers traced my shoulder, then the nape of my neck. It was a soft touch, but it was powerful. I fought to maintain a serene expression as I studied his features. He really was fiercely handsome. His fair skin was porcelain smooth. Charm oozed from him, along with a huge dose of raw sexuality. Against my better judgment, I was hooked.

"How was the rest of your run this morning?" he asked, hovering the bottle of beer in front of his sculpted lips. He parted them and waited for my response. I nearly slipped off the seat. He took a sip and smiled slightly.

"Fine."

"Just 'fine'?"

I shrugged. He touched my shoulder again. A surge of heat rushed through me.

"Sounds like you weren't able to achieve maximum satisfaction. Need a personal trainer?"

I held my breath and counted to ten before answering. *Jesus.*

"Let me guess. You think *you're* the perfect guy for the job," I smirked.

Alastair's eyes darkened. Whatever shield he had in place over them slid away unleashing a fiery intensity. We just stared at each other. I moistened my lips almost as a reflex.

"Do you have plans tonight?" he asked, not releasing me from his tractor beam stare.

"No," I answered, a bit too breathy. "Why?"

"Thought maybe I could show you around the city. Football and charity benefits aren't a proper way to see Glasgow."

"Hey," Darren interrupted, leaning forward. "I hate to cut this short, but I gotta go. We'll walk you girls back to the hotel."

"That's not necessary Darren. I'll walk Lia back when we're finished. You two can go." He leaned back, lowering his hands to his lap.

The calm, commanding tone he used sent a shockwave through me. I saw Stephanie's eyes widen in disbelief.

"I won't be too much longer," I said, finally finding my voice.

The three of them had a brief conversation but I wasn't aware of any of it. I was too busy focusing on the circular strokes he was making on my thigh. His powerful energy surrounded me, invading every fiber of my being. Thank goodness the table was wide enough to cover up his shenanigans. I snapped awake just as they walked off. The sounds and smells of the restaurant came roaring back, clanging through my brain.

"What are you doing?" I barked, jerking my leg away.

"Nothing," he muttered, pulling his wallet out from his back pocket. He dropped a handful of bills on the table. "Let's go for a walk."

We stepped out into the crisp evening air. I hoped it would knock a few degrees off my increased body temperature. Alastair placed his hand at the small of my back, guiding me down the sidewalk. I had no idea where he was taking me, but since it was a busy street, I figured kidnapping was out of the question.

He glanced over his shoulder before gently taking my elbow and moving me towards a cluster of trees next to a nearby building. There was a nice little park-like atmosphere with benches and shrubbery. My blood froze as his luminous eyes locked with mine.

"Can I see you again tomorrow?"

"We're supposed to be going to Edinburgh for the day."

"Change your plans." It wasn't so much a question as it was an order.

I crossed my arms and gave him a look. "I'm not going to ditch Stephanie."

"Is Darren going with you tomorrow?" he asked, moving closer to me.

"Yep."

"He'll be more than enough company for your friend." He pulled gently on the end of my braid. It resonated deep within me, setting off a spark. I had to get away from him.

"Alastair, I'm not—"

He held my face, the warmth of his skin washing over me. "Tell me you don't feel whatever this is between us, and I'll walk away now."

CHAPTER THREE

Blood pounded in my ears while Alastair traced his fingers along my jaw. His movements were smooth and controlled, as though he was afraid he'd spook me. I lost my ability to breathe as my mouth went dry. His verdant gaze made my knees shake.

Of course I felt whatever it was that hummed between us. I felt it since last night but I'd never admit it to him.

"I should get back to the hotel."

"Why?"

"Because I didn't come here looking for this," I snapped, my voice rising. "If anything, I want to get away from it."

"My kitten has claws." His smug grin irked me.

"I'm not your kitten. I don't want whatever it is you're offering," I grumbled.

Staring at me for several seconds, he stroked the curve of my cheek then dipped his mouth close to my ear.

"Your body betrays you, Lia."

Desire ran thickly through my veins as he slowly moved his hands down my neck, over my shoulders and onto my waist. I wet my dry lips, eliciting a small groan from him. It was a gorgeous sound, immediately conjuring images of him and I tangled together on the ground where we stood. I was in the middle of a busy city on a sidewalk, yet he made me feel like we were completely alone.

My walls finally went up with a resounding bang, enabling me to snap myself out of his powerful trance.

"I can't...I'm not interested in being a one-night stand for you."

I pulled away from him sharply and walked back to the hotel on wobbly legs. I willed myself to make it to the elevators. The concierge smiled warmly as I stumbled past. When the elevator arrived I jumped in like it was my salvation. Thankfully nobody else was around. I slumped against the wall and exhaled.

I didn't stop shaking until I was safely in the room.

"You're back already?" Stephanie yelled from the bathroom. "I'm taking a bubble bath. We'll talk when I'm done."

Collapsing onto the couch, I covered my eyes with my arm. My head pounded, my skin tingled and my heart raced. Never in my life had I experienced such a strong reaction to a person. A soft knock at the door startled me.

I shuffled over and opened it without looking through the peephole. A young man dressed in the hotel's concierge uniform smiled at me.

"Amelia Meyers?"

"Yes."

"This is for you," he said, handing me a small envelope.

"Thank you."

"Cheers, miss. Good night."

I closed the door, went back to the couch and opened it. Written in perfect block penmanship was a phone number and a simple request: *Call me. Please. Alastair x*

"That was some serious flirting I saw today. Well done." Stephanie perched on the edge of the couch, towel drying her hair. I quickly folded the note.

"What's that?" she asked.

Dammit.

"Nothing."

"Don't 'nothing,' me. The two of you flirted and circled each other like dogs all day. What happened after Darren and I left?"

"Nothing."

"You are the worst liar on the planet," she exclaimed, throwing her hands in the air. "That man is sex on a stick. *I* could feel the tension between you guys and I wasn't even taking part in the conversation. You were mentally tearing his clothes off all afternoon. And he's so primed and ready for you, it's not even funny."

"There will be none of that." I clenched the note, crinkling the paper.

"Oh come on. Enjoy it."

"Is there a particular reason why you want me to have what will most likely be a one-night stand with this guy?"

"He's hot. His entire physical being exudes wild, uninhibited sex. Do a little something for yourself for once. You need this. Grab him, throw him down and use him for his body."

"Gee, when you put it like that…"

"You're a fabulous, successful, *available* twenty-seven year old woman. But you've become too buttoned up and in control all the time. Where's my spontaneous Lia? My bold Lia? I miss her."

We exchanged glances. I sighed.

"She's still there, Steph. It's just taking me a bit to find her again."

"Sweetie, just because Nathan turned out to be a grade-A asshole doesn't mean you should let it rule the rest of your life. You have to live a little."

* * *

I stared at my cell phone. Ten-thirty. It was still relatively early, but Stephanie had already turned in for the night. I was sitting alone in the suite's living room, wide-awake and twitchy. The crumpled note beckoned me from the coffee table. It annoyed me that I couldn't get him out of my mind but I couldn't help myself. I reached for the phone, ignoring all of my instincts as they screamed in protest.

Taking a deep breath, I dialed Alastair's number and waited. It rang once. Twice. Three times. Voicemail. I hung up and went to bed.

A frantic, incessant beeping woke me out of a somewhat deep sleep. It was anything but restful anyway, so the interruption wasn't too unwelcome. I glanced at the time. Two in the morning? Only one person on the planet would have the balls to text me at this hour. *Nathan.* I cringed, wishing he would leave me alone. The phone beeped again. Grumbling, I grabbed it.

1:58am Hello, Amelia. Sorry I missed your call earlier. Do you always call someone and not leave a message?

Relief swept through me. It wasn't Nathan. The relief was soon replaced with anticipation. A tiny smile played at the corners of my lips.

2:00am How did you know it was me?

The phone rang in my hand, scaring the hell out of me.

"Hello?"

"I knew it was you because everyone else who has this number knows to leave a message."

I could almost see his smirk through the phone.

"You're up late," I said, stretching.

"I was working. What's your excuse?"

"Someone texted me at two in the morning."

He chuckled, low and deep. Lying like this and hearing his voice so intimately close was a turn on. I smiled in spite of myself.

"I don't want to keep you up. You have a busy day planned tomorrow."

Don't say it, don't say it, don't say it.

"I'm not going with them."

I squeezed my eyes shut, grimacing. *Eager, much?*

"You're not? What are you doing instead?"

My brain was apparently on hiatus, because my mouth spouted off whatever the hell it wanted.

"You tell me." I curled up on my side, closing my eyes.

"I'll call you in the morning," he paused. "Amelia?"
"Yes?"
"Sleep well."

* * *

Getting Stephanie out of the hotel while dodging her questions was an exercise in elusiveness at its finest. It wasn't that I didn't want to tell her what I was doing for the day, I just didn't know.

Riding down in the elevator proved to be more nerve-wracking than I had anticipated. I hadn't been this giddy and nervous to see a guy since, well, never. I reminded myself to play it cool, that it was just a simple afternoon out in the city. Besides, I could fake a stomach cramp if I wanted an easy way out. The elevator doors opened and I strode through the lobby. I could see Alastair standing on the sidewalk, looking hot in a t-shirt and jacket with his hands tucked in the pockets of distressed jeans.

This wasn't going to be easy.

"Lia." He slid his emerald eyes over me in his dangerously alluring way. My resolve to resist him weakened by the second. Holding my hand, he traced along the palm with his thumb. The sensation made my vision double.

"I like you with your hair down."

"Thank you." I twisted the ends, mentally kicking myself for enjoying his flattery.

"Let's go somewhere casual and fun. What do you say?"

"Do you even do casual and fun?"

He raised an eyebrow. "Depends. Would you like to go or not?"

I sighed dramatically. "Okay."

* * *

"The object of this game is quite simple really. You have to score more points than me." Alastair tossed a pale pink ball in his hand, looking smug. I folded my arms across my chest. We were at a pub attempting to play snooker. It didn't sound too difficult. I gathered it was similar to pool, only the balls weren't numbered.

Fifteen red balls were arranged in a triangle. The pink ball that Alastair nonchalantly tossed around needed to be placed at the top of the triangle but couldn't touch it. There were five other assorted colored balls. Each one had its own value. I grabbed my beer and circled the table.

Alastair grinned and leaned against it as I walked by. "Nervous, Meyers?"

"Not at all, Holden."

"Played a lot of English snooker while growing up in Florida then?"

"I didn't grow up in Florida," I corrected him, "I'm from Connecticut originally. And no, I didn't play it, but I'm a fast learner."

"While I admire your tenacity, you will lose."

He placed the pink ball on the table and reached for a cue stick. I watched him closely as he chalked it and leaned over the table. The tip of his tongue poked out of his mouth as he concentrated. In one smooth strike he broke the triangle, scattering red balls across the felt. He potted two of them immediately. His next shot wasn't so great. The white cue ball skated past the yellow one he'd aimed for. I snickered.

"So glad you find me amusing." Alastair handed me the cue stick, motioning toward the table. "I believe it's your turn."

His smile nearly knocked me off my feet. I raised the stick, leaned over and aimed. Just as I was about to strike, he hovered over me.

"You're not going to hit anything with the cue pointed so low."

His warm breath tickled my ear, sending tremors rippling under my skin.

"You're distracting me. That's not fair."

"Just trying to be helpful. Give you a sporting chance and all that."

"Sport yourself over there so I can take my shot."

The cue stick was difficult to hold thanks to my hands' obscene levels of clamminess. I blew a wayward piece of hair away from my eyes and bent over the table again. Even though I couldn't see him, I was keenly aware of Alastair's eyes roaming slowly down my body.

I aimed, striking the white cue ball. It skirted and snapped against two red ones, spinning them into the corner pocket. Feeling more confident, I took another shot. By some stroke of beginner's luck, I potted a green one and a brown one.

"Told you I was a fast learner," I bragged.

He sidled up close, leaving me eye level with his mouth. An extremely persistent pounding noise filled my ears. Alastair bowed his head and looked down at me over the bridge of his straight nose. "Then I'll have to teach you another game."

I clasped the cue stick close to my legs. He cupped his hand around my hip and squeezed. Staggering backwards, I knocked into the table. It wobbled violently. Both of our pint glasses crashed to the floor, scattering shards around our feet. Several people stopped what they were doing and stared at us.

"Sorry about that," Alastair called out. "We have a rather impassioned snooker player over here."

Completely horrified, I apologized to Alastair and anybody else within earshot. This wasn't normal behavior for me. But of course, being around him turned me into a nervous, twitchy mess. He pointed me to a nearby chair to sit while someone swept up the broken glass.

Un-freaking-believable.

"Are you alright?" he asked, bemused.

"I'm fine, thanks for your concern," I grumbled. "Don't think this is an excuse to get out of losing the game."

When the broken glass was cleared away, I grabbed the cue stick and prepared for another shot. Alastair never had a chance. I beat him swiftly and succinctly. We negotiated a bet for the next game. Loser buys the winner a drink of their choice. The competitive juices started flowing. I wasn't about to lose to this guy.

Four games and three pints later, it was clear I was out of my league against him. Apparently my beginner's luck had run its course. Alastair didn't seem to mind at all. He methodically made perfect shot after perfect shot.

"I didn't mean to scare you off last night," he said, leaning against the table. His statement was so out of the blue I stared at him in shock. *Scare me off?* I gripped my pint glass.

"You didn't. I meant what I said."

He clenched his jaw and rolled the cue stick between his hands. I couldn't tell if he was annoyed or not. Pushing himself away from the table, he stood in front of me, dominating my line of sight. The pub became a vacuum.

"I find you very intriguing," he stated.

"You do?"

"Yes."

"Why?"

"Do I need to have a specific reason?"

Caught in the emerald glow of his eyes, I parted my lips to allow more oxygen. Another foggy haze messed with my logic.

"I was, um, just curious. I'm pretty boring," I stammered.

"I highly doubt that."

"You probably say—"

He hovered his lips over mine, stopping me in mid-thought. I could practically taste him. And my God, he smelled delicious. Not of cologne but shampoo and body wash and…*him*. It made me dizzy. He curled his hand around my waist, pulling me closer. I put my hands on his toned abdomen to steady myself.

"Come with me."

It wasn't a request. Those three words sent a shudder through me. The intensity of his stare was enough to get me to move. He laced his fingers through mine, leading me out to the curb.

We hopped in a cab and went back to the hotel. My heart was beating a furious tattoo. As we walked through the lobby toward the elevators a daunting scenario took shape. What if Stephanie had already returned? *Then you sit in the living room like a normal functioning adult, you moron.*

When the elevator arrived, I stood as far away from him as the space would allow. It wasn't easy. That crazy gravitational pull he had was drawing me toward him, one cell at a time. Electricity buzzed between us so quickly we could have powered the building.

We both let out audible sighs walking into the hall. I was relieved to see an empty suite when I opened the door. Stephanie must have Darren running laps with all the shopping she had planned.

"What are you smiling about?" Alastair looked at me curiously.

"Oh, I was just picturing Darren trying to keep up with Stephanie and her shopping marathon through Edinburgh."

"I haven't known Darren very long, but he always speaks very fondly of his American friend."

"How long have you known each other?"

"His agency does the marketing campaigns for my grandfather's company. I know a few people who work there and ended up bumping into him at an event last year."

He moved toward me in calculated, controlled strides. That intense, undeniable pull ignited again.

"I had a lovely time with you today." He leaned so close to me I could feel his breath on my neck. Gasping, my eyelids fluttered closed. He was beyond dangerous. He was downright lethal. "Are you always so easily led back to a hotel with a stranger?"

"Do you always invite yourself into a strange woman's hotel room?"

"Cheeky."

"I have a feeling people need to be on their toes when they're around you," I grinned.

"Some might say that. But you're not the type to ever let your guard down, are you?"

My smile faltered a bit. Those luminous eyes of his were very observant. Too observant for my liking. He laced his fingers through mine.

"I made the mistake of letting my guard down too much once. I've been paying for it ever since." I swallowed back an acrid lump.

"Don't let the ghosts of your past haunt your future," he whispered. The look in his eyes betrayed the little pearl of wisdom he just dispensed. It was almost as though he said it more to convince himself than me.

"Your eyes are like butterscotch."

"What?"

"The color," he said. "I've never seen anything like it."

"Oh. Yeah. Amber, or something like that. I always thought they were just, you know, regular brown."

"There is nothing regular about them. Or you." He lightly fingered my hair, tucking a strand behind my ear.

"Does this charm thing that you've got going for you work often?"

"Charm thing?" The corners of his mouth curled up. "I've had some success with it."

"Have you?"

"It's working right now."

Someone is extremely confident. This spell he'd cast was messing with me.

"You're quite lovely, Lia. Pity you're leaving soon. I'd like to take you—" he paused, tracing his thumb over my lower lip. I shuddered. "—out. Again."

"You would?" I asked hoarsely.

Nodding, he stroked the curve of my cheek. "Are you coming back to Glasgow after the wedding?"

"Yeah…yes. Saturday."

Backing away from him, I bumped into the arm of the couch. I almost toppled over it, but managed to steady myself. Being in his presence made me so damn skittish, it was frustrating.

"I'm supposed to make an appearance at a cocktail party for my grandfather's company."

Oh good, he's busy.

"You should come. Or we could go out to dinner." Like an apparition, he was in front of me, stroking his fingers along my arm. "What do you say? Fancy spending the night with me?"

The unspoken promise behind that question nearly shattered me on the spot. This was supposed to be an easy trip across the pond. Go to the wedding, hang out with the family and go home. Not fend off an amazingly sexy, impossible-to-resist guy.

"Stop overthinking," he ordered.

Stormy, dark eyes carved a path through my skull. I wilted beneath the strength of his stare. A shaky breath escaped my lips as he traced his finger along my jaw and down my neck. He drew me into his hypnotic orbit with such ease. I was powerless to resist.

"This is inevitable, Amelia. Don't deny it."

Inevitable? Each stroke of his fingers left a fiery trail in its wake. The smooth, soft skin of his cheek brushed against mine.

"Come with me."

Oh Jesus, those three words. I jolted out of his seductive haze like I was on fire, trying to avoid his eyes. His expression was one of pure lust.

"No," I whispered.

His mouth fell open slightly in surprise. "No?"

"No," I repeated, louder. "Do you not hear that word very often?"

Impassivity dominated his features. He studied me as though I was the most confusing creature on the planet. We stood so close to one another I was overcome by his intoxicating scent.

"Why not?"

"Because," I sighed. "I'm not interested."

"In what, Lia? Food or drinks?"

"You know what I mean."

He looked right through me, down into my soul. I didn't know how it happened, but he pierced through my wall. There was something else behind his intense stare that made me flush. I tried to hold his penetrating gaze but dropped my eyes to his mouth. Not smart. It was very distracting.

"Tell me what you want," he coaxed.

"I…"

The damp warmth of his lips on my neck ignited my blood. He teased along my throat, methodically kissing it. This sensual assault wreaked havoc on me, making my insides liquefy. Unable to hold off my own yearning any longer, I moaned. Alastair stopped nibbling on my neck and focused his lusty stare.

"Next Saturday?" I asked as a hazy, sexually charged cloud fogged my brain.

"Yes."

"Okay."

I still wasn't thinking straight.

"Brilliant." He smiled. "Until we meet again."

CHAPTER FOUR

"You know, I found out some interesting things about Alastair while you were busy on your mysterious date," Stephanie glanced at me. We were sitting on the train heading down to Gretna Green. The Scottish countryside flew by in a blur of green and brown. I'd been quiet most of the trip, lost in my thoughts. Damn her for piquing my curiosity.

"And?"

She grinned. "He's thirty-one, single and filthy rich. His grandfather is Samuel Holden, owner and CEO of Holden World Media. It's a huge, billion-dollar corporation; TV, broadband, cell phones and music. Alastair is the chief financial officer and heir to the whole thing. You certainly have a way of attracting the high rollers."

I cringed, feeling nauseous. *Why does the universe have such a twisted sense of humor? Guys like that are trouble. They're controlling, jealous and possessive.* I just had an explosive break-up with one of them a couple of months ago. I refused to put myself through that again. But Alastair was…different? I wanted him to be.

"Sounds familiar," I sighed.

"Oh my gosh. Alastair is nothing like Nathan. He has manners. I'm willing to bet he'd treat you like a princess."

"It started like this with Nathan, too. Remember? He was all charming and fun, then wham! I couldn't even make eye contact with another guy if he was in the same room." I swallowed hard. "He broke me. I didn't see it coming, but it happened. When I realized it, I was in too deep and…"

I stared at the floor, annoyed. Even now, he still had control over me. Bastard.

"Give Alastair the benefit of the doubt," Stephanie said softly.

"We'll see what happens next weekend at the cocktail party. Why is it you two were discussing him?" Stephanie and Darren engaged in more gossip-based conversations than anyone else on the planet. It was an obsession with them.

"Because you won't. And because Darren knows him. He also overhears stuff from the girls in the office. They're all enamored with him. Remember that blonde from the benefit? Sarah? Apparently, she's been trying to get in Alastair's pants for years."

Jealousy cut through me like a hot blade. I had zero right to feel this way. He wasn't mine or anything but the thought of him even flirting with another woman made my skin crawl. I slumped into my seat, looking out the window. I still had to reconcile what happened yesterday. Now that I was away from his magnetic sphere, I could think rationally. *I shouldn't have succumbed so readily to his seductive charms.*

I stared out as green field after green field sped by alongside the train. I needed to quiet my mind and stop obsessing over this. My sister was getting married in a few days. That's where my focus ought to be.

When we finally arrived in Gretna Green, we were greeted by a very excited bride-to-be. Seeing my little sister was always a treat. I missed her terribly.

"Did you guys have fun exploring Glasgow this weekend?" Dayna asked as we piled into the cab.

"Your sister did," Stephanie volunteered. I glared at her.

Dayna fixed a curious stare on me. "What does she mean, Lia?"

"Nothing," I said firmly. My sister's eyes widened, but she didn't press the issue.

"By the way, mom is on the rampage. She's not real big on the wedding planner they have on staff at the castle. When I left to meet you guys, they were arguing over how the napkins should be folded."

I burst out laughing. "If I ever get married, I'm eloping."

"You will not." She playfully chided me. "Any imperfections that mom notices at my wedding will get totally micromanaged for yours."

"That's what I'm afraid of," I snorted. The cab came to a rolling stop in front of Auchen Castle. Despite the gloomy gray skies, it was like entering a fairytale. When we walked in to the main foyer, I immediately saw our mother talking with the wedding planner.

"My girls," Lillian Meyers exclaimed, hugging both of us. "Excuse me for a second." She strutted back to a short, stout woman holding cloth napkins.

"Celeste, we can't have these folded like that. People won't be able to see the silverware."

Dayna and I exchanged amused glances. Our mother was in her element. She loved planning a huge event. Spouting off orders to people was her other great love.

"Ah, the yin and the yang are here." Our dad hugged us and grinned. He'd nicknamed us that when we were kids.

"Dad, are you going to call us that forever?" Dayna scrunched up her nose.

"Yes, blondie, I am." He ruffled her hair, eliciting a squeal of displeasure from my sister.

"Joe, stop teasing her," my mother scolded.

Living in Florida kept me away from my family for most of the year. Dayna only saw us at Christmas, so it was rare that the entire Meyers clan was in one place at the same time. Being scattered around the world seemed to work for us though.

* * *

The days and hours flew by as the wedding grew closer and closer. Guests arrived on Wednesday, and by Thursday there was a palpable excitement in the air. I was arranging the seating cards in alphabetical order, lost in thought.

"How's work going Lia? Is it too stressful?"

I looked up from the letter Ks and smiled at my mom.

"It's good. Television people are television people."

"Too bad we can't see the program at home. It's no fun bragging about your big shot producer daughter with nothing to show for it."

I could practically taste the sourness in her voice. She loved to brag about me and Dayna to her circle of friends. The ladies she chose to spend her time with all had doctors, lawyers and business magnates as offspring. We were the lone creative types. With Dayna writing for a food magazine in London, my mother never failed to remind me how much easier it was to show the women back home her articles, than explain my broadcasts.

"It's regular, local news. No more intriguing than what you watch in Darien. Google the station. We stream the news live every night."

Her aquamarine eyes narrowed at the mention of watching something online. She looked just like an older version of my sister when she did that.

"I know you don't like watching TV online, but it's all the rage. If it'll make you feel better, I'll put something together and send it to you guys. I'm sure Dad would like to see it too."

"Your father would love it," she beamed. "How have you been doing since breaking up with Nathan?"

It only took her four days to ask, I thought, trying to smooth out my annoyance at the mere mention of his name. "Fine."

"Lia, you're trembling," she said softly. "It's okay to still be upset."

I clenched my fists so tightly that my nails left little half moons in my palms. Anger boiled through my veins.

"I'm not upset," I glowered, snatching another name card. "He's not someone I want to talk about at the wedding, if you don't mind."

Thankfully, my dad chose that exact moment to interrupt our conversation. "Hey, kiddo," he smiled at me. "Mind if I steal your mom for a bit?"

Salvation. He always knew when to diffuse a tense situation between me and my mother. He draped an arm around her shoulder and led her toward the hall. I finished with the cards and spent the rest of the night curled up in my castle hotel room.

* * *

A frigid wind swept through the courtyard on Friday afternoon. It rustled the trees and sent leaves swirling. We crowded close together by a fountain, dresses fluttering about and well-sprayed hair-dos fighting against the breeze. Dayna's sparkling cathedral veil slapped me in the face just as the photographer snapped a picture.

"Stay still ladies. Don't move….and smile," he directed.

I huddled in close to my sister, trying valiantly to keep a happy, relaxed smile plastered on my frozen face. Why she had to pick Scotland in April to get married mystified me. Castle staff members brought out a few platters of food for us to snack on, but it was difficult shoving bacon wrapped scallops in one's mouth while attempting a pretty smile at the same time.

The photographer dismissed the bridesmaids and groomsmen, but kept Dayna and her new husband, Andrew, for some couples shots. I trotted over to a plate lined with delicate rolls of raspberry and brie wrapped in filo pastry.

"Aren't those tasty?" my mother asked as she popped one in her mouth as well.

I managed a semi-enthusiastic nod while reaching for another roll.

"Your father and I can't wait to sit down and enjoy dinner. I had no idea being mother-of-the-bride was so exhausting!"

I grinned and watched the photographer finish up with the newlyweds. Dayna looked stunning in her ivory gown and Andrew was handsome in his tuxedo. Dayna squealed in delight, or shock, as Andrew scooped her off her feet. Her veil caught the breeze that was still blowing through the courtyard and soared over their heads, the crystals sparkling in the sunlight.

"Let's get this party started," Andrew Riley bellowed, carrying the new Mrs. Riley toward the reception hall.

Soft light glittered through the crystal chandeliers in the castle's main reception hall. The space was warm and inviting, with half a dozen decorated tables spread throughout. Dayna and Andrew had purposely kept the wedding numbers low, based on the distance guests would have to travel. Only immediate family and a handful of their closest friends were there, making the affair cozy and intimate.

Smiling guests filled the room. A low hum of conversation mixed with soft music. Some of Andrew's friends gathered around their newly betrothed mate, singing and chanting some soccer songs but changing the words for the occasion.

"These Brits and their soccer," Stephanie remarked, resting her arm on my shoulder.

"Yeah. Dayna told me he drags her to at least one game a month. I told her she should bring a magazine and read."

We laughed as Andrew sang along with his friends.

"By the way," Stephanie grinned. "You are a vision in sage, my friend."

The sage chiffon flowed effortlessly around my legs as I swished the gown back and forth. "The color doesn't look as dreadful on as I thought it would. Thank goodness."

After the main courses were enjoyed and dessert served, the DJ let loose and we partied the night away. My mom and dad danced to song after song. Stephanie managed to pair off with one of Andrew's friends. They sat huddled at a table by one of the massive picture windows. Her peals of laughter floated over the music.

Before the reception ended, all of us made our way to the back terrace for one final surprise for the bride and groom. Once everyone gathered outside, the night sky lit up with a dazzling display of fireworks. Glasses of champagne were raised and the bride and groom were toasted, as brilliant colors burst across the sky, illuminating the castle.

I stayed out on the terrace after everyone went back inside. Stars shimmered and glittered their way through thin tendrils of clouds in the night sky. A soft breeze tickled my skin. This was the closest I'd been to experiencing pure serenity in months. I wanted to bottle up this moment of peace and solitude forever.

"What are you doing out here all by yourself?"

I turned, surprised to see my sister.

"Admiring the view."

"What view? It's pitch black out here." Dayna gathered up her dress and stood next to me.

"I was looking at the stars. I don't get to see them much in Orlando with all the light pollution."

"I know what you mean. We don't see them in London either." She flicked a strand of my hair behind my shoulder.

"Why aren't you inside mingling with everyone?"

"They won't mind if I'm spending quality time with my big sister," she grinned.

"I know that look. What do you want?"

She sighed. "We haven't really talked since the break up. Is he still harassing you?"

The one person I could never lie to was Dayna. Sure, Stephanie could read me like a book, but Dayna knew what was on the page before it was written.

"Not anymore. Well, not since I moved. There's a guard stationed at the entrance gate, so he couldn't get in even if he tried. Plus, I have an alarm in my apartment."

"How about the texting and calling?"

"That cooled off last week."

"Are you sure he still doesn't have someone tailing you? He's a sneaky fucker."

I had to smile at Dayna's pissed off expression. It clashed so fiercely with her sparkly veil and wedding gown.

"You look like a demented bride with that grimace," I giggled.

"Lia, come on. I'm serious."

I leaned my head back, inhaling the crisp, fresh air. "There's nobody tailing me. There's no more harassing. I don't know what it means, but hopefully he got bored and moved on. Although, I wouldn't wish him on any girl."

"Guys like that think they own the world just because their bank accounts are bigger than their dicks. He'll find some willing gold-digger to boss around and tell what to wear and who to talk to. I'm just glad you finally saw him for who he really is."

We both turned our heads to see where the blast of music was coming from. Andrew had opened one of the French doors, waving to us.

"There you are. You coming back inside?"

"In a minute," Dayna answered. Her new husband nodded and closed the door.

"Go back to your reception. I'll hang out here a bit longer."

Bright blue eyes lingered on my face long enough to make me squirm. *I really wish everyone would stop fussing over me.*

"I know we're an ocean and a time zone apart, but if you need anything, *anything*, you call me, okay?"

"Dayna—"

"Just because you're my big sister doesn't mean I don't worry about you. We Meyers girls have to stick together."

"Yeah, I know. Thanks, Cinnamon."

"Ugh, you and Dad with the nicknames," she groaned. "Don't ever use it in front of Andy. I'll never hear the end of it."

"I make no promises." I smirked.

Dayna pulled me into a suffocating hug before returning to the reception.

* * *

I sat quietly on the cushy bed in my room, flipping through a magazine. The reception ended a couple of hours ago but people were still laughing and walking through the hallway. My sage dress rested on a chair by the window with the pair of sparkling heels next to it on the floor. *I have to pack at some point. Now is not the time.*

Leaning back against the pillows, I stretched my legs, wiggling my French manicured toes. Letting out a big sigh, I grabbed the magazine again. Nothing was coming into focus on the pages. It was all jumbled words and blurry images. According to my cell phone it was barely one in the morning. I idly wondered what Alastair was doing.

A stupid smile attacked my lips. *Really?* I thought back to what Stephanie said about my 'needing' this. She might be right but I wasn't ready to jump into something physical with anyone. Although, it could be fun. *He is awfully sexy.*

The door swung open, smacking against the wall. "Jesus, Stephanie. You just about gave me a freaking heart attack."

"Relax. I didn't do anything. These doors are so old and heavy, I had to push really hard." Stephanie kicked off her heels and flopped on the bed. "What were you thinking about so intently that I scared you so badly?"

I sighed, annoyed. "Nothing."

"Liar. You're thinking about your guy."

"He's not my guy."

"Are you nervous about seeing him tomorrow?"

"No."

"Oh my God," she snorted. Stephanie knew. Stephanie always knew when I tried to hide my feelings. Sometimes, being her best friend was a curse as much as it was a blessing. "Did I tell you Darren's company is hiring a graphic designer? He says I should apply."

"That's exciting. Isn't that your dream job?"

"Yeah, but I thought I'd be doing it in Orlando."

"You have to go where the opportunity takes you. Otherwise, you'll be cutting hair for the rest of your life."

Stephanie rolled her eyes. "I don't know."

"Apply. What's the worst that can happen?"

"You know if I do, Darren will make certain I get hired," she fretted, her face turning white.

"And that's a bad thing?"

"Well," she shrugged. "Not really. I mean, I have a built-in friend and stuff, but...I don't know."

"Do it. Darren wouldn't suggest it if he thought you weren't up for the challenge."

Stephanie's ice blue eyes lit up. I knew she couldn't back down from anything that remotely resembled a challenge.

"Maybe I will, Amelia Grace. That way, you can move here with me and go on fabulous dates with one Alastair Holden." She started digging through her purse. "What time are we getting up tomorrow? Will I have time to pack after breakfast, or should I do it now? I want to get to Glasgow at a decent hour. Darren's expecting us by mid-afternoon."

"There'll be time to pack in the morning. We'll catch the one o'clock train and be back in Glasgow by three. No worries."

"Perfect. I'll see you at breakfast. Sleep well."

Stephanie bounded out of the room as exuberantly as she entered. I leaned my head back a little too abruptly, hitting the headboard.

"Honestly," I grumbled, grabbing for my phone to set the alarm. It beeped the second I touched it.

1:06am I hope you had a cracking time at the wedding. I'll meet you at 8 tomorrow night. Wear something sexy.

1:07am Don't push your luck, Holden.

1:10am Fair enough. Good night, Amelia

1:11am Good night

I set the alarm and tossed the phone on the nightstand. Curling up under the blankets, I let my mind run a bit, thinking about what was in store for tomorrow night.

Sleep? Not possible.

CHAPTER FIVE

The cocktail bar was crowded when we arrived Saturday night. It looked very chic with its rich purples, deep grays and cocoa browns draped over velvet couches and leather booths. The whole room gave off a very seductive, captivating vibe. I was wound up tighter than a drum and needed something to take the edge off. Darren and Stephanie ended up coming too. His company was invited, so they took it as an excuse to have a fun night out. I followed them to a reserved table.

"Fancy a drink? I've already got us a bottle of Riesling." Darren motioned to the table.

That was more than enough for me. I poured a generous amount for myself and downed it. Stephanie rolled her eyes.

"Easy on the booze tonight, Lia. I know how you get when you're pretending not to be nervous."

Ignoring the ferocious tremor of nerves in my stomach, I poured another glass and took a sip. "I'm not pretending."

Some of Darren's co-workers joined us, saving me from Stephanie's scrutinizing glances.

"Lia, Steph this is Cassie Zanor. She's one of the graphic designers at the agency," Darren said.

Cassie smiled warmly and greeted us. Petite and curvy with dark cocoa skin, she was adorable. Stephanie chatted with her about the open job position. Another one of his co-workers took a shine to me right away. He seemed nice enough. I think he said his name was William, but it could have been Jack for all I knew.

Three minty flavored martinis later I was laughing at everything Bill-Jack said. He was cute in a scruffy way. His features were a bit too delicate for my taste, but he had extremely kind brown eyes. He'd recently gotten a buzz cut and was quite keen on getting me to rub his peach fuzz head.

"I bet you've never felt a head like this before. Give it a go."

"I don't want to be responsible for messing up your hair," I smiled half-heartedly.

"Ah, good one." He angled toward me. "Just once."

Christ. "Okay. Just once."

I brushed the palm of my hand across his head quickly. It tickled a little.

"See? Feels good right?" His eager smile made my skin crawl. *Your scruffy cuteness is fading, Bill-Jack.*

"Can I get you another drink?"

"I think I'm going to get the next one myself, but thanks. I need to stretch my legs a bit." I smiled at him and went over to the bar. While I waited for the bartender, I whipped my phone out. Nine. *I've totally been ditched.* Or was it stood-up? Either way, this wasn't a real date so it didn't matter.

"Why is such a pretty girl getting her own drink?" A dark-haired man with a friendly enough rasp to his voice was standing next to me. These Scottish accents kept getting more and more attractive each time I heard them.

"I felt like walking around a bit."

"Did you now? I'm Brent Garrison," he extended his hand. I shook it firmly and introduced myself.

"What brings you to Glasgow, Lia?"

"Vacation."

"How long will you be here?" He rested his arm lazily on the bar.

"I leave tomorrow morning."

"And I'm just meeting you now? That is a shame." He tilted his head, causing some of the wavy, chocolate brown hair framing his face to flop to the side. "What are you drinking? It's my treat."

"No, thank you, that's not necessary."

A hand suddenly found itself on my lower back. The sensation sent a crazy jolt through me.

"What's not necessary?" Alastair looked sharply at Brent who returned his chilly stare.

"I was just offering her a drink. Problem?" He smiled tightly.

Alastair remained silent for several seconds, keeping his hand pressed to my back.

"Not at the moment," he finally said.

Brent shook his head, chuckling.

"We were just having a friendly conversation. No need to get territorial. Nice meeting you, Lia." He tilted his glass toward me and walked off.

Alastair positioned himself so he was standing in front of me. "Was he bothering you?"

"What? No." A weird sense of déjà vu crept through my body. "Why?"

"He has a habit of hitting on anything in a skirt."

"So do most warm-blooded men." I smiled, moving my eyes along every well dressed inch of him.

"Enjoying the view?"

I glanced up at him through my lashes. "Maybe."

"Is there something I can do to make that a more definitive answer?" A lazy, sexy grin curled his mouth.

My heart took up residence in my throat, pounding furiously. I should be annoyed that he just showed up without an explanation for his lateness, but I liked flirting with him. A lot.

A pretty blonde server walked over and placed two drinks on the bar. One of them was the minty martini I'd been enjoying all night.

"How did you know I was drinking these?"

"I saw that guy you were with buy them for you."

"You've been watching me?" Panic seized my chest.

How is this happening again? I'm thousands of miles away from home. Being tracked and stalked by another over privileged, possessive rich guy wasn't on my vacation itinerary. The walls felt like they were closing in around me, crushing my lungs. I dug my fingernails into the velvet cushion on the barstool. He was watching me? *I've been here for an hour and he's been in the shadows keeping tabs...*

"Lia." His voice cut through the vacuum, snapping me back to reality. Heat radiated from his eyes, drawing me closer. It muted everything else in the room and calmed my nerves.

"I simply noticed you were here with your friends while I was sidetracked by some clients. That's all. Your sparkly dress is hard to miss."

He had a point. The dress did scream *look at me.*

"Sorry."

"It's alright."

He stared at me with an unreadable expression, making my insides twist anxiously. At least last week I knew he was staring at me out of lust. This was unnerving.

"Did you have a nice time at your sister's wedding?"

"Yeah, I did. How was your week?"

"Typical." He angled his body closer. "Except for the fact that I spent most of it thinking about you."

He's a smooth operator, this one.

"Did you?"

He nodded, running his knuckles along my cheek.

"Anything you want to share?"

Sliding his fingers down my arm, he skimmed them over my hip, settling on my waist. Goosebumps poked out all over my skin. I knocked back the martini like it was a shot. It went down much too easily for such a strong drink. My face was already a bit numb from the previous ones.

He scanned the room quickly before pulling me closer.

"There is a time and a place for sharing," he said, dipping his head closer to my ear. "This is not one of them."

A smile evaporated from his face as he backed away from me, leaving a chill in the air between us. Puzzled, I followed his frigid gaze. I saw nothing but people enjoying themselves.

"Is something wrong?"

Alastair didn't answer right away. His constant scanning of the lounge freaked me out a little. It was too bad that the blonde server hadn't been by to replenish my martini. I could have used another.

"Everything's fine," he finally said. I met his eyes and was floored by the hardness in them. Even his expression was stony.

"Are you sure?"

"Yes."

There was something about the clipped, almost dismissive way he responded which bugged me. I sat on the velvet stool, swiveling to face the crowd. The room wiggled a bit thanks to my fuzzy martini brain.

"I have to take care of something. I won't be long."

"Can it wait?" I asked, turning back to him. He slid his cell phone in his pants pocket.

"No," he looked at me coolly, "it can't."

I watched him disappear down a hallway toward the hotel entrance. Shaking off an unsettled feeling, I ordered another drink and went back to sit at the table.

"Having a good time, Lia?" Darren winked at me.

"Sure."

"Did Alastair leave?" Stephanie asked, frowning.

"No, he's taking care of something," I said, waving my hand.

"How many of those have you had?" She eyed the glass.

"Not nearly enough," I muttered.

A bunch of other people had joined the table, but I ignored the conversation. I had to know what he was doing. After a beat, I stood up and went to see what the hell was happening.

The hallway was quiet and empty. A handful of administrative offices lined one side. I walked down to the door leading to the hotel and turned around. Angry, I stormed back toward the lounge. *First he's an hour late, now he disappears. I'm all set, thanks.* Out of nowhere, Alastair appeared, all smoldering and hot. Without saying a word, he pulled me into one of the offices.

"What are you—"

"Are you involved with anyone?" he interrupted.

"This is a really bizarre time for you to be asking me that."

"Are you?"

I clenched my fists, blood churning through my veins.

"No. Why did you walk off like that?"

"It's not important."

He tensed, clearly uncomfortable with my question.

"Alastair, you can't—"

"Leave it alone, Lia."

The cold look in his eyes shut me up immediately. A detached, passive expression blanketed his face, rendering any charm or charisma obsolete. *And this is my cue to leave, jackass.* He grabbed my arm as I tried to walk to the door.

"Get your hands off me," I hissed.

He sucked in a breath, as though he'd woken up from a bad dream. His grip on my arm relaxed but I didn't leave. His eyes stopped me. They were pleading, apologizing for something far greater than just grabbing me.

"I didn't mean to do that," he atoned. "Did I hurt you?"

The culmination of all the martinis I'd had throughout the night paraded through my bloodstream with great fanfare, systematically shutting down my sense of logic and most motor skills. My legs wobbled.

"No. I'm fine. You just took me by surprise." My face and lips vanished, causing me to speak much slower than normal. At least it felt that way.

"You're going to pinch those right off."

He pulled my hand away from my mouth. I'd been tugging my lip without even realizing it.

"They're numb. You can feel them?"

He gently traced my lips with his thumb. "Yes. I hope you're not pissed."

"You think I'm mad at you?" I asked.

He tilted his head, grinning.

"Not mad. Drunk. I thought you said you knew British slang?"

"I do. I just…" I answered, trailing off. I was annoyed that I couldn't feel my face and probably sounded like a drunken idiot. *I should have just gone back to Darren's townhouse.*

"You really need to stop doing this. I can assure you, they are where they're supposed to be."

He pulled my hand away from my mouth again.

"I can't feel them," I complained. "Stop laughing at me. Now I'm pissed."

"So now you're drunk?" He folded his arms, raising an eyebrow.

"What? No. I'm *pissed*. You know what I mean."

Am I not making sense? Stupid alcohol.

"Oddly enough I do," he said, stroking my cheek. "Why are you upset with me?"

"For starters, you were late. Then you were snippy with that guy at the bar. And now, this whole walking away with no explanation."

"Is that all?"

"Yeah, I guess—"

He planted a lush, wet kiss squarely on my mouth. It was quick and chaste but enough to set off a spark.

"Good. Want to get out of here?"

"This office?" A noticeable tingle buzzed through the numbness, tickling the outer edges of my lips.

"This place in general. I never liked it here."

"And go where?"

He shrugged, grabbing my hand. Walking somewhat slower than a sloth in molasses, we made our way toward the lounge.

"You don't like many things, do you?" I asked.

"What do you mean?"

"Well, you don't like soccer, but you went to the game. And now, this place. Is there anything you do like?"

He remained quiet until we got back to the table. His only response was a quick squeeze of my hand before pulling out a chair for me to sit.

"Look what we have here," Brent announced, capturing everyone's attention. "The elusive Alastair Holden has graced us with his presence this evening for more than his requisite ten minutes."

I did not like the tone of that guy's voice. Alastair lowered himself onto the chair next to mine, never taking his eyes off him.

"Center of attention as usual, Garrison?" he responded smoothly.

"Don't be jealous, Holden. You can't have all the attention and all the…" he paused, glancing at me, seeming to reconsider his thoughts. "I'll give my sister your regards when I talk to her this week. She's looking forward to reuniting with you at your grandfather's retirement party."

"I didn't know she was invited," he said, in a menacingly calm voice.

"She's quite excited to see you. Keeps mentioning how much it would mean to her if the two of you—"

"That's enough, Brent."

I could feel the anger and tension seeping out of Alastair's pores. The room no longer had a defined horizon. Everything swayed and rolled as I let Brent's words snake through my mind. When I looked around the table it hit me that Stephanie wasn't there. Neither was Darren. *I have to leave. I have to get away from this.*

I stood up too quickly, sending the room into a rapid spin.

"Careful," Alastair said, rising to help steady me. "Let's go. You okay to walk?"

"I don't know where Stephanie is. I can't just leave."

"She's over there. Come on."

I was finally able to make out where Stephanie was standing as we got closer. She was still talking to Cassie. Her face lit up when she saw me.

"Oh my gosh, you'll never guess," she exclaimed.

"What?"

"Cassie is the manager of the graphic design team and wants to see some of my work."

"That's great, Steph." Warmth and happiness filled me from seeing her so excited.

"Y'all look like you're leaving. Where are you off to?"

"Just out for a drive," Alastair answered. "No need to worry. Have Darren text me when you're back at his flat and I'll drop Lia off then."

Stephanie scrutinized him. Great. She had that over-protective-friend look on her face.

"I'll be fine," I said. "Go find out more about this job and fill me in later."

"Keep your phone on," she said, raising an eyebrow, before rejoining Cassie.

A blast of chilly night air gave me a brief dose of renewed energy when we walked outside. My brain was still much too cloudy from all the martinis though. I was surprised when Alastair bypassed the valet and went straight for an idling Mercedes SUV. *What are the odds this is the one I practically fell onto last week?*

I climbed in as gracefully as I could, settling into the soft, leather seat. Alastair climbed in next to me.

"Paxton, this is Lia."

The driver turned and smiled at me. *Yep. It's the same guy from last week.*

"Nice to see you, miss. Where to Alastair?"

"The cottage, please."

Unable to fight off the boozy fatigue, I rested my head on Alastair's shoulder for what felt like a split second.

He nudged me gently, waking me up. "We're here."

I sat up, looking out the window. He got out of the car and offered me his hand. I stepped onto the ground, my heels sinking into the soft earth. It was dark and quiet, with no discernible landscape. But, oh, when I looked up. The sky was a swirl of onyx and fluorite with bright stars dancing through it. I'd never seen anything like it, not even as a child at the science museum. The dark expanse was huge, stretching far and wide. Staring at it filled me with an even greater serenity than I'd felt last night on the terrace.

"Come inside," Alastair whispered, holding my hand. He led me toward a small, two-story thatched cottage. The dark wooden front door creaked as he opened it. Once inside, I immediately felt at home. Soft lights glowed from the end tables as Alastair walked through, flipping switches.

"Make yourself comfortable." He pointed to one of the crimson couches. "I'm going to get you some water."

I kicked off my heels and scrunched my toes in the plush throw rug before sitting down. I heard him moving around in the kitchen, opening the refrigerator. A few moments later he handed me the bottled water.

"Is this where you live?" I asked, watching him settle onto the couch next to me.

"No. It's just where I come when I want to get away."

I nodded, sipping the water. I hadn't realized how thirsty I was from all the martinis. My lips were still mysteriously among the missing though. Being in this cottage had a soothing, calming effect on me. I couldn't put my finger on it, but it just felt…right.

"What are you thinking about?"

The look in his eyes made me melt. There was no veil, no hard edge, which had been there earlier. They were soft, almost gentle.

"What was all that with Brent before? Why was he being such an ass?"

"That's just the way he is," he said, stiffening.

"Are you dating his sister?" I pushed the words out in one rushed breath.

"No."

He looked me dead in the eye, not flinching. His stare tore

through me the same way it always did, only this time I didn't want it to stop.

Tilting his head, he leaned closer. The parts of me that weren't numb from alcohol shivered in anticipation. Swallowing hard, he backed away. I unclenched my hands, not even realizing I'd fisted them. He didn't want to kiss me. I should be relieved.

Keeping my eyes downcast, I fidgeted with my dress. I felt his hand run over my shoulder and down my arm. His touch was incredible but I had to keep a level head. A one-night stand was the last thing I needed, especially after having so many drinks.

The constant touch of his skin on mine did nothing to help convince me otherwise.

"You've successfully lured me to your house, Holden. What do you plan to do now?"

Oh no. The alcohol speaks.

He tilted my chin up so our mouths were just about touching. "Nothing, Amelia. Not this way."

The logical side of my brain was satisfied with his answer. The drunk part? Not so much. Getting a handle on my breathing was difficult. The fact that he was now stroking my cheek and staring at me with such yearning made it nearly impossible.

That mouth. I wanted it on me.

I'm loaded. This isn't smart.

"Maybe you should just take me back to Darren's place. It's late and I have an early—"

Pressing his mouth to mine, he stopped my rambling. I inhaled his warm breath in shock. Tangling his fingers through my hair, he pulled gently. I leaned my head back, gasping. With stormy restraint, he took advantage and slid his tongue past my lips, kissing me slowly and deeply. My mind went blank. I was lightheaded, unaware of anything but him.

Caressing his face, I ran my fingers over his cheeks and jaw. He groaned, kissing me harder, setting my blood on fire.

Abandoning my trepidations, I straddled his lap. Grasping my lower back, his fingers dug into my skin. I shoved my hands in his hair, pulling it and slanting his head so I could fully taste him. His moan was low and sexy, reverberating through me.

His body stiffened as he fisted his hand in my hair, trying to regain control. I relaxed my grip and surrendered to him.

"We have to stop," he rasped against my lips.

"Why?"

His chest heaved and fell as he sighed. My mind and sense of logic were wrapped in a boozy blanket, obscuring any distinction between *stop-it-now* and *this-feels-good-keep-going*.

The alcohol won again. I kissed him greedily. He was too good not to. I got a rush from how he savored me with the long slow strokes of his tongue. Lust throbbed ferociously through my body. No man had ever gotten me this hot and bothered with just a kiss.

Working fast, I pulled up his shirt, scratching my nails down his chest. His muscles twitched and contracted under my touch. He brushed my hair back, cupped my jaw and pulled his mouth away.

"Don't," he said rather unconvincingly.

"I want to."

His quiet moan drove me wild. My hand disappeared into the thick, dark red softness of his hair.

"No, Lia." His eyes hardened in a determined stare.

He was rejecting me? Everything spun wildly. I broke out into a cold sweat as my vision tripled and stomach churned. Seconds later it rolled again as nausea spread through my body. *No, no, no.*

CHAPTER SIX

I could count on one hand how many times I'd been sick from drinking too much. This was going down as the most mortifying one in history. My entire body lurched as all the minty martinis flew out into the toilet. At least I had enough presence of mind to flush it immediately.

Disgusted with myself, I rested my head on my arm to quiet the pounding.

This is attractive. I bet he loves having drunk girls on their knees in front of the toilet.

Someone gathered my hair into a low ponytail.

Oh my God. Please don't let me puke with him kneeling beside me.

Too late. Another horrific wave of nausea overtook my body. Alastair knelt quietly beside me, stroking my back. I prayed to the gods of porcelain thrones to keep his clothes free from any splashback. When it seemed I'd completely emptied my stomach, I slumped against the wall and whimpered.

"Don't move. I'll be right back," he said.

Where else could I possibly go? I cradled my head in my hands. What a disaster. A few minutes later Alastair walked back in carrying a toothbrush, a washcloth and the bottle of water.

"Come here." He knelt next to me and pressed the washcloth to my face. "I've run it under cold water. Sorry if it's a bit chilly."

The cool cotton felt good against my flaming skin. Tears flowed down my cheeks in thick streams.

"No tears, love. You've nothing to be ashamed of."

I looked at him through watery eyes. I was so embarrassed. I must look like such an asshole to him.

"Drink this." He handed me the water.

"Thank you."

Alastair tucked a strand of hair behind my ear. "You're welcome. I'll let you finish up in here. Come find me when you're done, alright?"

"I'm sorry."

"For what?"

"This."

Tilting my chin up, he started to say something then stopped. We stared at one another for a couple minutes.

"I'll be in the bedroom down the hall. Take your time."

Once he was gone, I stood up and brushed my teeth quickly, then splashed more cold water on my face. I caught a glimpse of my reflection in the mirror and grimaced.

I walked cautiously into the hall. A nasty headache pounded between my ears. All I wanted to do was lie down. There was light spilling from a nearby room. I staggered toward it, willing the rumbling in my stomach to settle down.

My vision doubled and I had to reach for the doorframe. He was at my side immediately, helping me to the bed. A t-shirt and flannel boxer shorts were folded on the pillow. I wasted no time changing into them. Yanking the dress over my head, I stood with it tangled around my arms. Some of the embellished sequins caught on my lace undergarments.

"Here. Let me help you." Alastair gingerly loosened the sequins from the lace. As valiant as he was, his fingers did brush against my bra a couple times. One of the sequins was stuck on the lace edge, right at the swell of my breast. I held my breath as he moved deftly to get it off.

"No touching, Holden," I breathed. He stared hungrily at me and tossed my dress to the side.

"You're not making it very easy."

He grabbed the t-shirt and pulled it over my head. Holding out the boxers so I could step into them, he inadvertently brushed my thigh and muttered something incoherently.

"Come. Lie down."

I crawled on the bed and snuggled into the pillows. All I needed was a warm body close by. "Lie down next to me. Please."

Alastair squeezed his eyes shut and swallowed hard. "You need to rest. I'm going to call Darren."

"No. Stay with me."

He ran both hands through his hair and looked at the ceiling. "Please?"

Looking positively torn, his brows knit together in concentration as he climbed on the bed. I moved closer and ran my hand down his chest. He flinched.

"Lia, don't."

He took my hand and curled it under my chin, then draped his arm around my waist. I felt so safe, so secure. This was what I craved. I closed my eyes and passed out cold.

* * *

Everything was fuzzy and dim. I peered out from the blankets and tried to make sense of the shadows and shapes on the wall. It wasn't my bedroom, that's for sure. Ah, I was in Darren's townhouse. Bits and pieces of the previous day started creeping back. The train. The cocktail party. The martinis. *Oh shit.*

These sheets smelled so damn good. *Like Alastair.* My eyes flew open. The room zigged and zagged when I sat up. This wasn't Darren's townhouse. I clutched the fluffy comforter, waiting for my eyes to focus. The bed was empty, so that was a good sign. I looked down, relieved to see I was fully dressed, although the t-shirt was a little too big and I knew for a fact I didn't own any green plaid boxers. Glowing red digital numbers confidently told me it was nine in the morning. A very weird feeling settled in my bones.

This wasn't the same room I'd fallen asleep in last night. Panic snaked its way through my veins, trying to derail my attempt at a logical thought process. I stood in the middle of this very well decorated bedroom. It was immaculate, almost too perfect, like a model home used for an open house. What happened to the cozy cottage?

I peeked into the hallway. It was dark, except for a sliver of light coming out from beneath a door. I padded down and leaned my ear against it to see if anybody was inside. Soft music was the only thing I heard at first; then, the subtle tapping sounds of fingers hitting a keyboard.

Knocking on the door, I turned the knob. Alastair looked up from a desk in surprise.

"Good morning. How are you feeling?"

"I don't know. Fine, I guess. My head hurts."

Alastair closed his laptop and folded his hands on the desk. He motioned for me to sit in the oversized gray chair I was leaning against.

"Do you remember much of what happened last night?"

"Some of it. Where am I?" I felt stupid asking it out loud, but what else could I do.

"My house."

"So, this isn't that cottage you took me to?"

"No. After you passed out I called Darren. He and Stephanie drove out to get you." He cleared his throat and continued. "Needless to say, there was a rather heated discussion about your flying home this morning. Stephanie wasn't too pleased about my offer to let you sleep here and then get you home later in the afternoon. She's stubborn, that one."

"Can you blame her? No offense, but you're practically a stranger and now I'm all alone in a foreign country with you.

How the hell did you convince her?"

"With a little help from Darren."

"He must have likened you to the Pope or something. She would never agree to this unless she was one-hundred-fifty-percent certain—"

"It's not for you to worry about. Everything is taken care of."

"You like to interrupt me a lot." I furrowed my brow, tapping my fingers on the chair.

"I do? Sorry. I don't mean to be rude."

I shrugged, waving my hand in the air to dismiss the notion. I should be more upset with the whole situation, but as crazy and random as all this was, everything still felt...right. I got up and strolled around his home office. The heavy, dark lines of the furniture contrasted greatly with the light walls and cream window treatments. Everything was perfectly in its place. *He's a neat freak,* I grinned. I could certainly appreciate someone who liked to have things organized. The room was so smart it wore its windows like wire-rimmed glasses at the tip of its nose.

"How fancy," I said, pointing at his framed diploma hanging on the wall. "Oxford University." I scrutinized it. "What does the 'R' stand for?"

"Reid." He wrinkled his nose.

"Alastair Reid Holden? I like it."

His lips curved. "Thanks."

"My being here hasn't interfered with your plans for today has it?"

"No."

"No rugby thing this weekend?"

"No," he said, rubbing his eyes. "Maybe next."

A wave of nervousness washed over me. The embarrassment from last night started creeping in. *Did I really jump on his lap and kiss him like that?*

"You are far too deep in thought," he observed. "Would you like some breakfast? I don't know about you, but the morning after a night of serious drinking always calls for a cheesy omelet with toast. At least for me it does."

My stomach growled on cue. It never turned down food. Alastair stood up and headed toward the kitchen.

"It's settled then. Follow me."

He prepared two very cheesy omelets for us to eat. I waited patiently at the table, sipping tea while he laid out the plates, silverware, toast and butter. Everything smelled divine. I ate enthusiastically, savoring each bite.

"What?" I arched an eyebrow.

"I'm rather enjoying watching you eat."

"Are you?" I brought the fork to my mouth. So help me, his entire body just trembled. Or was he just shifting in his chair? Either way, his subtle movements drove me crazy. "How's yours?"

Without missing a beat, he flashed a broad smile and ate a forkful of cheesy eggs. If there has ever been a more distracting mouth on the planet, please show it to me because damn, he made eating an omelet look illegal. "It's okay."

Inexplicably, his expression hardened and he paled slightly. He was quiet for several seconds. Our flirty little eating game was apparently over. We finished our breakfast in silence.

I helped clear the table and leaned against the doorframe in the kitchen as Alastair loaded the dishwasher. He was even mind-numbingly gorgeous being domestic; hair all disheveled, dark blue pajamas bottoms hanging perfectly at his hips, a long sleeved cotton shirt clinging to his toned torso.

"I took the liberty of placing all your toiletries in the bathroom for whenever you'd like to shower. There are towels as well." He put the last plate in the dishwasher. "I have some work to finish, so the house is yours."

As he passed by, he reached out and squeezed my waist gently, making me jump.

"Someone's ticklish," he grinned, walking down the hallway.

I took a second to recover, then scurried off to take a shower.

Alastair wasn't kidding about leaving my things in the bathroom. Neatly lined up on the counter were my shampoo, conditioner, shower gel, razor, shaving cream, pretty much my entire supply of beauty products. His bathroom was stunning. I stared enviously at the large, egg shaped tub wondering if he ever used it... *and who with.*

The shower alone was the size of a walk-in closet. Wrapped in limestone tile, it had a rain head, a hand spray and multiple wall sprays. There was even a bench that, I would imagine, comes in handy for shower shenanigans.

Stop thinking about him like that.

After taking a leisurely, hot shower, I packed the rest of my belongings. I could still catch a late afternoon flight back to Orlando if we left for the airport in the next hour or so. Once I finished dressing, I went back to his office. Alastair was still typing away.

"What are you listening to?"

"John Field. He's an Irish pianist and composer. Do you like it?"

"I like classical music. It's very soothing."

Alastair nodded with approval. "I couldn't agree more."

Watching him work in such a casual atmosphere intrigued me. Dressed in his pajamas, he sat with perfect posture. His head tilted slightly to the right as he typed out a few quick lines. Intelligence and professionalism reflected in his eyes and serious expression. All that was missing was a three-piece suit. The visual gave me goose bumps.

"I'm not bothering you, am I?"

"Not at all. Just finishing up an email." He closed the laptop. "You seem to be much better."

"I am, thank you. Not to inflate your ego or anything, but that omelet had something to do with it."

His throaty laugh filled the room. "Consider my ego fully inflated."

A cluster of framed photos hanging by the window caught my

attention. I walked over to get a closer look. Some of them were very old, others were more recent. One in particular caught my eye. A little boy, no older than five or six, was throwing a handful of leaves over his head. He was sitting on the grass alone, looking up as the leaves fluttered around him. It was a joyful photo, except for the lack of any happiness on his face. Especially in his beautiful eyes. They were listless and sad.

"Is this you?"

"Yes," he answered tightly, walking towards me.

The pain behind his eyes was immense. He stared at the photo of his younger self, clenching and unclenching his fists. His despair filled me with sadness. I wanted to see him smile.

"You used to be cute, Holden. What happened?"

Mischief replaced the pain in his eyes a split second before he grabbed at my waist and squeezed. I yelped like a scared puppy and tried to break free. He mistook my genuine reaction of panic for carefree joy and tickled me faster. I tried like hell to stop him, but the expression on his face halted me in my protests. His shielded eyes were free. They were gleaming and happy and full of life. Alastair's radiant smile lit up the entire room. When he finally stopped with his tickle assault, I giggled myself right into a bookcase sending several books tumbling off the shelf.

"Oh. I'm so sorry." I scrambled to pick them up.

"It's okay. I'll get them." He knelt down and gathered the escaped novels. Seeing him bent down on his knees made my heart flutter a little. When he glanced up at me, insecurity possessed his features for the briefest of seconds. He stood up quickly and shelved them.

"I've never had to rescue my books from a hysterically laughing, stumbling girl before."

"There's a first time for everything, right?"

The window into his soul snapped shut as he regained his calm, impassive demeanor. "I've arranged for your flight home, in case you were wondering."

His switch to all business was a little jarring.

"Which airline?"

"My plane."

Of course he has a plane. What normal, billionaire CFO in his early thirties doesn't? I hated that this was my initial reaction.

"Let's go for a ride to the hangar. That way you can see for yourself and I'll introduce you to the flight crew. If the plane looks too dodgy for your liking, we'll get you set up on a commercial airliner. Alright?"

He sounded so sincere; I'd be remiss to thumb my nose at his kind gesture.

"Sure."

"Brilliant. I'm going to shower. Wait for me in the living room."

* * *

Our drive out of Glasgow started off benignly enough. I settled into his gray Mercedes SLK55 Roadster comfortably. The interior was gorgeous; black with soft leather seats. Very sporty.

"Have you ever driven a car while in the UK?" He glanced at me out the corner of his eye.

"Nope."

"Would you like to try?"

"Driving? Here? No way."

"Why not?"

"First of all, I can't drive a stick. Plus, I don't want to be responsible for crashing your sexy little car."

Alastair laughed good and loud. "Sexy little car? Never heard it referred to that way before."

"So, do you always fly complete strangers thousands of miles on your private plane?" I asked as nonchalantly as I could.

"Not generally," he shrugged. "Why do you ask?"

"I was just wondering. Do you use it for business travel?"

"Mostly."

"You never just hop on it and tell the pilot to take you somewhere remote?"

"Hasn't crossed my mind to do that," he admitted. "Where would I go?"

"I don't know. Fiji?"

"You ask too many questions, kitten," he teased.

"Come on," I pressed. "You mean to tell me you don't go anywhere?"

"My life isn't as glamorous as you may think, Lia."

I grumbled to myself and got lost in the music for a bit. I knew what was coming. My curiosity was rather insatiable but I had a crazy need to know everything, especially when it came to people in Alastair's position. *I can blame Nathan for that.*

"Why didn't you tell me you were the heir to your grandfather's company?"

"I didn't know I had to."

"You didn't. But it's not a small detail."

"You clearly found out on your own," he answered stiffly, tightening his grip on the steering wheel. Up until this point, I'd been enjoying the way he handled the car; fluidly, controlled and confident. Now, he seemed annoyed.

"It just would have been nice if you'd told me yourself."

"Why does it matter?"

"I have my reasons," I said, grinding my teeth. "Or don't you know them already?"

"What are you talking about?" His voice was even and calm, but I could sense he was keeping something from me.

"People in your position often have an insatiable urge to investigate anyone who wants access to their inner circle."

Getting involved with a high profile person wasn't for the faint of heart. Not that we were 'involved.' My breakup with Nathan was still fresh and the emotional scars hadn't healed yet.

"I've been around this before," I continued. "You probably sent my name to your security team the day we met."

The blank expression on his face should have stopped my ramblings. Unfortunately, my insecurities were running wild.

"Lia, you're being—"

"What?" I interrupted, nearly shrieking. "I'm being paranoid? Ridiculous?" Anxiety hijacked my thought process. All my pent up hostility and hurt bubbled to the surface. "You're all alike. You guys turn stalking into a recreational sport."

Heavy silence filled the car. Only the growling drone of the engine made a sound. I sunk my nails into the leather seat, trying like hell to regain some semblance of my dignity.

We didn't speak for what seemed like ever. A burning lump slowly worked its way up my throat. I swallowed it down, wincing from the discomfort. Why did I have to say all that?

"Sorry," I whispered. Alastair nodded, keeping his eyes glued to the road.

A young man dressed in a security uniform greeted us at the airport's security gate.

"Hello, Mr. Holden. Nice to see you again." He leaned down to the window and peered in. Alastair greeted him and the two exchanged pleasantries. The guard pointed to a parking area by the hangar and directed Alastair to leave his car there. "Enjoy your flight, sir."

Apprehension seeped out of my pores. I wanted to kick myself for being such a lunatic with all my ridiculous questions and accusations. Goosebumps rose across my skin as a cool breeze gently blew across the tarmac. I stood next to the car, staring at the hangar. Alastair placed his hand at the small of my back, leading me inside.

Pointed toward the exit was a sleek, white Learjet. Two men were having a conversation by the wing. I blinked and swallowed hard, scanning the plane. It was stunning, like the kind celebrities used when they're jetting off to a premiere in the south of France. On the fuselage written in bold black letters was the name *Holden World Media*.

"Alastair, you don't have to do this. I can fly home on a regular plane. This is completely unnecessary."

"I promised your friend I'd get you home safely. I'm a man of my word." He waved someone over. "Kevin, this is Amelia Meyers. She'll be flying with you tomorrow."

Kevin smiled politely, extending his hand. I shook it firmly. "Good to see you, Miss Meyers. I understand you live in Orlando? I may schedule a longer layover for myself once we arrive. The beaches must be lovely this time of year."

I laughed in spite of myself. *Everyone loves the beach.* Alastair and Kevin talked shop for several minutes, so I strolled around the plane. In a word, it was huge. Avoiding coach with screaming kids and cramped spaces was a tempting idea.

"What do you think?" Alastair's velvety voice cut through the air.

"It's not that dodgy." I grinned.

"I'm glad you approve. It's all yours if you want to use it."

"I don't deserve your generosity."

When I looked into his eyes, they darkened. He grabbed my shoulders and brought our foreheads together. "Jesus Lia, just accept the gift," he whispered.

I froze. Even after all the bullshit I spouted off in the car, he still wanted to do this for me?

"If I agree to this, I'll be in your debt for, well, probably forever. I can't accept it, Alastair. I just can't."

I glanced at the gleaming white plane and sighed.

"Consider it, then? The crew knows to be ready if they're needed. You don't have to give me an answer now."

At some point, I had to believe that not every guy was a substandard human.

CHAPTER SEVEN

I curled up on the bed, snuggling into the pillows. Alastair was in the kitchen making us some tea. The floor creaked in the hallway as he made his way into the bedroom. The wooden tray he carried held the mugs along with milk, honey and sugar.

"I'm not sure how you take your tea, so I brought in everything."

"It's fine with just honey." I sat up and criss-crossed my legs.

Alastair squeezed a teaspoonful of honey into one of the mugs. He blew on the steaming drink and handed it to me carefully before sitting on the edge of the bed. We sipped in silence for a few minutes. The atmosphere in the room was heavy. Not uncomfortable, but certainly tinged with a level of uncertainty. A familiar pain began to grow and spread through my chest, suffocating me. For no good reason, my fingertips and toes turned into ice cubes. A distinct crushing sensation prevented any air from getting into my lungs properly.

"Hey," he whispered, noticing the change. "What's wrong?"

I sat as stiff as a board, clasping my hands around the mug until the knuckles turned white. Of all the times to have a panic attack, this had to be the worst.

"I'm fine."

"You are not fine," he admonished, taking the mug. "Your hands are freezing and you're pale."

My heart pounded, frantically trying to escape. I couldn't look at Alastair, not when I was in this state. Only the touch of his skin on mine kept me from going off the deep end. Closing my eyes, I focused on the warmth and softness of his hand on my cheek. It soothed me in a way I never expected.

The mattress jostled as he repositioned himself. Pulling me into his chest, he wrapped his arms around me, holding me tightly. I slid my arms around his waist, wanting to stay like this for the rest of the day. I wasn't even aware that he'd been whispering to me until his breath tickled my ear. Being surrounded by the feel and scent of him tamed my furious heart. I sighed heavily, nuzzling into his shirt.

"Your heartbeat slowed down," he said, unwrapping me from his embrace. I opened my eyes, stunned to see clear, bright emerald irises focused on me.

"How do you know?"

"I could feel it." He put my hand on his chest. "Right here. Hammering away like a scared rabbit."

That little grin could melt the polar ice caps. I smiled, feeling my cheeks heat up.

"I've made you smile. That's a good sign."

"Don't push your luck, Holden," I grinned, pushing him back gently.

"Feisty."

He pressed a small kiss to the corner of my mouth. The gentleness surprised me, making my brain go fuzzy.

"I have to go finish up some work. You can stay here and rest if you want, or roam around the house."

"Work? On a Sunday? I take it this isn't one of your free weekends?"

"Not quite as free as last weekend, no. We have some investors coming in tomorrow and I have to do a presentation. It won't take me long, I promise." He gracefully lifted himself off the bed and left the room.

I grabbed my phone and scrolled through a few emails. Nothing from Stephanie yet. It was only quarter past four. She still had another few hours before arriving in Orlando. I decided to do a little exploring, as Alastair suggested. I hadn't really been able to see the whole house yet, and since he was busy, I could snoop around uninterrupted.

Slipping off the bed, I walked to the hall and through the kitchen. For some reason, I really wanted to see his living room, which I assumed was where he'd spend the majority of his time relaxing.

Plush cream carpets spread from wall to wall. On the far side of the room was a fireplace. Two oversized, charcoal gray couches were set in the center. Neutral tones were prevalent throughout, with subtle, rich accents of color.

It was gorgeous, but lacked the cozy, homey feeling I felt at the cottage. Aside from a large black and white photo of London, there weren't any personal effects. No photos of friends, no photos of family, and, most notably, no photos of a girlfriend. I leaned against one of the couches, grazing my fingers on the material. *Beautiful, but too perfect.* A person's home should reflect who they were, inside and out. All I gathered from Alastair's home were things I already knew about him: pristine, elegant and well put together. *Another mask to hide his true self.*

Sighing, I went back to the bedroom and read a little. Once the sun dipped below the horizon, I couldn't ignore the hunger pangs gnawing at my stomach.

I crept down the hallway to Alastair's office. The door was wide open. He was leaning back in his chair reading through a folder with his feet propped up on the desk. He looked almost regal as he pinched his lips between his thumb and forefinger. Even in jeans and a sweater, he was the epitome of quiet control and power. It was sexy as hell.

"Hi."

"Hello." He placed the folder down, waving me in. "Did you

have a nice time snooping around?"

"I wouldn't call it snooping. More like a self-guided tour. Did you get all your work done?"

"More or less."

Something in his stare made me flush. He looked at me with such longing it unnerved me. I averted my gaze and turned to the cluster of photos hanging on the wall. I was still so drawn to the sad little boy in the leaves.

"What are you doing?" The deceptively calm intonation in Alastair's voice caught me off guard. When I spun around, a bone-chilling stare greeted me. "These photos aren't that interesting."

"They are to me."

"*Why?*"

"Well, this photo—"

"Forget about the damn photo for now, please." Alastair's brows slashed down. His entire body was rigid and unyielding. Mask or not, he suddenly appeared uncomfortable in his skin. Except for his eyes. They were securely shrouded.

"Sorry," I mumbled.

"Be careful, kitten. You know what they say about curiosity." He approached with slow, calculating strides. I was his prey, he was my predator. The crazy thing was, deep down, I didn't mind. I wanted him to pursue me. I wanted to be chased. It was the being caught part that scared me.

There were so many things about him I still didn't know. Those eyes had a story. They were veiled for a reason. He kept himself just open and friendly enough to lure everyone in. He only let people see what he wanted them to see.

"You're so deep in thought again."

Without warning, he grabbed my shoulders and kissed me. Next thing I knew, the wall was at my back and every toned, beautiful inch of him was pressed against me. His kiss was searing and unapologetic. I arched my back, pushing myself into him. A delicious, body-melting tingle coursed through me as he deepened the kiss.

Before I could put my hands on him, he lifted both my arms over my head and held them firmly against the wall. Not being able to touch him drove me insane. I groaned into his mouth and wrapped my leg around him. Alastair tore his lips away from mine and stared at me. He released my arms to slide his hands along my jaw. Adrenaline spiked through me. His animalistic stare was white hot.

"That was unexpected," I said, panting.

"We're even now," he declared.

"Are we?"

He nodded, brushing his lips against mine. As I lost myself in the lingering softness of his kisses, I couldn't help but wonder if his heart was racing as fast as mine. He ran his hand through the back of my hair, pulling it. Need and want overpowered me. My addiction to him was irreversible.

We stared at one another, muddled in a lustful haze. I ran my thumb back and forth over his lips. He leaned his forehead on mine, his expression softening. I touched his jaw, his cheeks and ran my fingers through his hair.

"You're so beautiful, Alastair."

"I'm glad you like what you see." He straightened his spine, staring through me. A myriad of emotions twisted through his handsome face before disappearing abruptly. My skin reacted negatively to the loss of heat when he pushed away from me. Craving his closeness, I followed him as he walked toward the cluster of photos, stroking my swollen lips. I couldn't tear my eyes away from him while he stared at the photo of his younger self. His reticent expression gave nothing away. He cleared his throat, not moving his eyes from the photograph.

"My parents and sister died when I was very young. We were hit head on by someone who'd fallen asleep at the wheel while driving home from a family picnic."

Tears flooded my eyes. He saw them and winced.

"Please don't pity me, Lia. I can't take any more tears out of pity."

"I'm sorry," I whispered. "I didn't know. I really...I didn't know."

Disbelief washed over his face. It disappeared quickly as he reattached his stoic mask.

"I wanted for nothing growing up. My dad's brother, Jason, and his wife, Katherine, raised me as their own."

"How old were you?"

"Six."

"So that photo—"

"It was taken several months after the accident."

I hastily brushed away tears, not liking the wary glances he was shooting at me. "Thanks for—"

"What happened before shouldn't have," he interrupted. "It won't happen again."

What? The kiss? He must be joking. I was completely dumbstruck. Not to mention catastrophically disappointed. He kept avoiding my gaze. It was beyond annoying.

"Alastair—"

"You're a beautiful, sweet girl. You have no business being with someone like me."

"Stop interrupting me." I folded my arms, giving him a look. The corner of his mouth ticked up into a slight smile. I worked fast to capitalize on his softened mood.

"Listen, you can't be all flirty and charming and kiss me like that, then put restrictions on it. I mean, you can, but—"

"You think I'm flirty and charming?"

"Again with the interrupting."

Apparently teasing me was more than just a pastime for him. I smiled in spite of this baffling conversation. His pretty eyes dropped their impenetrable shield just a bit.

"Don't be coy with me, Holden."

"Wouldn't dream of it," he said with a sly grin.

"You're an enigma. You're lucky I know how to handle people like you."

He laughed loudly, the tension and discomfort dropping away from him in bits and pieces. "Are you hungry?"

"A little."

"Care for some dessert?"

"Dessert?" I became all giddy and excited. "Sure."

Alastair instructed me to wait for him in the living room. He set out a bottle of vintage port and a couple of glasses before retreating to the kitchen to prepare dessert. I found myself staring at the large black and white photo hanging on the wall. The entire picture was devoid of color, except for a double decker bus passing in front of Big Ben. It was colored with a vibrant red.

"Do you like that?" The silkiness of his accent massaged my senses.

"It's amazing. Where did you get it?"

"I took it myself."

"Really? Wow. It looks so professional."

"Thank you." He looked at the photo, then at me. "I also took the one of the skyline hanging in my bedroom. It was just a little hobby of mine."

"Do you have any more?"

"Not here. They're in storage back in England."

"One of the guys I work with in Orlando is an amateur photographer. He's always sticking a lens in my face when we have parties. It's annoying at times, but he does a really nice job, so I don't mind."

"I don't think I ever asked you what you did for a living."

"I produce the local news. Nothing exciting at all," I shook my head, turning back to the picture.

"You must photograph beautifully."

I snorted. "What? No."

"I beg to differ. You have such delicate, soft features. Full lips." He pressed a kiss to them. "Perfect little button nose." Another kiss. "Expressive eyes. Those alone would make a gorgeous portrait. Maybe I'll get the chance to photograph you one day."

Snaking his fingers behind my neck, he kissed me so passionately my knees almost gave out. This was happening too fast, but I didn't want to stop him. I cherished the way his lips moved so effortlessly on mine. The tender warmth of his tongue stroked mine with such reverence it made my insides quiver.

"I thought we weren't supposed to do this anymore," I whispered.

"We aren't," he said, kissing me again. "You make me--"

A buzzer went off somewhere in the universe. I jolted out of my daze and watched Alastair move toward the kitchen. *I make him what?* Only one thing dominated my thoughts; him. He consumed me. My body ached for him in a way I didn't know was humanly possible.

"It's ready," he poked his head into the room. "Join me, won't you?"

I shuffled into the kitchen. The breakfast bar was set with two napkins and a steaming bowl of chocolate bread pudding. The sweet scent of buttery cocoa surrounded us. I climbed onto the stool next to him.

"There's only one spoon."

"Nothing gets past you," he said dryly and handed it to me. "Here."

I took the spoon and scooped out a gooey hunk. It was warm and sweet and sinful. I passed the spoon to him and watched impatiently as he dug into the pudding. He lifted the spoon to his lips and paused briefly. The way his mouth wrapped around it forced me to cross my legs. A small dab of chocolate on the corner of his mouth distracted me. I impulsively reached over and wiped it away, sucking it off the pad of my thumb.

"Chocolate and Alastair. Quite the flavor combination."

Our eyes locked and a noticeable change in atmosphere engulfed us. He ran the spoon through the pudding, holding up another scoop. A sultry, dark veil cloaked his eyes.

"Open," he commanded quietly.

My lips parted as he traced my bottom lip with the spoon before smoothly moving it over my tongue. We never broke eye contact. Closing my mouth, I grabbed his hand to keep it in place. Alastair shifted on his seat, watching me suck the pudding off the spoon. His features lost some of their hard edge, revealing more of his youthful beauty. When I finally released his hand, he exhaled.

"Something on your mind, Lia?"

"Not particularly." I licked my lips. "You?"

He grinned alluringly. "I'd like to finish this first before we share any private thoughts." He took another slow, deliberate bite of the bread pudding. "Would you like more?"

"Yes, please."

Alastair lifted another steamy scoop. A little dab of chocolate threatened to fall off. Holding the spoon up, he stroked his tongue against it, capturing the wayward pudding. Perspiration misted over my body as my breathing became labored.

"Open."

My jaw went slack waiting for him. I trembled, anticipating his closeness. The way he fed me was so effortless and careful. There was no way in hell I'd be able to eat dessert normally ever again. He kept feeding me spoonful after spoonful. I wasn't even hungry anymore; I just wanted this to continue. He brushed a few strands of hair out of my face and fed me one last time.

"You're a messy eater." Hooded, lustrous eyes pierced through me. He leaned in, pulled my bottom lip into his mouth and sucked off the pudding. An animalistic, full-bodied groan came from somewhere deep inside me. I clutched the back of the stool as he licked along my lips.

"Dessert tastes divine on you," he said, sliding his hand up my thigh, kissing me deeply. I couldn't concentrate on anything. *We can kiss, we can't kiss, we can kiss. What the hell…?*

"You're making my head spin." I barely got the words out.

"Imagine what you're doing to mine," he whispered.

CHAPTER EIGHT

The cold water shocked my skin as I waited for it to warm. Alastair was in the kitchen cleaning up. I grasped the edge of the marble counter, concentrating on the air as it filled and expanded my lungs. Doubt tickled and flickered through my innermost thoughts.

I finished washing my face and gathered the rest of my toiletries. Alastair was sitting on the bed when I walked back into the room. I quickly put my belongings on the suitcase. He reached out his hand, looking at me intently. Hesitating, I went to him, wedging myself between his legs, my head still spinning.

He kissed the palm of my hand, then seemingly searched the room for some type of divine intervention. It unnerved me. A sense of dread pricked along my skin. Tons of questions swirled in my mind while butterflies fluttered through my stomach. His smoldering intensity was still there but it was muted.

I bowed my head, unable to look directly at him.

"Don't do that." He tipped my chin up. "I need to see your eyes."

"Why?"

"It's the only way I know what you're really thinking."

Flustered, I sucked in a breath.

"What are we doing? I'm…I'm leaving tomorrow. I can't—"

"I know," he said, verdant eyes flashing. "We shouldn't take this any further."

His words ripped through my soul with a searing intensity far beyond anything I expected to feel. My heart dropped into a bottomless pit at the exact moment my walls went up, echoing through my mind. I jerked my hand away from his, nearly losing my balance.

"Let me explain," he said calmly.

"Explain what?"

"This," he gestured to himself and me. "I can't give you what you need, I can only give you what you want."

"What I want? You have no idea what I want," I glowered.

"Yes, I do. It's in your eyes. It's been in your eyes since the moment I caught you."

I stared at him, annoyed by his nonchalant arrogance. "So if you claim to have known all this time, why did you come on so strongly? Even after I told you I didn't want to be a one-night stand for you. You sure as hell laid it on pretty thick. Is this fun for you?" I stopped short, an unpleasant realization dawning on me. "You have a girlfriend, don't you?"

"No. I don't date. Relationships are too messy."

"So, what then?" I lashed out, my thoughts scattered. "You thought you'd get some action from a tourist? Seduce me with your little dessert stunt, then fuck me and drop me off at the airport?"

He looked at me, stunned, almost as though I'd slapped him across the face. Wow. My filter was long gone. But I was emboldened. This seductive dance we'd engaged in was obviously just a game to him. I could feel him withdrawing from me. The humid heat between us disappeared, leaving me chilled to the bone. I tried to let my emotions settle but knowing I was being irrational wasn't enough to stop me from careening off Mount Hysteria. I was in full defense mode; strike first and get out, before getting hurt.

Tilting his head, he regarded me cautiously. "There's always a woman out there who thinks getting close to me physically translates into a meaningful relationship. It doesn't. I have…" he paused, hesitating, "rules when it comes to this."

"What does that even mean?"

A distant, detached expression slid into place so fast it mesmerized me.

"The women I'm intimate with are just that. There's nothing above and beyond the sex. They get what they want, and so do I. If they don't like it, they can walk away at any time. Or I'll end it."

I was horrified. He treated what was supposed to be a mutual closeness between two people like a merger with provisions. I glanced at him. He looked as he did sitting in his office; serious, focused, professional. The small glimpse I'd seen of his vulnerable side was securely locked behind his shield once more.

"You're in luck then because I don't want anything from you. Clearly, I've perfected the art of being attracted to the wrong people."

Clenching his jaw, he sighed heavily. "Wrong how?"

I groaned and gave him a look. "Just *wrong*. I don't know what your deal is but this sex-with-no-attachment-thing isn't the type of relationship I'm into. It sounds too cold."

"This is the way it has to be."

"And you don't deviate from this rule?"

"No."

I must be a magnet for people like this. Either that, or I was so awed by his well-rehearsed charm I'd neglected to pay attention to my instincts. *Dumb, dumb, stupid, dumb.* He studied my face, gauging my reaction.

"I don't know what you want me to say, Alastair. You're like two different people. Which one of you is real? The one I met last week or the one I'm being introduced to right now?" I bit out. "You've managed to screw with my mind. Is that what you were going for? Or were you going to take it all the way and, oh, how did you put it. 'Get what you want?' I am sick of being used and tossed aside by guys like you."

"Lia." His husky whisper demanded my attention. "Look at me."

Shaking, I looked into his seraphic, emerald eyes. The night was slipping away from me and I was powerless to stop it. *What am I doing? Control, Lia. Get control.* "I need to get out of here." My voice quivered and broke.

"Hush." He leaned his forehead against mine. I closed my eyes, fighting every instinct I had to bolt out the door. "Quiet your mind."

Every caress he made soothed me. I held onto his shoulders to steady myself. Being so close to him silenced the persistent, overbearing voices of insecurity. Little by little, my muscles relaxed, my mind stopped racing and I found my equilibrium.

"I…" he started, then paused. "You've seen more of the real me than anyone."

The small tremble in his voice shook me to the core. There it was again, the flash of vulnerability. A hot, salty lump formed in my throat.

"My ex-boyfriend is a controlling, possessive bastard who stalks me," I blurted out. "I was nothing more than an accessory to him; someone to control and decorate with fancy dresses and sparkling jewelry and use for sex only when he deemed it necessary." My soul laid naked on the floor, shocked that it was released so haphazardly.

Alastair's body stiffened. He loosened my grip on him, looking up at me. He sat so quietly and still, I wasn't sure he was even breathing. Discomfort filled every muscle and cell in my body.

"Did he hurt you?"

"Not physically."

I still couldn't get a read on what he was thinking. His expression was so blank. Being caught between his thighs wasn't very comfortable anymore.

"What's his name?"

"It doesn't matter."

"The hell it doesn't," he hissed. "Tell me his name."

"No. I've had enough of people telling me what to do." I pushed away from him, walking to the center of the room. Seconds later, a hand grasped my shoulder. I spun around, knocking Alastair's arm away. "Don't."

"I didn't mean to upset you. I'm only trying to help."

"You really want to help me? Forget this guy exists."

"Lia, you're shaking," he whispered, reaching for my hand. Closing my eyes, I let him slide his fingers through mine. His touch had become a soothing balm, which as much as I hated to admit, I needed. The warmth of his body surrounded me as he held me. I needed to be closer. I needed to touch him. Resting my head against his chest, I ran my fingers along the waistband of his jeans, sliding them up beneath his sweater. He sighed when I made contact with the skin at the small of his back, a low moan vibrating in his throat.

How could he be so comforting and so frustrating? I wanted to believe that I'd seen more of who he really was than anyone. I lost myself in the increased rhythm of his heartbeat and deep, heavy breaths. Nuzzling his nose into my neck, he whispered something unintelligible on my skin. As I lifted my head, his lips met mine. I ached for him, craving his touch. I sighed into his lush kiss, melting in his arms.

Sliding his hands over my hips, he snuck them under my shirt. My skin welcomed his touch, warming immediately. It was a rush, a frisson of excitement that sent tremors through me. He groaned, sucking my bottom lip into his mouth, biting it gently.

"What are you thinking about?" he asked, pulling my hips into him. The friction from his arousal rubbing against me made me gasp.

"Why?"

"This look you have right now," he growled. "Flushed cheeks with gleaming eyes. This is how you looked when we met. Do you know how hard it is to control myself when you look like this?"

"Keep kissing me." I didn't recognize the sound of my own voice. It was so low and breathy.

Alastair looked me in the eye steadily. I held his electric gaze, not breathing. He crushed his lips to mine, banding his arms under my backside and lifting me off the floor. I was barely aware of the movement. I sank into the plush softness of the mattress as he laid me on his bed. Hovering over me, he dragged his eyes down my body.

He lowered his head, kissing the crook of my neck while unbuttoning my jeans. I tilted my hips up so he could pull them off without much difficulty. Pressing his lips and tongue harder on my neck, he sucked a soft patch of skin into his mouth.

"Are you trying to mark me?" I buried my fingers in his thick hair. His only response was a muffled grunt. As good as it felt, I wanted his mouth somewhere else.

He traced his fingers along the edge of my lace boy shorts. "This," he whispered, inching his finger along the thin material, "is too wet to stay on." My toes curled as he deftly ripped it off.

"We should— oh my God!"

He slipped a finger inside me so quickly I lost my train of thought and all command of language.

"It's my turn to take you by surprise, love." His stare was fiercely sensual and dark. "We should what? Is this what you want?"

"Yes," I moaned while he slid his finger in and out, excruciatingly slowly. Clasping his shoulders, I focused on nothing but his touch. A second finger joined the unhurried, rhythmic movements of the one already tantalizing me. As he massaged me, my eyelids fluttered closed.

"Look at me," Alastair ordered thickly. I snapped my head up and held his dominating stare. It was all too much; his eyes, his fingers, his ragged breathing. I closed them again.

"Open. Your. Eyes."

His breath tickled my ear, awakening parts of me I didn't know existed. My lids popped open. He kissed me, curling his fingers.

All my muscles clenched viciously. I gasped, breaking our mouths apart. His eyes glittered a vibrant green as he watched me lose myself in him. The delicious, warm climb that I hadn't felt in ages ravaged me. Pressing his cheek to mine, he stroked my inner thigh. "Don't come yet."

I writhed beneath him as he repositioned himself between my legs. The second his tongue flicked against my hypersensitive skin I jerked my hips up. He splayed his fingers across my stomach, holding me down. A slow burn spread through me, blossoming out from where he expertly worked me with his mouth. I clawed at the sheets.

"Alastair." I arched my back, rolling my hips.

Hooking his arms under my thighs, he clamped his hands down on my legs, preventing any further movement. I dug my heels into the mattress. The velvet warmth of his tongue entered me once, twice, then withdrew, circling my clit. He sealed his mouth against it, sucking softly. The exquisite sensation seared me. I grabbed a handful of his hair and pulled. He sucked harder, setting off an orgasm so powerful I launched myself backwards and smacked into the headboard.

He wouldn't stop. I tensed and shook with anticipation before descending into another fuzzy oblivion, moaning his name. Euphoria trickled through me, relaxing each and every muscle. I sank further into the bed, enjoying the soft kisses he placed along each inner thigh and up to my stomach.

The heaviness of his body surrounded me. Pressing his hands into the mattress on either side of my shoulders, he lowered his head so his face was inches from mine.

"That sounded like it hurt," he grinned lazily.

"What?" I looked at his amused expression, totally baffled.

He rapped his knuckles on the headboard before stretching out next to me. "That was a pretty big whack. I hope you don't get a lump."

"I...this...are you seriously making fun of me right now?" I rolled over to face him.

"Not at all," he answered, kissing my nose. "You okay, love?"

"I'm fine." I narrowed my eyes at him. "You should really come with a warning label. 'May cause embarrassing, uncharacteristic episodes.'"

The bed shook from his laughter. I could only fight back my own giggles for a few seconds before I joined him. I savored this moment, reveling in his sexy playfulness. Tiny slivers of insecurity tried to spoil the delicious morsels of pleasure that still flowed through my body. Alastair lay quiet next to me, his laughter subsiding into a satisfied smile.

"You're staring."

"Am I?" I propped my head up in my hand. "Your eyes are closed. I could be making a face at you for all you know."

"I know everything, kitten." Moving fast, he pinned me on my back, sitting on my legs with his hands at my waist. His mischievous stare was scintillating.

"Alastair Holden, don't you *dare*."

He smiled so widely I was afraid his face would split in two. God, I loved the way he looked poised above me, ready for anything. I squealed in shock at the quick squeeze on my waist.

"There's that look again."

"What are you going to do? Tickle it off my face?" I smirked.

Dipping his head so our noses touched, he grinned. "I'll save that for another time." He leaned back, climbing off me to sit. I pushed myself up so we faced each other, our knees touching.

My brush with euphoria dissipated the second I saw his expression. He was pale. The frantic thumping of my heart ceased.

"What are you doing to me?" He directed his question more toward the mattress than me.

"Excuse me?"

"You make me…" he said, his eyes widening.

"What? I make you what?" I swallowed back a healthy dose of fear.

He clasped his stomach and for a minute I thought he might be sick. I didn't know where to look or what to do. I tried not to let my mind race again, but he looked so lost.

"I booked you on a flight in case you were wondering."

He switched gears so fast, I half expected to get whiplash.

"Right," I said quietly. "On your plane."

"No. A commercial airliner. It leaves in the morning. I can— Lia, it's done. No arguments. I can drop you off at the airport on my way to work."

I folded my arms, marveling at how he switched from hot to cold and back with almost zero effort. "Fine. Thank you."

"You're welcome. Sleeping arrangements, then. You can have my bed again and I'll camp out in my office."

What? A streak of desperation surged through me. "You're not staying with me?"

He didn't answer right away, which sent me back into panic mode. I rubbed my head to quiet the dull ache.

"I'll stay," he murmured, avoiding my gaze. The nagging sliver of insecurity gained some momentum. I became acutely aware that I was naked from the waist down and my underwear was in pieces somewhere on the floor.

"Um, I just need to get some pants or something," I muttered, getting off the bed. Rummaging through the suitcase, I grabbed the first thing I touched. Gray yoga pants. Jackpot.

I crawled under the blankets, waiting for him to join me. The bed shifted as he moved closer, curling up next to me. Ignoring an impulse to wrap myself around him, I folded my arms up under the pillow instead.

"Thank you for letting me stay here. I um, I hope I haven't been too much of a burden."

"My pleasure," he said, brushing his knuckles down my cheek. "And you've not been a burden."

"Next time you're in the States, you'll have to come to Orlando."

"Would you like that?" he asked, almost with a touch of uncertainty.

"Yes."

He stared at me, expressionless, a hazy film covering his eyes.

My heart twisted. *He's withdrawing again.* He sighed, pulling me flush against his chest. Sliding his hand over my waist, he rested it on my backside. I hooked my leg between his, fitting with him like a puzzle piece. We were intertwined in such a way that there was no telling where he ended and I began.

"Sleep, my Lia. I'll be right here when you wake up."

* * *

Whimpering and moaning filled the room. Rousing from sleep, I found most of my face buried in a thick mass of dark red hair. Alastair's head was nestled on my chest, his body blanketing me with warmth. The grip he had on me was borderline uncomfortable. I attempted to reposition myself without disturbing him too much.

He whined, strengthening his hold. "You always *leave.*"

I moved again, trying to free myself. His fingers dug into my back. I pressed my hand against his chest, gently pushing him away.

"*No.* Don't leave," he hissed through clenched teeth. "It was my fault."

Shit. He's dreaming.

He continued muttering incoherently, becoming more frantic. I was afraid to wake him in the throes of a nightmare but he was crushing me.

"Alastair," I whispered. "Wake up. Please."

"*DON'T LEAVE!* I didn't mean to! I'm sorry. I'm sorry. *I'm sorry!*"

He pushed away from me, sitting up gasping. I scrambled to the edge of the bed. Moonlight streamed in through the windows, casting a pallid glow on the sheen of sweat covering him. The t-shirt he had on stuck to his damp skin. His breathing was harsh and ragged. An overwhelming urge to comfort him flowed through me.

I sat up, keeping my eyes glued to him. He stared straight ahead, his eyes still smoky with sleep. The sheets were fisted in his hands.

A few moments later, full consciousness took control. He inhaled deeply and looked at me. Tears stained his face, breaking my heart.

"Why are you looking at me like that?"

I raised my eyebrows in surprise. "You've had one hell of a nightmare."

"Oh." The muscles in his jaw twitched. "Sorry."

"Don't apologize. Want to tell me about it?"

"No." He threw off the blankets and stormed out of the room.

His reaction left me stunned for a minute. I was about to follow him, when he came back in with a glass of water. He drank a bit then slid under the covers. Nothing about his demeanor revealed that he'd been crying out in his sleep. The tear-stains were gone along with any signs of distress. He was the same calm, cool-as-ice guy as always. I climbed back into bed and crawled closer to him, hugging into his body. I kissed along his neck and jaw, before pressing my lips to his forehead.

"Hey." He tangled his fingers through my hair. "What's wrong?"

I looked into his tired, questioning eyes. I could only imagine how many nights he'd woken up alone, screaming in the dark.

"Nothing." I kissed him. He rolled us over, the weight of his body pressing me into the mattress. He nuzzled into my neck before leaning his cheek to mine.

"I'm glad you're here," he whispered, wrapping himself around me protectively. I held him close, stroking his hair. He blew a shaky sigh against my neck before relaxing into my embrace. I whispered to him until his breathing became slow and heavy. The peace and refuge of sleep dissolved any veiled edge his face held when he was awake. *How many people have seen him this way? Unguarded and vulnerable.*

I watched him sleep until the first rays of sunlight poked through the windows.

CHAPTER NINE

Telephones rang in a disjointed symphony, a cacophony of sound so jarring it could wake the dead. I glanced up from my computer and stared out into the newsroom. It was the second week of May and we were in the middle of a breaking story.

A short, blonde haired woman ran toward me, clutching her bouncing chest.

"Amelia."

"Yes, Jeanie?"

"I need you. Louise is already in the booth, the writers are up to their ears in video and copy, and Vanessa is freaking out about her package. She's looking for a sound bite from the transportation presser. Can you find it? Thanks."

She waltzed off without waiting for an answer. I fumed, aiming a laser stare at her departing backside. I watched her return to her desk, sit in her little slouched position and stare blankly at the computer screen. *Yes, you're so very busy. Don't want to miss the online early bird sale at Beals?* I normally didn't mind helping out a co-worker, but Jeanie Arrington grated on my last nerve.

"She's something, isn't she?"

I flicked my eyes to Sydney Makeeda, my co-worker and cubemate.

"Yep. 'Something' fits her perfectly."

Sydney laughed. "Bet you ten bucks she'll take the credit for finding the sound bite."

I sighed, clicking on the file labeled *media*. The transportation department was dealing with a nightmare on I-4, the main freeway that everyone in Central Florida used at least once a day.

One of the lanes on the eastbound side, midway between Orlando and Lake Mary, had developed a good-sized sinkhole, paralyzing traffic. They were scrambling to get it fixed so people didn't have to spend two hours in their cars for a drive that usually took thirty minutes. I found something decent and emailed it to the editor.

The set was lit up under bright television lights as our evening anchor team, Cynthia Steele and Vance Winters, meandered to the desk fidgeting with their microphones. They droned on about the sinkhole when the show went live.

I glanced at the rundown for the eleven o'clock show and started rearranging some of the stories. The hair that was piled loosely on my head started to slip. I reached up to adjust the makeshift bun, but it was being disobedient so I yanked out the elastic and tossed it on the desk.

"Giving up on the all-business look?" Tyler Garrett mused, sauntering over.

"Shouldn't you be at the assignment desk on a pretend phone call?" I smiled.

"Probably. Are we all going out? You've been back since last week and still haven't told us about the big trip to Scotland."

"I know, I know," I said, pulling my hair back into a ponytail. "We're going to The Cottage, right?"

Meeting at the local bar and restaurant was a Friday night ritual for us if we had to work on the late broadcast.

"Yep. Wes is coming too. I'm assuming you'll be there, Sydney?"

"I'll go for a little while," she said.

"Hey, Tyler," Gus yelled from the assignment desk, his voice ricocheting through the rafters. "Cops are on the phone. They have new details about the highway."

Leaning his body against my desk, Tyler exhaled until his lungs were empty. "If either of you get there before me, order me my regular."

He threw his head back and plodded his way to the desk. A chronic chain smoker and whiskey drinker, Tyler was the hub of cynical fun. As he'd put it, "*Not bad for a chubby Jewish kid from Atlanta.*"

Sydney leaned forward, clasping the small divider between our desks. "You have been way too quiet about this vacation. If there's anything you don't want the boys to know, spill it now."

I feigned an innocent look and glanced at her. She smiled, drumming her fingers.

"There's not much to tell."

"Come on, Lia. I'm married with two kids. My husband thinks switching from Coors Light to Heineken is exciting. You were surrounded by hot men in kilts for a week. I live vicariously through you."

I laughed, continuing my dissection of the evening's rundown. "I'd hate to disappoint you, seeing as you think my life is so exciting, but the only kilts I saw were in display windows on mannequins."

"Fine," she pouted.

I hadn't spoken a word about Alastair to any of my friends at work. The last thing I needed was a barrage of questions from nosy journalists, producers and writers about the media heir I'd been cozy with. Especially since the news broke that Holden World Media bought several network affiliate stations in the U.S., including one right here in Orlando. It was all everyone talked about since I'd been back.

Plus, I hadn't heard from him at all. We'd exchanged email addresses the morning I left, but I didn't expect him to write. He'd been distant and preoccupied on the ride to the airport. After getting my suitcase out of the car, he'd stood with me on the sidewalk, memorizing my face as though he'd never see me again.

"Go to the terminal," he'd finally said.

"Walk with me?"

A pained expression blanketed his features. I hooked my fingers through his belt and pulled him closer. His muscles strained when we made contact.

"Lia. You have to go."

I'd wrapped my arms around his waist, pressing my cheek to his chest. He'd smelled so good. The clean scent of body wash had filled my lungs. The rapid beating of his heart hypnotized me. I didn't know how long we'd stayed like that, mostly because I'd had a bad feeling that if I let him go, he'd run. He'd get in the car, drive off and I'd be nothing but a distant memory.

He'd tilted my chin up, a tiny smile curving his mouth. Seeing it calmed me down, but not much.

"Have a safe flight, love."

That had been it. He'd released me from his embrace and got in the car.

Two piercing, high-pitched tones shook me free of my thoughts. It was an alert from the Associated Press. I clicked on it, expecting to see something about the debt crisis or new unemployment rates. It was from the international wires and it was all about Samuel Holden's retirement party. My curiosity shot off the scales. I opened an internet browser and searched for any stories on the event.

What I saw hit me like a truck. There was a photo of Alastair, smiling and looking gorgeous. Next to him, or rather, draped on him like an over-styled, over-designed blonde ornament was Sarah. She was touching him, and not in the way people do when they're casually posed in a photo. Her hand was resting against his stomach, the way lovers who know one another intimately touch. His arm was wrapped around her waist, providing an excuse for her body to press into his side.

Bile rose high enough in my throat to threaten an oncoming tidal wave. I swallowed hard, forcing it down through my burning, constricted esophagus. *I'm so fucking stupid.*

"Ooh, who is that?"

I jumped, scrambling to minimize my browser.

"Nobody, Sydney." The thick layer of dread coating my throat made my voice sound deeper.

"He's hot. Look at all that gorgeous hair," she said, leaning over my shoulder. "Alastair Holden – *yum* – grandson to British media tycoon Samuel Holden, arrives at his family's estate in Ascot, England for his grandfather's retirement celebration. He's accompanied by Sarah Everett, Vice President of the prestigious Finley Marketing and Advertising Group based in Glasgow. Well, well. What a fancy schmancy little party that must have been."

I exhaled as soon as she stood up straight.

"Holden…Holden…Didn't they just buy WTDO a couple weeks ago?"

"I don't know."

Go sit down. Please go back to your seat and sit down. Sit. Sit. SIT.

"Yeah, they did," she confirmed more to herself than to me. "You were on vacation. I overheard Bruce talking to Vincent Jennings about it. Apparently some of the higher ups are flying over from England this weekend. Maybe that young stud will be one of them."

Oh thank God, she finally sat down.

"You should call Grant and see if he can…."

Sydney yammered on and on about how I should try to work my contacts so we could go to the HWM event on Sunday. I told her to stop being ridiculous.

"We're the competition, Syd. The last thing they want is one of us snooping around their backyard."

"It wouldn't be snooping." She tapped the desk with her pen for emphasis.

"Whatever," I muttered, closing the tab so I didn't have to see that picture anymore. My inbox was now staring me in the face, and I had a new email.

To: Amelia Meyers <ameyers@wmzb.net>

From: Alastair Holden <aholden@holdenworldmedia.co.uk>
Subject:

Hello Amelia,

I see you're having a busy night at work. Sinkholes? Sounds dreadful. Sorry you haven't heard from me. Work was busier than I anticipated. As you've no doubt heard, we are the proud owners of some news stations in the States. One is even in Orlando. It's not yours though, I checked.

I'm just relaxing now after my grandfather's retirement party. Was thinking of you and wanted to say hello.

Write when you have a chance.

Yours, Alastair x

A tsunami of emotion flooded me. There were too many things in that email for me to process.

He's thinking of me?

Heat blossomed through my lower abdomen, giving me an unexpected rush. An image of his gorgeous mouth popped into my head, along with what he did with it.

Stop it. You're being ridiculous.

"Are you okay?"

I looked up, surprised to see that I was clutching the desk.

"I'm fine, Sydney."

Two icky, sweaty palm prints marked the spot my hands occupied on the desk after I lifted them. I closed my email account and went back to the rundown. I had to; otherwise I'd spend the rest of the night obsessing over everything. I didn't stop revising scripts for the next two hours. By the time the late night news team signed off the air, I was ready to claw out of my own skin. I grabbed my car keys and walked out into the muggy night air.

If I hadn't agreed to go to The Cottage, I would have hightailed it home.

Tyler was nursing a Jack and Coke at the bar and shoving nachos in his mouth when I got there. An old school Journey song pulsed from the speakers.

"Well, well. Look who's already drinking their troubles away," I remarked.

Tyler rolled his eyes and took another long sip. He sized me up, opened his mouth to give one of his trademark responses, but put the glass to his lips again. I ordered a sparkling water with lime and sat down. Sydney waltzed through the door with Wesley Jenkins not too far behind. They were bickering about the broadcast.

I spent the next hour telling them about my trip. Being inquisitive news people, they had a zillion questions. I answered everything as best I could, even the ridiculous ones from Tyler.

"So, like, what exactly did you eat for food over there? Don't they like sheep guts in Scotland?"

"It's called haggis," I retorted. "And it's not sheep guts. It's more like a savory pudding."

"Yeah right. A pudding served in a sheep's stomach lining," Wesley snorted.

"Okay, that's enough. If it makes you feel any better, I ate nothing but neeps and tatties."

"Lia, I don't understand your crazy British talk. The least you could have done was wave hello to the Queen for me." Tyler stood up and saluted at us. "I'm off people. See y'all Monday."

It was nearly one in the morning when Sydney, Wes and I walked out, yet the steamy Orlando weather was still bearing down on us.

"It feels like I'm walking into a sponge." I tugged at my t-shirt and frowned. "Bye, guys."

My little yellow Fiat sat all by itself under a light in the parking lot. By force of habit, I walked to it quickly, remotely unlocking it as I approached so the interior light popped on. There had been many times over the course of the last year that I'd have a note or a rose waiting for me on the windshield, courtesy of Nathan. I thought it was cute at first. Then it became creepy, especially when stuff would be waiting for me when I hadn't told him where I was going. At one point, I'd considered renting a car so he wouldn't know where to find me.

Scanning the car with a quick walk around it, I checked the back, then sank into the leather seat and sighed. I pulled out of the parking lot, turned the radio up and tried to sing along with Coldplay about ruling the world.

Once I got home, I grabbed my laptop and collapsed onto the couch. It was so quiet in the living room I could hear the air scraping through my lungs. Against the better judgment of almost anyone else on the planet, I opened my email. His message was still sitting there, daring me to open it and respond. Did I? No. I did the next best thing. I searched online for more photos from the party. *Yes, Lia. This is healthy. Torture yourself over someone who was no more than a one-and-done fling.*

I hated that photo of them. I hated myself for hating it. Bitterness and hurt wrapped their iron-clad hands around my heart.

This is what you get for letting him squirm his way in and see through you so easily.

Angry with myself for being so gullible and eager, I saved the photo to my desktop, opened the email, attached it and hit reply.

To: Alastair Holden <aholden@holdenworldmedia.co.uk>
From: Amelia Meyers <ameyers@wmzb.net>
Subject: Re:

It certainly does appear that things have been "busier than you anticipated." Hope you were both able to get what you wanted.

CHAPTER TEN

The stupid whiteboard needed to be broken in half and thrown out the window. Bruce Singleton kept writing more and more story ideas on it; computer hacking, child pornography, embezzlement. I was sitting in the conference room surrounded by the other producers, reporters and assignment editors. Cynthia and Vance huddled at the head of the table, scribbling furiously in notebooks.

For a Monday, my attention span was somewhere between nonexistent and barely functioning. I drew little corkscrew patterns on my notepad as Bruce droned on about an investigative piece on business owners in Deltona trying to cheat the government out of millions in taxes.

Riveting.

The rest of the meeting was spent brainstorming and planning for the week. One good thing about May was the busy workload. I had zero time to obsess over anything but how many stories I could cram into each night's show and if the special projects pieces stayed on time without any glaring mistakes. By Wednesday, I was ready for the week to end. The day started with a bang. Literally.

One of the light fixtures in the studio broke loose and crashed to the floor. We were just about to pre-record an interview when it happened. The poor woman who'd come in had nearly passed out from fright. Vance unleashed a barrage of profanity so spectacular I stood and listened to him in awe. Sydney laughed and nudged me.

"We haven't seen one of those in a long time."

"He's rather artful with his language," I remarked. "Come on. Let's go see if the set in the back studio is interview ready."

We walked down the hall to a smaller studio. There were some plush chairs and a couple of tables strewn across the set. Sydney and I positioned them nicely and grabbed some plants to dress it up a bit. Vance came in a few minutes later with a much calmer looking guest. I chatted with them briefly and was relieved to see them both in good spirits. The crew filed in and within minutes the interview was underway.

Bruce popped his head in the control room, summoning me to his office. I signaled I'd be there in a couple minutes.

When the interview ended I strolled up the hallway. Cynthia was coming out of the green room, looking TV ready as usual. Her perfectly arranged auburn hair looked like it could survive a hurricane and a trip through a wind tunnel without breaking formation.

"Hi, Lia. On your way to Bruce's?"

"Yep. You too?"

"Yeah. Excited for the big gala on Saturday?" she asked as we walked to the news director's office.

"I am. How's your speech coming along?"

"It's not. That's probably why Bruce wants to see me." She stopped at his door and leaned closer to me. "If he asks you to help me write it, say no. You have enough stuff going on with sweeps."

Bruce was typing intently and squinting at the monitor. His bright blue tie sat in a crooked slant against his crisp white shirt. He resembled a mad scientist with disheveled curly black hair and wire rim glasses.

"Come in, you two," he said, waving his hand.

Cynthia and I sat on the old school, aluminum framed office chairs. I'd be willing to bet a week's paycheck Bruce had owned these since his college days. The leather cushions were practically flat.

"We're sending out a camera with you for Saturday. Freddie will be there early to get the arrivals."

"Why?" I asked.

"Senator Greyson will be there. His press secretary confirmed with me this morning. Cynthia, you'll have about fifteen minutes to sit with him for an interview. Lia, I'll need you to be on site by six to field produce and get the room set up…"

Cynthia and Bruce continued to chat about the interview. Whatever they said went over my head and out the window.

"Lia. Lia?"

I looked up and swallowed. "Got it. Six. I'll be there."

Bruce handed me a folder loaded with talking points and kept Cynthia with him to work on her speech. Saturday's banquet was an important annual fundraiser for the children's hospital downtown. Up until this moment, I'd been excited to go. The minute I got back to my desk I dropped the folder and called Stephanie.

"Hey, girlie. You caught me at a busy time. What's up?"

"Shoot. Sorry. Call me when you're free."

"You're on the early show today, right? Come over when you're done. I feel like I haven't seen you in years."

"Okay."

I sat down with a flourish and opened the rundown. There were a few notes in the system from the assignment desk, plus my email inbox was littered with publicists vying for coverage for their clients. Oh, and of course there was a message from Alastair. There had been messages from him since the weekend. I glared at his name and hit delete.

* * *

"Greyson is going to the gala." I said in a rush.

Stephanie swirled the wine around in her glass, looking at me shrewdly. "The dad?"

"Yep."

We were sitting at her kitchen table, making our way through bottle number two.

"Well," she paused. "It's in a big ball room. You probably won't even see him."

I squirmed in the chair, tapping my fingernails against the glass. "They're having Steele interview him. I'm field producing."

"Christ in a wheelbarrow. Are you going to be alright?"

"I'll be fine," I said, rubbing my eye.

"What if Nathan shows up? Want me to cancel my trip and go with you?"

"No, no. You've been looking forward to this conference. I'll be fine."

"You said that already."

"Yeah, well, what can I do? It's my job. It'll be quick. The interview is only supposed to last fifteen minutes."

My eye started twitching. If the earth chose this moment to open up and swallow me whole I wouldn't object.

"So," Stephanie pursed her lips. "Have you heard from Alastair at all?"

"Yep."

"What does he have to say for himself?" she inquired, eyes wide and glossy.

"I wouldn't know. I've deleted every email he's sent."

Stephanie's jaw dropped. "Really? You're not curious about what he has to say?"

"Why should I be?"

"Because you like him," she proclaimed.

"No, I don't."

Stephanie tapped her well-manicured nails on the table and looked me up and down.

"I've known you what, five years? I have never, in all that time, seen you light up the way you do about Alastair. I don't care how hard you try to hide it, I see it. He dazzled you."

"He's not good for me." The words sounded unnatural coming out of my mouth.

"Why?"

The twitching in my eye got worse. *Because he sees me. He gets under my skin and into my soul too easily.*

"Lia," she said, shifting in the chair. "I'm all for self-preservation, trust me. He's still on my shit list for being so friggin bossy about wanting you to delay your flight home, but you said yourself that he treated you really well. As far as the photo or whatever, hear him out."

* * *

Flashbulbs popped as reporters, bloggers and casual on-lookers watched guests arrive at the Peabody Hotel for the Black and White Ball. I stood just inside the main doors waiting for Cynthia to finish posing. As soon as she got inside we dashed off to the conference room that was designated for the interview. I was in full-on work mode, scrutinizing the lights and making sure nobody tripped over any cables. I had even made six copies of the talking points in case Cynthia lost hers.

The senator and his entourage arrived on time and as scheduled at six-thirty.

"Good to see you, Lia," Kenneth Greyson clasped my hands, smiling. "You look beautiful."

"Thanks," I said, guiding him to a high-backed leather chair. "Would you like some water or anything?"

"No, thank you."

"Okay. Cynthia will be sitting across from you. This shouldn't take much more than fifteen minutes. Thanks again for this, Senator."

Kenneth adjusted his jacket before sitting down. I'd forgotten how much he looked like an older version of Nathan. They both had the same square jawline and dark blue eyes.

"Think nothing of it, Lia. It's my pleasure. Actually," he paused, regarding me thoughtfully, "I'm glad I have this chance to see you. I'm sorry things didn't work out with you and my son. Samantha and I adore you and were hoping…well, you're missed. That's all."

He patted my shoulder and sat down. I wanted to throw up, but forced a smile instead. Pushing all the discomfort to the pit of my stomach, I focused on the task at hand and made sure Cynthia's interview went without a hitch. Senator Greyson was gracious and personable, answering questions ranging from the economy to immigration reform.

They went well over the fifteen minute target and only stopped when one of the event organizers came in to ask when he'd be ready to address to the ballroom.

After everyone said their goodbyes, I lingered in the empty conference room for a few minutes before going to the gala. This section of the hotel was relatively quiet. The sound of my heels clicking on the marble in the hallway echoed and bounced off the walls. As I got closer to the ballroom, applause filled the hallway.

Walking in was like entering an enchanted land. Everything was decorated in black and white. Guests were also urged to wear those colors. It was a good excuse for me to wear my favorite black cocktail dress and sparkly red heels. Making my way to the table, I noticed each place setting was adorned with a small, white mask. *Nice touch.* I joined Cynthia and several other media personalities at a table close to the main stage.

The whole room sat enraptured during the senator's remarks. I half-listened to him, playing on my cell phone instead. I'd received a few texts from Stephanie and replied, letting her know that everything was fine. Senator Greyson talked forever. Everyone at my table was either eating or whispering to each other. I only had to stay until Cynthia was finished with her speech. Time could not pass by fast enough.

A hand pressed into my shoulder, warm and strong.

"Hello, Lia."

The low cadence of that voice paralyzed me from the inside out. Gathering what strength I could, I looked up to my right and locked eyes with Nathan. The smug smile that crossed his lips drained the life out of me.

"So nice to see you again. Come, walk with me."

He squeezed my shoulder, not really giving me the option to say no. Cynthia glanced at me as I stood up. Not wanting to make a scene, I gathered my clutch, smiled weakly and let Nathan lead me out of the room. Scattered applause rippled through as the senator wrapped up his speech.

"This way," Nathan instructed, pointing me towards the hall I'd come from earlier. The minute we turned the corner and were out of sight, he caged me against the wall.

"I thought you'd be happier to see me."

My chest tightened. The last time he was this close it hadn't ended well.

"What do you want?" I tried to sound forceful.

"Nothing. I was just here enjoying the event. Imagine my surprise when I saw you." He leaned closer. "You haven't forgotten about me already, have you, Lia?"

The strong scent of musk turned my stomach. Pieces of his sandy blond hair tickled my forehead. It'd grown longer since the last time I saw him. Heat radiated off his body, suffocating me.

"You must want something. If not, I'm leaving." Flattening my spine against the wall, I wriggled a bit to the left, pushing away from him. Before I got very far, he grabbed my arm, tugging it hard. My heels slid on the floor, rolling my ankle. Pain shot through it at lightning speed.

"Why do you want to get away from me?" he asked, bewildered.

"You're kidding, right? Let go of me."

He tightened his grasp on my arm, making me wince in pain.

"I know you're here alone. What's the hurry?"

"I'm. Working," I said through clenched teeth.

"You're babysitting that hair-sprayed kewpie doll. How far up her ass does she need you to be to make a speech?" he sneered.

"Let. Me. Go." I glared at him, tugging my arm.

"Not so fast." He pushed me against the wall again, gripping me tighter. "We still have unfinished business."

Whiskey coated his breath. Voices ricocheted down the hall. I tensed, hoping they'd come down here and interrupt whatever 'business' Nathan thought we had. The voices grew silent, signaling they'd turned toward the main lobby.

"We have nothing to talk about," I seethed.

"Lia, baby," he condescended. "You threw your little fit, I let you have some space and now we need to talk."

"About what, Nathan?" I yelled. "We're done. Finished."

"We're not finished until I say so." His dark blue eyes flashed. I couldn't believe there was ever a time I found him attractive.

"Oh really? You no longer have any say in what I decide," I taunted.

"Don't push me."

"You're drunk, Nathan. Go back to your friends or whoever you came here with and leave me alone."

"Not until I get something from you first. You look good, baby," he moaned in my ear, sliding his other hand under the hem of my dress. He groaned again when he skimmed over the lace trim on my thigh-high stockings.

"I always liked it when you wore these," he said, kneading my thigh. I could feel his erection pressing into me. "See what you still do to me? You drive me wild."

"Stop."

"That's it, baby. Beg."

He pushed his hips into me harder, digging his fingers in my arm. I cried out, expecting no sympathy from him. This was what he wanted; to exert complete control over me and my body. Tears rolled down my cheeks, fast and hot.

"I like that no one else has been here," he rasped, cupping his hand between my thighs. "It's still mine."

"You're disgusting," I said, repulsed. "It's not yours. I'm not yours. Let. Me. Go."

I tried to wrestle away from him.

"Not so fast, Lia."

Twisting my arm, he shoved me, knocking my head into the wall. My vision rattled. There was no escape. He had me trapped. I couldn't move. I couldn't even breathe.

The echo of heavy footsteps moving quickly cascaded down the hallway. A blast of cold air shot through my lungs as Nathan's body was ripped away from me.

"Get your filthy hands off her."

That voice. It's not possible.

Shocked and scared, I turned my head to see what happened. Nathan was in a chokehold, flattened against the wall, glaring venomously at Alastair. A defiant laugh gurgled in his throat.

"Who's the British prick?"

"I'll be more than happy to tell you who I am." Alastair's face twisted into a sinister smile. "Let her go. Now."

The second he dropped my arm I crumbled to the floor. *This has to be a nightmare. What is even happening?*

"Get your goddam hands off me," I heard Nathan utter. "Do you have any idea who I am?"

"Don't like being roughed up? Tough shit. I don't care who the hell you think you are, but if I so much as hear you breathe the same air as her, it'll be the last thing you do," Alastair threatened. "Get the fuck out of here."

Shoes scraped and scuffled along the floor as they moved. I lifted my head in time to see Nathan straighten his jacket and shoot a deadly glance in my direction before he walked away. Resting my head on my knees, I closed my eyes and surrendered to more tears.

CHAPTER ELEVEN

Someone kept talking to me. Their voice floated around me like a halo, penetrating my senses. I opened my eyes, a flash of red catching my attention. It was my shoe. One of my ruby sparkled heels laid on its side on the bone white floor. I didn't even know I'd taken it off. Painful, deep breaths burned my lungs as I tried to compose myself. The floor was hard and cold, but something warm and soothing held me close.

He's here. It can't be.

"Are you okay, love?"

Hearing Alastair's voice sent me into a tailspin. I tensed, choking back a sob. A feathery kiss landed on my forehead, beckoning me to look up. He knelt in front of me, concern bleeding from saucer-sized emerald eyes.

"You're here," I whispered.

"That I am," he replied, wiping away my tears. "Can you stand?"

"I...yeah, I think so."

Straightening his lean frame, he offered a hand to me. I held it, standing on shaky legs. Dull pain rattled through my left ankle. It dawned on me that I was uneven. *Right, my shoe.* Still holding Alastair's hand, I turned to locate the sparkly heel.

"Here. I'll get it."

He bent down and picked it up, handing to me. I held it for a few seconds, not entirely sure if I wanted to put it on.

"You can take the other one off, if that's more comfortable."

"No, I have to go back to…Cynthia is supposed to give her speech and…"

"That's not important right now."

"What? I'm working. It's my job to make sure…" A weird murkiness clouded my vision. Putting my shoe back on took longer than necessary.

"I'm sure the organizers have everything under control. What's important now is getting you out of this hallway and somewhere comfortable."

The fact that he was right irked me. I wanted nothing more than to climb into bed, wrap myself in layers of blankets and shut out the world. Fatigue draped itself over me, making me woozy. Alastair's fingers tickled my arm before holding my hand.

"Let's go."

I was too drained and scattered to argue. I let him lead me through the lobby to the elevators. He dug in his pocket for a key card, slipped it into a slot next to the floor numbers and pressed the button for the penthouse suite. It didn't even faze me. Where else would he stay?

The doors slid open, revealing a private hallway.

"Come with me." Alastair tugged my hand and walked the very short distance to the suite door. He held it open as I tentatively walked in.

Beautiful views of Orlando were visible from the large dining and living area. Plush furniture in earthy hues of creams, blues and tans filled the room. Alastair removed his jacket and laid it on the table, then loosened his tie and untucked the tails of his shirt. Everything had happened so quickly downstairs; I didn't even notice his impeccable black suit.

"Are you alright?" he asked as we settled onto the couch.

"I'm fine."

"Lia," he sighed, rubbing his eyes with the heels of his hands.

"Your ex-boyfriend assaulted you in that hallway. You are not *fine*."

Unbridled anger flared from his eyes as he looked at the bright red markings along my arm. A faint bruise was starting to bloom in vivid purples and blues. I covered it up with my hand.

"Can we not talk about this now, please?"

Tears welled in my eyes again. They were hot and frantic, ready to unravel me in front of him. My lungs constricted and burned, making it difficult to maintain control of my emotions. *I will not let him see me this vulnerable.*

"Why are you here, anyway?"

He exhaled slowly. "I emailed you and told you I'd be here starting Thursday to visit with the news director and vice president at WTDO. I emailed you several times this past week. Did you not get any of them?"

"I deleted them."

He nodded, seeming to know the reason why.

"Fair enough."

We sat in silence for quite some time. Neither one of us moved, let alone looked at the other. Being in the same space as him again reignited all the sparks I'd extinguished after leaving Glasgow. There was a definite hum in the atmosphere. I pulled at the layered ruffles on my dress. The skin Nathan had touched crawled, making me nauseous. Stealing a glance at Alastair, I noticed he was fidgeting with his onyx cufflinks. Other than that small movement, he remained stoic.

I couldn't get the image of him throttling Nathan out of my mind.

"Why did you do that?"

"Do what?" he asked, staring at the floor.

"Put yourself in a position to get the shit beaten out of you."

The cushions shifted under his weight.

"My well-being isn't important," he responded, staring blankly at me. "That bastard had his hands on you and needed to be stopped."

"I can handle myself with him. He—"

"Can you?" Hard, stony eyes tore through me. "He's twice your size and had you pinned to a wall. He overpowered you and would have done God knows what to you if—"

"You shouldn't have put him in a chokehold," I shouted. "He would have no problem bashing your face in, given the chance. You need to think about that the next time you sweep in to save the day."

"I told you, my well-being isn't important," he said, fixing his gaze on me. It was blistering and made me lose my train of thought. I didn't want to argue with him. Not after all that happened downstairs. *If he hadn't been here...* The thought was too much to bear.

Exhaustion cloaked me, both mental and physical. The cushions were so soft they nearly swallowed me up. All I wanted to do was crawl into my bed. I felt Alastair curl up next to me. He draped his arm across my shoulders, tucking me securely into his side. His other arm snaked around my waist, holding me tight. Overcome by emotion, I choked back another sob. I didn't realize how much I needed to be held.

"Thank you."

"You're welcome." His breath tickled my temple. I snuggled into his warmth, feeling safe and protected. Half an hour must have passed before I raised my head, meeting his soft gaze. I'd seen that look before, but only a handful of times. It quickened my heartbeat and...

He kissed me. It was so sudden and passionate; it left me breathless. Lacing my fingers behind his head, I leaned back, pulling him into the cushions. The intensity of his desire shocked and amazed me. Far beyond his yearning, I felt his fear. The force was astronomical, as though he thought I'd disappear if he let me go.

Gasping, he jumped back.

"I'm sorry. I shouldn't have done that," he stammered, getting up.

First he folded his arms, then planted his hands on his hips, pacing in front of the couch. I ran my finger over my burning lips, watching him. The placid exterior that he so carefully kept under control was cracked. It lasted only for a second though. I witnessed the subtle shift in his expression as he reattached the protective shield that blocked any entrance to his deepest thoughts.

"Sarah didn't go with me to the party. We happened to arrive at the same time."

The hairs on my nape stood up. I wanted to believe him.

"Convenient," I snickered.

He stopped pacing, holding out his hands. Refusing to give in to him so easily, I crossed my legs and remained on the couch.

"Come to me. Please." He reemphasized the fact that his hands were outstretched.

"Fine," I muttered, grabbing them as I stood.

Tucking a strand of hair behind my ear, his look penetrated through me.

"It was convenient. For her, not me. I wanted it to be you on my arm in that photo." He trailed a finger along my cheek and down my neck. Softness filled his eyes once again, making my heart race.

"You were so distant when you dropped me off at the airport. I figured you didn't want to talk to me again. The way you were looking at me, it was like...I knew as soon as I let you go, you'd disappear." I nearly choked on the words.

A haunted expression ghosted across his face, clouding his eyes. "I'm sorry."

He kissed me again, his lips now a familiar warmth that I craved. I slipped my hands under his shirt, grazing my nails along his back. The low growl that vibrated in his throat was such a damn turn on. I kissed him harder. He responded immediately, tasting and worshipping me. Savoring every move, I held him tighter.

His entrance into my life was so thorough and...*right*.

Hovering his lips over mine, he leaned back. Not wanting to let go, I nibbled on his bottom lip, eliciting another moan from him.

Subtle flashes of vulnerability passed through his eyes. Somehow, I knew I was the only one who had ever seen it. Just as he'd done with mine, I was the only one who'd broken through his shell.

"You're sure you're okay?" he asked.

I didn't know if I was or not. Being in his arms helped. "I'll be fine."

"Seeing him hurt you," he pulled our foreheads together, "made me want to rip to his head off. You don't deserve to be treated that way."

Exhaling sharply, I pressed a kiss to his mouth.

"Lia. You make me..." he whispered, swallowing hard.

"Tell me," I whispered back.

Shaking his head, he broke our embrace.

"We need to sort this out," he cleared his throat. "You know my position on relationships."

Great. Back to the whole *I-don't-date-I-just-get-laid* thing. *Way to kill the mood, Holden.*

"I've wracked my brain since you left Glasgow trying to figure out how I can see you again," he eyed me cautiously. "I don't play games, Lia. I don't like coy answers. But I don't...I don't ever do relationships. This is –"

"Listen, I don't want to be a convenient plaything for you or anyone," I blurted out. "Sex is just sex. I want it to mean something."

God, I was so frustrated. The night had been draining enough; I didn't need his ridiculous hang-ups to complicate things even more. Nothing had changed since Glasgow. He was still messing with my head. I felt like I was being pulled in twenty different directions.

"That sounds reasonable enough. I'm not asking you to be a plaything, Lia. I don't want that. And I certainly don't want other men pursuing you if I can help it."

The strength of his dark stare left me speechless. *He doesn't want anyone else pursuing me? It's not like I have a line forming down the street.* Logic finally cleared the fog from my brain.

"Right, I forgot. You just get what you want and move on to the next one."

He steeled his expression. "That's not fair. You make me sound cold and calculating."

And very direct. I'd never encountered anyone who approached relationships or sex like this. He viewed it in such a clinical way; no attachment, only physical satisfaction. If he'd been any other guy I'd have kicked his ass halfway to Australia by now.

I make him what?

"Look at me," he murmured, tipping up my chin. "Can we at least try this? Give me that."

That friggin accent had special, superhuman powers. I never pegged myself to be one of those girls who swooned over anything, but dammit, the way he spoke was so flipping sexy.

"You live in Scotland. I live here. How would this even work?"

The corners of his mouth perked up into a smile. It was the first time I'd seen him do that all night.

"Someone asked me once if I used my plane for anything other than business trips. Starting now, I do." He kissed my forehead. "If I were to ask you out, on a proper date, what would you say?"

"Isn't that against," I made air quotes, "the rules?"

He shrugged. "I'm making an exception."

"A proper date? What does that mean exactly?"

"It means I take you somewhere nice, like a fancy restaurant or the opera."

The opera? Oh, Alastair.

He tapped his foot, giving me a look.

"I'm okay with, you know, dinner, a movie and a stroll through the park or something."

"Long walks on the beach, too?" He lifted an eyebrow, stifling a laugh.

"Cheeky," I grinned, playfully shoving him. The lightened mood didn't last long. His expression grew serious.

"Promise me something?"

"Okay."

"If your ex gives you any trouble again, let me know."

"Alastair, that's—"

"I'm serious," he interrupted. "I will not have him treating you like that. Ever. Promise you'll tell me."

Swallowing hard, I searched his probing eyes. The veil was locked in place again, but there was also a firm resolve behind them.

"Okay, fine."

"Good. Now, come with me."

He turned and walked toward the master bedroom. I stood, frozen in place. Too much had happened tonight, I wasn't ready for more. Anxiety churned through my body making me break out into a cold sweat.

"It's not what you think, love. I want to do something for you. Come."

Standing in the doorway with his hand outstretched, he looked so sincere. I went to him, no longer anxious about what he wanted. He led me toward the bed, turning me so I faced him.

"Please take off your dress and your shoes."

I stiffened. "You said this—"

He pressed a finger against my mouth, silencing me.

"I did and it's not."

Sliding his finger off my lips, he reached around my back and pulled down the zipper. His eyes were bolted to mine the entire time. Leaning his cheek against mine, he whispered, "Trust me."

What did I have to lose? He'd already seen me in my underwear once, and that was in a drunken stupor. Nodding, I let him glide the material over my shoulders, feeling the dress skim down my body. It pooled at my feet.

"Hold my shoulders," he said, crouching down. I did, but looked at him funny. He grinned, tapping my right foot. *Of course. Shoes.* He removed each heel, then looked up at me.

"Do you want to keep these on?" he asked, running his finger over my thigh-highs. I nodded.

"Alright." He sat on the edge of the bed, patting it. "Lie on your stomach, please."

Hesitating briefly, I obliged. Moving some of the pillows out of the way, I stretched out, sighing into the mattress. The bed moved as Alastair repositioned himself.

"Close your eyes. Relax."

The second his fingers started moving slowly down my back, my skin warmed. He caressed all the way down to my backside and legs, leaving goose bumps sprinkled everywhere. A small groan of appreciation escaped my lips.

He swept my hair off to the side, exposing my back. Loosening the bra straps, he slid them down my arms. A heightened awareness prickled at my flesh. I tried to anticipate his next move. Soft lips glided like silk along my shoulders to the nape of my neck. The stress and unpleasantness of the night melted off me as he kissed and nipped his way down to the small of my back. Placing his hands on my hips, he flicked his tongue on my skin, kissing just above the lace edge of my underwear.

Exhaling with great pleasure, I sank further into the mattress. His gentle touch and feathery caresses transported me to a level of relaxation I'd only dreamed about. My mind emptied for the first time in months. All that mattered, all that existed, was his skin on mine. I barely knew him, yet couldn't imagine a moment without him.

He traced what I thought were shapes and letters along my spine. I couldn't figure out what, if anything, he was actually spelling. More goose bumps rushed to the surface as he smoothly ran the palm of his hand up from my backside to my shoulders and down again. Time no longer applied to this moment in the universe.

I wasn't even aware that he'd stopped. Struggling to open my eyes, I saw him lying next to me, our faces inches apart.

"Finished already?" I mumbled into the pillows.

"No, love." He pressed a kiss to my forehead. "This is only the beginning."

CHAPTER TWELVE

I awoke to Alastair nuzzling my neck. His hand was warm and comforting on my stomach. Opening one eye, I saw sunlight pushing its way through the curtains. It glinted off the dark red hair lazing against me.

"That tickles."

"Hmm?" he hummed, the vibration echoing beneath my skin.

"Your hair."

"Does it?" He lifted his head, pressing a light kiss to my cheek. "We can't have that, now can we. Did you sleep alright?"

"Yep. Like a rock. Why do you sound so much more English now than you did last night?"

What the hell am I saying?

"Do I, m'lady?" He nipped at my earlobe, making me laugh.

Traces of cologne lingered on him. Inhaling it, I wondered if waking up with him was always this tantalizing. He'd been among the missing when I'd woken up at his house. I stretched, rubbing my eyes. "What time is it?"

"Time to eat," he said, a playful grin spreading across his face. "Breakfast arrived five minutes ago. Meet me out in the living room."

Alastair pushed his sinewy body up off the bed and walked toward the door. He was wearing his plaid pajama bottoms and dark blue t-shirt. I got a nice eyeful of a cotton-clad derriere as he walked out. *Yeah, waking up with him does not suck at all.* Pushing the covers off, I sat up and stretched again, wincing a bit from the soreness in my arm. The red markings were gone, but a couple of small bruises were visible.

Still in my black lace underwear and thigh-highs, I poked around the bed looking for my clothes. His white dress shirt caught my eye. It was draped across the nightstand, so I grabbed it, shrugging it on. It smelled delicious. Buttoning it, I walked into the main living room.

Breakfast looked more like a full buffet fit for the royal family.

"Did you order the entire menu?" I was floored.

Pausing to take an unhurried look at my choice of clothing, he grinned.

"Would you have preferred my cheesy omelet?"

"Maybe."

"Unfortunately for you, this," he gestured to the table, "will have to do. I ordered a bit of everything. Eggs, pancakes, bacon, toast, fruit, erm, cereal, too, I think. Not quite a full English breakfast, but it'll do."

I loaded a plate with scrambled eggs, two pancakes and bacon, along with some fruit. Alastair chuckled, watching me eat everything with aplomb. I hadn't been for a jog since Thursday and should probably have cooled it with the pancakes, but they were too good to ignore.

"Aren't you going to eat?" I asked between mouthfuls.

"I'm waiting to see how much food you leave for me."

I balled up the cloth napkin as best I could and threw it at him. "Muppet."

"What?" Alastair started laughing.

"You heard me. Would you prefer I use 'numpty,' instead?"

He laughed good and hard for another minute. Sitting there in his cotton pajamas, smiling and carrying on, he looked so relaxed and carefree. It made me happy to see him that way. Hard to believe I was angry with him twenty-four hours ago. It felt like a lifetime had passed. Tiny goose bumps rippled over my skin at the memory of his sweet caresses. He'd been so caring and comforting.

Part of me wanted to remain cautious and take everything as slowly as possible. But it was times like this when I had difficulty listening to that part.

"I've lost you to the depths of your mind again, haven't I?" he asked, nudging my foot. I hadn't even seen him switch to the chair next to me.

"Yeah, sorry."

"It happens. However, today I want you to try something."

"Oh?"

Inching the chair closer, he grasped my hands. Oh for crying out loud, the solemn look on his face was priceless. I chewed the inside of my cheek to stifle a laugh.

"First, I know you're mocking me. Those eyes of yours are a dead giveaway."

I tried to feign a serious expression, but ended up giggling. *Giggling? What am I, sixteen?*

"As much as I adore your girlish little laugh, I'm serious." He squeezed my hands, giving me a stern look.

"You're awfully bossy, Holden."

"So I've been told. Now, in light of your propensity to get so wrapped up in thought that I lose you to the far corners of your mind, I'm proposing the following." He paused, scanning my face for a reaction before continuing. "For the rest of today, and hopefully into tomorrow, you are not allowed to overthink anything."

"But I don't—"

"You do. We both know you do. I offered to buy you a drink the night we met and you thought about it for three days before answering."

I gaped at him. Not the most attractive thing, but he had me pegged.

"Are we in agreement?" He arched a brow.

"You have got to be kidding me."

He dragged the chair closer. "Do I look like the type of man who kids about things?"

I wilted. He didn't look like the type of man who took too kindly to the word 'no,' even if this was probably nothing more than a game to him.

"I'll ask again. Are we in agreement?"

That stare was hot. Too hot. It hit a few buttons in me that I didn't know existed. Shifting a bit in the chair, I leaned closer, not breaking eye contact.

"Whatever. You. Say." I squeezed his hand, engaging him in a challenging stare.

"Watch yourself, kitten," he responded, in a voice as smooth as silk. "It starts now."

"Does it?" I was way too distracted by his mouth. He ran his tongue along his bottom lip before capturing it between his teeth. The move caught me off guard, sending a surge of heat through my body. I wanted to bite him.

"You don't play fair."

"I never claimed to. Kiss me, Lia."

I hesitated, my breath hitching. This wasn't going to be as easy as I'd hoped. Or was it? Tearing my eyes away from his mouth, I pressed a quick kiss to his nose. He looked so disappointed, I had to laugh.

"You didn't say where," I shrugged, turning back to my breakfast.

A phone call interrupted us, so while he took care of some pressing matter, I gathered up my clothes and redressed. A black ruffled cocktail dress with five inch ruby red Louboutin heels seemed a bit much for a Sunday morning. Shaking my head, I had flashbacks to college and the ever so popular walk of shame. Although, I had nothing to be ashamed of with this walk.

Alastair's agitated voice sliced through the air the closer I got to the living room.

"Who took them? Are there any more? No. I told you why.

That's not your concern. You will do no such thing. Wait until I return. Because I said so. That's your answer."

I shrank against the wall so he wouldn't see me. He stalked around the room.

"I told you, no," he barked. "She's my responsibility, I'll take care of it."

Panic coiled around my heart. His responsibility? Who? I heard a dull thud, assuming it was the phone hitting the table. I saw Alastair pacing the room, his footsteps vibrating through the floor.

"Hey there," I said, walking into view.

He turned, his expression steely. It softened when he saw me.

"Everything okay?"

"Right as rain," he replied, avoiding my gaze. "I was just about to shower. I'll only be a few minutes, then I'll follow you to your flat."

* * *

I showered so fast not even the water knew if it actually hit my skin or not. Alastair was waiting in my living room and I didn't want to take forever. His mood had been a little chilly since the phone call. Rummaging through the closet, I grabbed a bright yellow sundress and some sandals. I loosely pulled my hair into a low, side braid before scurrying out of the bedroom. *Ten minutes. Not too shabby, Meyers.*

I paused, watching him soak in the photos hanging on the wall. Arms folded, head tilted, he stood as though he was at an art show instead of in my living room.

"Where were these taken?" he asked, pointing to several pictures.

"Lake Eola, last July. Those are my co-workers and, obviously, Stephanie."

He reached for my arm. Two oblong purple splotches marred the skin near my elbow. They didn't hurt, not even when Alastair brushed his thumb over them.

"You look different in that picture. Happier. You weren't with him back then?"

"Um, yeah, I was. He just wasn't at the lake that day."

Nodding, Alastair's expression remained blank as he looked at my arm.

"It doesn't hurt, if that's what you're worried about." I tried to divert his attention away from the bruise. All the staring made me uncomfortable. He was so much better at masking his emotions than I. His ability to shut down and remain so dispassionate was, for lack of anything better to say, impressive. Sad, too. The few times I'd seen him unguarded made him human.

"Ready to go?" he asked, tugging on my braid.

"Where are you taking me?"

"Somewhere," he smirked.

* * *

Corn dogs. He wanted us to have corn dogs for a late afternoon snack. I sat on a bench, shaking my head, while Alastair stood in line. We were at the county fair of all places. Not quite what I imagined as a 'proper date' destination, but he got points for creativity. I would imagine he'd also get a severe stomach ache after eating every single deep fried morsel of food that was for sale. *He must have steel-lined intestines.*

A breeze carried the sweet scent of cotton candy, funnel cakes and caramel apples on its back. County fairs were a guilty pleasure of mine. I wondered if he ever went to things like this as a child in England. I imagined his aunt and uncle wanted to make sure he had as normal a childhood as possible. He never talked about any of it though. Then again, I never asked.

"Here you go. One corn dog."

He handed me the stick and sat down. Anybody else looking at him would see a random young guy in khaki cargo shorts and gray t-shirt. I think he liked the anonymity. The way he was chowing down on the corn dog led me to believe he liked that, too.

"Where are you putting all this food? You haven't stopped eating since we got here."

"I didn't have much breakfast, if you remember."

"Oh come on. I barely made a dent in that spread. We could have fed the entire hotel."

He grinned, grabbed my uneaten corn dog and took a bite. This boyish, almost goofy, side to him was captivating. I hadn't forgotten about the tense phone call I overheard at the hotel, but seeing him like this made my heart swell. It gave me hope that I'd be able to piece together all the different facets of who he was deep down. Not knowing left me vulnerable to unpleasant surprises.

We strolled in comfortable silence past vendors and gaming booths.

"Let's get a photo." Alastair stopped, pulling his iPhone from his pocket. He asked a woman standing nearby to snap the picture. I leaned against him, wrapping an arm around his waist. The woman cooed in delight at the photo.

"What a beautiful couple you two make," she remarked while handing the phone back to him.

Couple? Not quite. Neither one of us said anything as we walked toward a secluded spot near some trees behind the performance tent. Music from local musicians floated through the air.

"Dance with me," he whispered in my ear. Apprehension shot through me but I managed to nod. Still under strict orders not to overthink anything, I really didn't have a choice. Well, I did, I just didn't have the option to debate it. I knew as soon as we embraced for this dance, the last remnants of any resolve I had to resist him would disappear.

"You're tense. Relax, Lia. Let me guide you."

Swaying his hips to the music, he banded his arms around me. The physical closeness made me tremble. The way his body moved against mine kindled a deep seated fire that was hard to control. I couldn't relax. I couldn't melt into his arms the way I wanted. He sensed it, I knew he did. Hugging me closely, he tried to assuage my fears by caressing them away. It had worked last night, but failed this time.

"What is it? Tell me." He pulled back, twisting the end of my braid.

I couldn't speak. Longing and desire overpowered me. I wanted him too much. That was the problem. I wanted every aspect of him; his controlling nature, his vulnerability, his darkest secrets, his brilliant smile. Given my track record, he was exactly what I should avoid. Einstein said it best about insanity: Doing the same thing over and over again, expecting different results. As independent and strong-minded as I believed myself to be, I was drawn to men like him.

At what point was I willing to admit that I'd never find the perfect balance?

"Hey," Alastair's quiet voice and soft touch brought me back to reality. "Where'd you go?"

"Take me home."

"Now? What's—"

I kissed him to avoid any questions.

"Please. Take me home."

He nodded, confused. I walked to his car in a fog. The ride back to my apartment was stone silent and crackled with tension. As I expected, he was fully enclosed in his impenetrable shield. We didn't exchange words until we stood in front of my door.

"Do you want to come inside?" I asked, unlocking it.

"I don't think that's wise." His strained answer was unconvincing.

With very deliberate movements, I grabbed his hand and pulled him into the living room toward the oversized couch. The element of surprise worked in my favor. He collapsed onto the cushion in stunned silence. Straddling his lap, a charge roared through me. I ran my nails down his chest, feeling his muscles.

When I reached the waistband of his pants, I slid my fingers under it before unbuttoning them. Staring straight in his eyes, I reached down into his boxer briefs until I felt what I wanted. He gasped and quivered when I wrapped my fingers around him.

"What are you doing?"

"What does it look like?"

"This wasn't—"

"You told me not to overthink anything today." I squeezed him. Alastair groaned and crushed his mouth to mine. Goosebumps poked out all over my skin the second he slid his hands under my dress and up my thighs. I shuddered and sighed into his kiss. He traced his fingers along the edge of my underwear, setting fire to the kerosene that was coursing freely in my veins.

"Jesus. You're almost ready." He ripped the material off, tossing the tattered pieces on the floor.

"You like destroying my clothes."

"No talking." He slid his tongue past my lips, melting into me.

Shifting his body to the left, he pulled something out of his pocket. I heard the sound of foil tearing.

"Slide back a little," he instructed. I did as I was told, trying not to watch too eagerly while he rolled on the condom.

The second his hands grasped my thighs again I sat up on my knees. I watched his expression shift while I guided him inside me. The fullness and pressure was exquisite. Alastair closed his eyes briefly, euphoria and agony rushing across his face. I took him in, inch by inch, reveling in the way he felt against my tender skin.

A low, gravelly moan vibrated in the back of his throat, spurring me on. He was a little bigger than I anticipated, but the slight discomfort was worth it.

"Easy. Go easy. I don't want to hurt you."

"You're not going to hurt me," I whispered.

Rolling and grinding my hips, I clutched the back of the couch. I sheathed him completely, becoming bolder in my movements. He thrust into me, unleashing a wave of ecstasy so powerful I cried out, almost coming on the spot.

"You feel too good," I moaned. Perspiration misted over my body. Alastair grabbed my hips and held me still. His deep, methodical thrusts nearly split me in two.

Our eyes locked. He was more beautiful now than I'd ever seen him. Gone was the veiled, guarded barrier. I saw into his soul, wanting more. He snapped his eyes shut as though he revealed too much. Pure, carnal desire took over. I wanted, no, I needed to lose myself completely in him. My pace quickened, taking him faster and harder.

"Slow, Lia. I want this slow." He bit his lip and slid his fingers around the back of my neck, bringing our foreheads together. Pressing his other hand to my lower back, he held me in place.

I tangled my fingers in his hair and pulled it. His low moans were erotic as hell. I was so intimately entwined with him it nearly brought me to tears. Our bodies moved in perfect rhythm. He was holding onto me so tightly, I couldn't escape. I was at his mercy. He was everywhere – beneath me, inside me, around me.

I slanted my head, kissing him long and slow. Being so completely connected with him sent a surge through me. With a gasp, he laid his head back. Seeing him so gloriously sprawled beneath me, losing himself with each avaricious movement, was empowering.

He brought our foreheads together again, holding the back of my neck. His grasp on my lower back tightened, intensifying every thrust.

Each one hit me perfectly, turning my mind into a delightful mess. An orgasm came fast and ruthlessly, seizing my body in a frenzy of tingling waves. I clenched around him, calling out his name. It was possible I dipped out of consciousness. The next thing I knew, his body went taut, then relaxed beneath me.

Raspy, heavy breathing filled the room as we both tried to collect ourselves. Our foreheads were still pressed together in an ardent, heated embrace. I cupped his face, kissing the salty sweat off his lips. He returned my gentle kisses tenfold, stroking my cheek with such reverence that it unnerved me. Feelings that I wouldn't allow to surface fought ferociously to reveal themselves.

His other hand was still pressed against my lower back, keeping us fused together. I moved gently.

"Not yet," he moaned.

The longer he stayed inside me, the more I wanted to have him again. I was sensitive, but still aroused. He seemed to sense my thoughts and released his grip. I climbed off him aware of how silky smooth he was pulling out of me. I couldn't help myself and looked down at his magnificent body.

I knelt on the couch next to him. My legs were nothing but trembling noodles. Alastair peeled off the condom and tied it in a knot. Once he got himself situated, he fetched me some tissues from the box on the coffee table so I could clean myself. It was an incredibly intimate gesture. He even half-turned his back to give me some privacy before sitting.

"You surprised me," he said, running a hand through his hair.

"Did I? How so?"

Swallowing hard, he clasped his hands together, turning the knuckles white. When he looked at me, I stopped breathing. His eyes were naked and raw, filled with emotion.

"You make me feel," he whispered.

"Feel what?"

"Everything."

CHAPTER THIRTEEN

A crackling boom reverberated through the apartment. Light illuminated the room, throwing jagged shapes across the walls and floor. I jumped, burrowing deeper into Alastair's chest. Orlando was notorious for lightning strikes and they never ceased to scare the crap out of me.

"Scared of a little thunder and lightning?"

I could hear the smile in his voice. Aside from the bright intrusion courtesy of Mother Nature's megawatt smile, it was dark. We hadn't moved from the couch for an eternity. I supposed at some point I should get up and turn on the lights, but staying tangled with him was much more appealing.

"I'm not a fan. Although I should be used to it by now. Storms like to pop up uninvited all the time."

The shrill ringing of a cell phone made me jump again. I sat up so Alastair could reach into his pocket. The second he saw the screen, he groaned with annoyance.

"Duty calls. I won't be long." He stood with all the grace of a king and walked toward my bedroom to take the call.

Wasn't it a bit late for work? What did I know. I wasn't in charge of the finances for a global media company. *He must get calls at all hours of the day and night.* Since his grandfather retired, he was probably taking on more work seeing as they hadn't named a new CEO yet.

I flipped on the lights and stopped at the windows. Rain pelted the glass in a furious crescendo. A single vein of lightning cracked through heaving black clouds, sending a shiver straight down to my toes. The storm's billowing rage gave me pause, almost as though it was warning me that I'd tempted the fates and lost.

Shaking off the weird feeling, I curled up on the couch and turned on the television. There was a plethora of stupid movies on to choose from. I settled on one about a ginormous shark battling an even bigger snake.

"I can see the last of your brain cells running for help," Alastair chided, appearing from the bedroom.

"All done with work?"

He nodded, folding his lean body onto the cushion next to me. "Yes. A good thing too. This so-called entertainment will stunt your intellect."

"Well, excuse me. I had no idea you could be so persnickety."

"Persnickety?" Alastair grabbed my waist and squeezed, a drowsy smile playing at his lips.

Another loud ring echoed through the room. This time, it was my phone. I squirmed out of his grip and grabbed it.

"Hey, Steph."

"Ah! You're there. Did I catch you at a bad time?"

It was so good to hear her melodic voice.

"Nope. How was the conference?"

I held up a couple fingers to let Alastair know I wouldn't be long. He stretched out on the couch, folded his hands behind his head and winked at me.

"It was alright," she answered. "Anything exciting happen there?"

I hesitated. "No."

"You're even a bad liar over the phone. What's going on?"

"Nothing." I turned away from Alastair and walked into the kitchen.

"Did Nathan show up at the gala? Don't lie to me."

"Yeah."

"Asshole. Did you see him?"

"It's a long story. We'll talk about it later."

"Why not now?" Her voice rose an octave. "Oh Jesus, he's not there, is he? I'll—"

"No, no, he's not here." I'd never get her off the phone if she got wind I wasn't alone. *Think, Lia, think.* "I was just about to hide under the blankets and watch bad movies to distract me from the storm." *Weak. She'll smell right through that pile of fertilizer.*

"I don't believe a word coming out of your mouth." *Shit.* "What's going on over there?"

I sighed, not wanting to have to explain everything to her. "There was a…I had an incident at the gala with Nathan. I'm fine. Um, Alastair was there… he intervened and took care of everything. He's here now."

Glancing over at the couch, I noticed he wasn't stretched out anymore. He was sitting up watching me closely, elbows on his knees, fingers steepled in front of his mouth.

"Alastair is there? At your apartment? What do you mean an incident?" Stephanie sounded more and more upset.

"I promise I'll tell you about it. Just, not now, okay?"

Silence. I closed my eyes, willing her to speak.

"Be careful, Lia. You're vulnerable. Don't let him take advantage of you."

"I won't."

"Call me tomorrow. Or call me later if you need anything."

I hung up, preparing myself for the inevitable questions that were coming. A rumble of thunder, like a distant avalanche, echoed outside. *How appropriate,* I thought, sitting on the couch.

"Would you mind if I undid this?" Alastair asked, tugging on my braid.

Not quite the question I expected.

"Oh. Sure. Go ahead."

He inched closer, kissing my forehead. I watched him with great interest as he concentrated on freeing my hair. His fingers moved slowly, loosening the elastic and untwisting the strands. Running his hand through the dark waves cascading over my shoulders, he kissed me again. Sparks rustled in my stomach, signaling that all systems were go.

"Wait." I pulled back.

"What's wrong?" Lowering his head, he licked at the soft skin below my ear. Hooking his arm around me, he urged me closer, kissing my collarbone and clavicle. I couldn't think straight. Thunder roared outside mirroring the thumping of my heart. His hands roamed freely over my body, touching and exploring.

"Lia," he moaned, his breathing labored and ragged.

We collapsed onto the cushions. The heaviness and warmth of his body surrounded me. Alastair hovered over me, his right knee on the cushion and left foot planted on the floor. Using one arm to support himself, he grabbed my thigh with his right hand, sliding up my dress.

My throat burned with desire when the friction from his pants rubbed against my bare skin. I grabbed a handful of his hair, pulling his mouth to mine. The atmosphere was thick with lust and need. Which one had me kneeling at the altar? I'd already lost control and let lust have its way with me. Now it was need's turn.

"I want you," he murmured against my breast, kissing it through the cotton.

I wanted him, too. Even more, now that I knew how he sounded and felt during sex. I still couldn't believe I'd been so intimate with him already.

Stop. I have to stop. I'm doing everything too fast again.

His fingers grazed the sensitive flesh between my thighs, making my toes curl. It felt too good. He felt too good. When paired together, lust and need were a powerful duo.

Gliding my hands along his back, I felt each knotted muscle through his t-shirt. Teasing my needy skin, he came dangerously close to driving me over the edge with the flick of his fingers. *He could make me orgasm with just a kiss if he wants.*

"Alastair...I..."

Crystal clear green eyes met mine, boring into me. Poised above me like a beautiful, tragic angel, he smiled.

"Hush. I want to feel you. I want to feel this way a little longer. Then we can talk. I promise."

I closed my eyes, surrendering to him. Rain slammed against the windows, thunder rolled overhead and lightning snapped while he peeled off what few clothes I had left. Each nerve ending stood at attention, waiting for his next caress. I was a ball of sensation. It was far too easy for me to get lost in the haze of Alastair.

Don't let him take advantage of you.

Stephanie's words and my own scattered thoughts weren't enough to distract me. I'd been so starved of genuine affection for too long. Tracing the contours of my body first with his hands, he then covered me in velvet kisses. Every brush of his lips was laced with reverence and adoration.

"My Lia," he said, his voice thick with emotion. "You make me feel too much. It hurts."

Pressing his forehead to mine, he shuddered. I moved a bit so he'd have room to lie next me. The tortured expression that seized his face broke me.

"It's okay," I cooed, holding him close. Wrapping himself around me, he hugged me fiercely. Whispered words fluttered through the air like silken strings, barely touching me before disappearing. The strands were enough to remind me of his nightmare and his screaming.

Don't leave.

Who? Who didn't he want to leave?

Brilliant white light filled the room, followed by an earsplitting crash, making us both jump. The storm was far from over. Alastair held me so tightly I thought I'd shatter into a thousand pieces.

"Don't break me, Holden."

Loosening his grip immediately, he apologized.

"Did I hurt you?"

"No."

"You would tell me if I did?"

"Yes, yes, of course," I answered, poking him in the chest. "No harm done this time."

He sat up, running both hands through his hair to tame the thick mess. I reached for the blanket draped over the back of the couch and covered myself. I didn't mind being naked, I was just a little chilly.

"I should go."

No. Don't run from me.

"It sounds pretty bad out there. At least stay until the storm ends," I offered weakly, hugging the blanket closer. History can't repeat itself again. I didn't want it to happen. I'd spent too many nights alone, cast aside after being used by Nathan. That was the problem with controlling personalities. They could do as they pleased with no regard for who got left behind.

I wished I could be as detached emotionally. That way, I'd be able to give an easy, breezy response and wave goodbye.

Settling back into the cushions, Alastair looked at me. I flashed a crooked smile, curling up next to him.

"Do you want me to spend the night?"

I nodded against his chest, content with listening to the rhythmic beating of his heart.

"I'll stay, love," he acquiesced. "Did you have a nice time on our date?"

"It was okay." I sat up, facing him.

"Just okay?"

"No pouting, Holden."

The most beautiful, shy smile curved his mouth. His guard was still down. I'd never seen him go this long without retreating behind the mask. Maybe we'd crossed some invisible threshold. Draping his arm over my shoulder, he leaned in close.

"Thank you for going to the fair with me."

I kissed him. I couldn't help myself.

"You're welcome."

Another dramatic alteration to his expression took my breath away. He looked desolate. Complete and utter sorrow filled every inch of me. He opened his mouth to say something, then stopped. I sat quietly, not moving, not wanting to force anything. I was so curious about the thoughts and feelings he hid so well.

"Ever since…I haven't," he stammered before regaining his composure. "You're so different from the people who've surrounded me all my life."

"Different? In a good way?"

"For the most part," he smirked.

He's teasing me. Sneaky.

"Do you enjoying being a smart-ass?" I folded my arms, suppressing a grin.

"Only at your expense."

"I see. In that case, I'll be right back."

I popped off the couch without looking back and waltzed into the bedroom. Grinning like an idiot the entire time, I changed into some yoga pants and a tank top. He was opening up, albeit slowly, but he was opening up. I snuck a glance at myself in the full-length mirror by the closet. My eyes glowed a molten caramel color.

Keep your head on straight.

Returning to the living room, I saw Alastair standing by the photos on the wall. This time, he stared intently at one of me from last autumn. I remembered it well. Sydney had invited me to her lake house for a weekend. I'd had a particularly tough fight with Nathan and needed a relaxing getaway.

She'd snapped a photo of me while we were out on her husband's boat. I'd worn a ridiculously huge straw sun hat with my bathing suit and cover up. It'd been a brief moment of fun and silliness during the most stressful time of my life.

Alastair turned when he felt my hand on his back.

"You have quite the collection of photos," he remarked, snaking his arm around my waist. "I like this one. That hat is a bit daft, but it suits you."

"I thought you'd be used to seeing ridiculous hats since you grew up in Ascot."

He chuckled. "Fair point. Come here. I want to show you something."

Leading me back to the couch, he waited until I was settled before reaching in his back pocket. Visibly shaking, he removed something from his wallet. Seeing him like this was too much. Every barrier he used was broken. He sat with a sigh, staring at the floor.

I eyed what appeared to be a folded piece of paper with interest. Alastair handed it to me.

"Open it," he said in a hushed tone.

As soon as I touched it, I knew it was an old photo. The paper was soft and worn from being folded. Faded ink on the back was hard to read, but I managed to make out a date – December 1984.

I unfolded it and gasped. An attractive young couple cuddled two children in front of a Christmas tree. The man had dark brown hair, brown eyes and a very familiar smile. The woman's long, dark red hair fell softly over her shoulder. Her green eyes sparkled.

The little girl in the picture looked to be about ten or eleven years old. Her curly blonde hair rested just above her shoulders. Mischief glinted in her brown eyes. She was hugging a boy who looked no older than five. Smiling proudly, he was clutching a toy helicopter. Those emerald eyes and chocolate-red hair were unmistakable.

"Oh my gosh," I whispered.

"That picture was taken the Christmas before the accident." His voice tightened. "As you can see, I was quite excited about that toy helicopter."

Trying to keep myself together, I rested my head on his shoulder. A door to his past had opened.

"What are their names? Your mom and dad?"

"Daniel and Rose," he answered thinly.

"You have your dad's smile."

"Think so?" His breath tickled my forehead.

I nodded, soaking in their joyful faces.

"What's your sister's name?"

He inhaled sharply, tensing. "Grace."

I lifted my head, catching his gaze. The raw emotion that spilled from his eyes drowned me. All these years later, he was still hurting. I wanted to be a pillar of strength for him, show him that he could talk to me about anything.

"That's my middle name."

Smiling briefly, he cocked his head to the side. "Is it?"

"Mmhmm. How much older was she?" I placed the photo on the table.

"Um." He shifted nervously. "She was five when I was born."

The sudden openness about his family shocked me. Not wanting to make him uncomfortable or have to reveal too much, I decided to keep things light.

"Speaking as the older sibling, I took great pride in torturing my sister, Dayna, when we were kids. I convinced her that since the carpet in her bedroom was dark blue, it meant sharks lived in it. She was petrified to walk on it."

"You're awful." Alastair squeezed my waist, pausing to think. "Grace dressed me up as girl once. I was four. She told my mum and dad she'd rather have a sister. They went right along with it. Called me Allison for days."

"You have got to be kidding me. That's hilarious." I burst into a fit a giggles.

"I've never told anyone that before. Thanks for being so sensitive."

"Did she put a little wig on you?"

Alastair narrowed his eyes, a salacious grin curling his lips. "You're on thin ice."

Grabbing at my waist, he tickled me fast and hard. I shrieked, but made no real effort to stop him. If anything, I wanted to draw this side out of him even more. Catching me off guard, he grabbed my hips and flipped me back on the couch so he could sit on my legs.

Leaning in for a quick kiss, he whispered, "Thank you."

Climbing off me, he offered a hand to help me sit up.

"You must miss them terribly." I cringed at my own stupidity for saying that out loud.

"I try not to dwell." The muscles in his jaw twitched. I felt awful for making him talk about it.

"I'm sorry."

"Don't be. It's different talking about this with you. I just…" He paused, wetting his lips. "There's a lot about me you don't know."

I took that to mean he was finished with the heart to heart.

"Thank you for sharing this with me," I said, folding the picture and handing it back to him. Once it was securely tucked in his wallet, he enveloped me in a warm embrace. We sank into the cushions, arms and legs entangled. I focused on the softness of his hair, running my fingers through it. So much had happened since last night. Alastair hugged me tighter, sending sparks shooting through me.

You make me feel too much. It hurts.

Was this what he meant? Did he not allow himself to properly grieve over the loss of his family? I wanted to know everything. I wanted to crawl inside his mind and watch the movies of his past. The man who sat next to me was more than the aggressive, cool-as-ice guy who pursued me relentlessly in Glasgow. He was broken. *Damaged.* But so was I. My own insecurities were too deeply engraved for me to ignore. The outer shell I wore wasn't as fortified as Alastair's. He'd strengthened it over decades. Mine was new, a badge I'd earned from two years of being told that I wasn't living up to someone else's idea of what a 'real' woman should be.

Two years of trying to see the light in someone who embraced the dark. Two years of being a possession, an object to control and manipulate. In relationships, I was weak. Alastair needed someone strong.

CHAPTER FOURTEEN

The first text message came during the middle of Monday afternoon's editorial meeting. I grabbed my phone, turning off the sound. Bruce didn't mind if we always had our phones attached at the hip, he just preferred the volume to be turned off during a meeting. By the time I got back to my desk, I had notifications for six new texts.

Feeling uneasy, I looked at the messages. Most of them were from Stephanie. Breathing out a relieved sigh, I responded to her. She wanted to have a girls' night, complete with Chinese take out and bad reality television. We hadn't done that in a long time, so I told her to be at my place for eight. Alastair was tied up with meetings and conference calls until late and told me he'd stop by later. I'd given him the extra key to my apartment and left his name at the guard's gate.

The other two texts were from Dayna, just to say hi and fill me in on her new promotion at the magazine.

I couldn't shake the weird feeling all those notifications gave me. I hadn't been bombarded with texts like that since the week before I left for Glasgow. Those had all been from Nathan, telling me how much he missed me and wanted me back. He'd been suspiciously quiet since Saturday's incident. I assumed he would have called or texted or shown up unannounced to be a jerk about it.

Maybe he's finally moved on and cares less about what I do in my spare time.

I shivered.

The remainder of the afternoon flew by. A steady stream of good stories kept the newsroom humming. Days like this were rare, so we took advantage of as many of them as we could. About half an hour before the show went live, Vance walked over and plopped himself down on the corner of my desk. My phone beeped. Another text from Stephanie.

4:27pm PS - I sent my portfolio to Darren's company. Eek!

"Message from a secret admirer?"

I looked up at Vance, nearly blinded by his ultra-whitened teeth.

"Nope. Girl talk." I grinned.

He nodded, holding up two ties. "Which one?"

"Uh…" *They're both hideous.* "I thought you were going to wear that chocolate brown suit?"

"I was," he complained, "until Jeanie told Cynthia to wear orange."

"Orange?" I wrinkled my nose. "Oh, you mean that burnt orange suit she just bought. Yeah, I can see why don't want to wear brown."

"I may not know much about clothes, but I do know I don't want to look like a Halloween display in the middle of May."

I laughed and helped Vance pick something that wouldn't clash too horribly with Cynthia's outfit. In the end, we decided on charcoal gray. It probably wouldn't win us any points in the world of high fashion, but for local television news, it was going to have to do.

The broadcast was a good one, chock full of informative and interesting stories. Vance and Cynthia were in rare form, cracking jokes and engaging in effortless banter when appropriate. Everyone usually dragged on a Monday, but I left the newsroom feeling great about the start of the new week.

Dropping the mail on the kitchen table, I tried to tidy up the apartment before Stephanie got here. It wasn't huge by anyone's standards, but it was cozy. The high ceilings helped make it appear open and airy.

Stephanie arrived with the food, excited and flushed about her new job prospect.

"I can't believe I sent them my portfolio," she squeaked, scooping out a hefty serving of lo mein.

"This is so exciting. Did you send it to that girl, Cassie?"

She nodded. "She gave me her business card at the cocktail party. We've been in touch ever since. She sounded really serious about my going back out there for a formal interview."

"Do you already have one set up?" I took a bite from an egg roll.

"No. Cassie said she'd email me as soon as she showed the department head my work. I'm dying. I mean, look, my palms are sweating."

I reached over and felt her hands. "Ew. Yep. They're clammy and gross," I teased.

"Argh, Lia," she exclaimed. "This is life changing. What if they want me? I can't leave Orlando."

Dropping my chopsticks, I leaned back in the chair. "Stephanie Ann Tempe, stop talking shit. You can and you will leave Orlando, especially if you're offered your dream job." She blinked at me. "Oh my God, it's only Scotland. It's not like you'd be shipping off to Antarctica. And what about Darren? He must be over the moon about all this."

"I talked to him at least thirty times today. He's so excited. He said he'll clean out the spare room at his townhouse so I'll have a place to stay."

"See? You already have a built in support system. It's perfect." I popped the rest of the egg roll in my mouth and grinned. My phone beeped. Assuming it was Alastair, I checked it.

8:33pm Still need to settle our unfinished business.

Jesus. I stopped chewing to prevent the egg roll from lodging in my throat. I deleted the message, stabbing at the touch screen to make sure it disappeared forever.

"What's wrong?" she asked, nudging the food on her plate.

I finished chewing. "Nothing."

"You're doing it again," she stated. "That was Nathan, wasn't it?"

The food didn't taste good anymore. A piece of shredded cabbage got stuck between my teeth, aggravating the situation. I swished wine around in my mouth to free it.

"Lia, I'm not going to pry or anything, but I'm worried."

My temper flared. "Worried about what?"

"I think you're keeping something from me about him."

She was so blunt I almost dropped the glass. My stomach knotted. "What would I possibly be keeping from you?"

"I don't know," she sighed. "It's just a feeling I get every time something like this happens. You clam up. I mean, you brushed me off the other night when I asked you about the gala."

"I wasn't in the mood to talk about it." Tension billowed through the room, stifling the atmosphere.

"Okay, okay, fine." She put her hands up in retreat. I slumped my shoulders, guilt washing over me. She'd been there for me during my darkest hours, a fierce ally and steadfast force to help me climb out of a never-ending abyss of despair. A lifetime wouldn't be long enough to repay her for all she's done.

"Hey," she brightened. "How about we veg out and watch some ridiculously bad television."

We cleared the table and spread out on the couch to watch the best of the worst reality shows we could find. The two of us loved insanely stupid programming, so we spent a good chunk of the next couple hours mocking the shows. By the time eleven rolled around I could barely keep my eyes open. I said my goodnights and hugged Stephanie goodbye. I changed into some pajamas and crawled under the covers. I was out like a light within seconds.

The mattress dipped slightly, waking me up. Terror froze me for a second before I realized who it was curling up next to me. In an instant I was securely wrapped in a pair of toned arms. Alastair's body was warm against my back, a comforting sensation that I happily snuggled into.

"What time is it?" I mumbled, rolling over to face him.

"Late. Go back to sleep," he answered in a low, husky whisper.

I peeked over his shoulder at the clock on my nightstand. *Two in the morning? Why even bother coming here at this hour?* I listened to his steady breathing, not wanting to bug him with questions, but my curiosity was insatiable as usual.

"I hope you weren't working this whole time."

Silence. *Is he asleep already?* Impossible. I couldn't even hear him breathing anymore. Shrugging off my suspicions, I nestled into the pillow.

* * *

He was too close. His body was too strong. Angry words flew out at me but I couldn't avoid their wrath. I was immobile, pinned against the wall again. A shadowy figure loomed in front of me, shouting and ranting in soundless bursts. I wasn't going to let it happen this time. I was going to get away. Plaster cracked and shattered next to me. Bits of white dust circled my head like a sinister crown. I'd lost again. I'd never win…

I shivered, opening an eye. Next to me, sleeping peacefully on his back, was Alastair. Shivering again, I watched his chest rise and fall with each measured, deep breath. I was always so cold when I had that dream, even with the blankets swaddled around me. Deciding to be proactive in my sleepy state, I snuggled against him, resting my head on his shoulder. His body heat definitely helped.

"Hmm," he hummed, shifting on the mattress. I didn't want to wake him, so I remained still, listening to the low, sexy grunts he made in slumber. How ironic that I was the one waking up thanks to a bad dream.

"Are you alright, Lia?" His question was encased in a deep, gravelly tone from sleep. My cheek warmed when his fingers brushed against it. "You're safe with me, you know that."

Confused by his concern, I slid my hand across the soft cotton t-shirt he wore, resting it on his stomach. Sighing, he leaned his head on mine. I listened as his breathing became heavy and deep before closing my eyes.

* * *

"I'm driving you to work today."

I stopped smearing cream cheese on my bagel and stared at Alastair. He strode into the living room, smoothing down his tie. The suits this man owns were ridiculous. Today's ensemble was a navy blue three-piece Burberry. I fought an urge to peel it off him with my teeth.

"Why?"

He shrugged. "It seems like a nice thing to do."

I finished with the cream cheese and bit into the bagel, never taking my eyes off him.

"Stop looking so suspicious," he grinned. "I have plans for us tonight right after work. It's just easier if I drive you and pick you up."

"You do realize that I don't get out until seven, right?"

Nodding, he slid into his jacket, completing his stunning ensemble. Abandoning the half-eaten bagel, I gathered my things and walked with him out the door. A Mercedes SUV was parked next to my car. His driver, Paxton, kept a watchful eye as we walked toward him. I was annoyed, but greeted him pleasantly. He smiled and opened the passenger door.

"Good morning, Miss Meyers."

"Hi, Paxton. I wasn't expecting to see you here." *Especially since I gave the guard Alastair's name and not yours...*

"Official business," he stated.

Alastair slid into the car next to me, folding his tall frame gracefully into the leather seat. Not saying a word, he grabbed his cell phone. Brows creasing in frustration, he tapped against the screen, either writing an email or a text. I rolled my eyes and watched as the city came to life. Orlando had its own ebb and flow; not nearly as chaotic and frantic as New York, but certainly not calm.

Since I normally drove myself, I never took the time to observe the morning rhythm. Tourists moved at a snail's pace, but didn't slow the practiced stream of businessmen and women merging onto the sidewalks. Quite the opposite was taking place in the backseat. Alastair didn't utter one word the entire time. When the car stopped in front of my building I was more than happy to get out.

"Thanks, Paxton."

I walked with purpose toward the entrance. Just as I was about to open the door, Alastair gripped my elbow and pulled me aside. I snapped my arm away.

"Let go of me," I hissed.

"Hey, whoa," he ceded. "I'm sorry. You walked off so quickly."

"Yeah, well, you were engrossed in your phone." I folded my arms.

"I had to take care of a few things," he said, his eyes hardening. "Make sure you meet me here at seven."

Oh no, no, no. He will not take that tone with me.

"You," I poked him in the chest, "are not my master and commander. I will come out when I'm done, and not a minute before. If you don't like it, I'll call a cab."

The muscles in his jaw flexed. Something was going on and I didn't appreciate being kept in the dark.

"What's the real reason you wanted to drive me to work?" I glared at him.

"I told you," he answered calmly, "I'm taking you out tonight and it's easier."

Veiled eyes darted across my face. My temper flared.

"Why is Paxton here and how did he get into my complex?"

Alastair stiffened. I'd hit a nerve.

"I'm here on company business. He's my driver and personal security detail."

"So how did he get into my complex this morning if I left *your* name at the gate?" I was livid.

Remaining still as a statue, Alastair stared me down. "He gave my name when he dropped me off last night, that way he'd be able to get back in this morning. We can fix all that later if it'll make you feel better."

Red flags shot up in unison as we stared at one another. *He's hiding something.* My instincts were on high alert, petrified at the vast unknown path I was navigating.

"You're scaring me," I whispered.

"That wasn't my intention," his expression softened. He twisted my ponytail through his fingers. "Don't be upset. Please."

Broken shards of distant memories tried to cut into my current reality, taunting me. I knew, on some level, Alastair wasn't stalking me, but it was all too familiar. The wounds were still too fresh.

"Lia," he breathed, cocking his head to the side. "You're overthinking again."

I bristled slightly, catching a glimpse of his little grin. "So what if I am?"

The corners of his mouth curved as he leaned in for a kiss. Ugh, I'd become *that* girl; easily distracted by a grin and a kiss. My insides liquefied, leaving me at the mercy of his lips. It didn't even register that we were still standing on a sidewalk in front of a building teeming with professionals on their way to work. I grabbed his tie, holding him close. He slanted his head, deepening the kiss. The world around us disappeared.

"Have a good day, kitten."

"Thanks, chief," I called after him.

The morning flew by. We were fast approaching the final week of sweeps, which meant the lure of vacation days and time off was strong. Sydney plopped on the corner of my desk a little after one, chattering away about her daughter's upcoming birthday party.

"Are you still baking those cupcakes? Violet has been pestering me all week," she said.

"Of course."

"Oh! I wanted to ask you what gym you used. Ray's on a health kick and wants to start lifting weights or something."

"I'm a member at Pure Fit, but haven't been in a couple months." I tapped the pen on my desk. "Is he just looking for general workout stuff or a personal trainer?"

"General workout stuff for now. Who knows, maybe I'll sign him up for some sessions with a trainer," she grinned.

"Pure Fit is perfect then."

A shrill ringing interrupted us. I looked at my cell phone.

"Hey, Steph."

"Your picture is all over the internet," she blurted out.

CHAPTER FIFTEEN

Son of a bitch. I opened the web browser and searched the local gossip columns and society pages. Lo and behold, there I was, sucking face with Alastair in front of this very building. Someone had been all too eager to whip out their smart phone and snap away.

"Thanks, Steph."

"If it makes you feel any better, you guys look hot."

"Not what I was going for, but thanks."

Sydney eyeballed me as I placed the phone down with a thud. I started a mental countdown to when the entire newsroom would find out. My best guess was five minutes.

"Is something wrong?" she asked.

I sighed, drumming my fingers. The caption below the photo gave me hives.

Ratings High: WMZB's producer Lia Meyers gives the competition a tongue-lashing. An eagle-eyed passer by caught her in a racy lip lock with British media mogul Alastair Holden. His company purchased the city's second place news station, WTDO, in recent weeks. Meyers recently broke off her two year relationship with Nathan Greyson, son of Florida Republican Senator Kenneth Greyson. Stay tuned…

I almost hyperventilated.

"Oh my God, Lia." Sydney stood next to me, staring at the screen slack jawed. "Is that really you?"

Grinding my teeth to within an inch of the gums, I responded as evenly as possible.

"Yes."

"Wow. I didn't know you were dating anyone."

"I'm not. We've been out a couple of times. It's nothing to get too excited about."

I stared at the screen for a few more seconds before closing the page. A brief scan of the newsroom revealed everyone still working diligently. Sydney kept talking to me while she sat down at her desk. Half paying attention, I answered some of her questions. The messaging line on the rundown dinged.

Well, well. So nice of you to grace us with your presence today, Ms. Society Section.

Rolling my eyes, I glanced up and caught Tyler smirking in my direction. *Great, here he comes.*

"You enjoy this crap way too much, Tyler."

"Did you pick him up in a souvenir store?"

"Ha, ha."

I tried to convince him and Sydney, and by this time the handful of reporters that had gathered around my desk, there wasn't any need to get all worked up over the photo. It wasn't a big deal.

Whatever.

Even I didn't believe the load of shit coming out of my mouth.

Thankfully we had a show to produce, providing a much needed distraction for everyone. I kept my phone with me in the control room during the broadcast. I hadn't heard from Alastair and was curious if he'd seen the photo. He was such a private person, I'd imagine he wouldn't be too thrilled. I sent him a quick text.

6:10pm Seems we're internet famous

6:12pm So I've heard

6:13pm Have you seen it?

6:16pm No. But I hear I'm one lucky guy. Everyone is talking about the knockout in the purple dress

6:18pm Knockout? I saw her. She's alright. And the dress is lavender, FYI

6:21pm Duly noted. Aren't you supposed to be producing a live show now?

6:23pm I am. I'm a multitasker

6:24pm Focus on your job. I'm coming soon.

He was even bossy via text. I shook my head. I planned to get to the bottom of a few things with him tonight.

The final few minutes of the show were a blur. An excited drone of goodbyes filled the control room. I slipped out and went back to my desk to gather a few things before leaving. For the time being, the inquiry into my salacious morning snog on the sidewalk ended.

Paxton waited for me next to the car. He stood in that casual-but-ready-to-jump-into-action stance; hands loosely clasped below the waist, feet shoulder length apart. He smiled as I approached and opened the door. Alastair scrolled through his phone while I settled in next to him. He seemed relaxed. The atmosphere was much calmer between us than earlier. He slid the phone into his pocket and grabbed my hand, kissing the knuckles.

I let out a huge sigh.

"Rough day?" he asked.

"Not particularly. Just dodging questions from everyone under the sun about you and our public display of affection."

"Sorry."

"It's not your fault. It's the nature of the news beast," I commented as we pulled into traffic. "How was your day?"

"Better now that you're here." He stroked my palm. As much as I adored his caresses, something was still off. We sat quietly for the duration of the ride. Alastair hopped out to open the door for me when we arrived at the restaurant.

"Are you hungry?"

My stomach rumbled. "Always."

"Well then," he chuckled, "let's get inside."

The hostess sat us in a corner booth, tucked away from everyone. The menu looked amazing. There was everything from pizza to pasta to seafood to sandwiches. When the server came over to take our order, Alastair piped up quickly, requesting bruschetta and a margherita pizza to share. He also ordered himself a McEwan's Scotch Ale and a glass of red wine for me.

"Do you always order for others or did you think I'd be too indecisive?" I grumbled.

"I don't want you to have to worry about making any decisions tonight. That includes dinner."

Shaking my head, I glanced around the restaurant. It was warm and friendly, with rich dark wood floors and soft, red velvet covered booths. No sooner had we placed the order, the food arrived at our table. We both dove into it. True to form, I managed to stomach two pieces of bruschetta and one and a half pieces of pizza, much to Alastair's immense pleasure. I was craving carbs, so this food was heaven in a hand basket.

"Been for a jog recently?" he teased.

"Hey, be nice," I warned.

We finished the rest of our meal in comfortable silence. Alastair paid the bill and led me back out to the waiting car. I had no idea where we were going next and watched the artificially illuminated scenery fly by. Lost in thought, I didn't even notice when Paxton parked along the curb near Lake Eola.

There were some people strolling through the park but not many. It was close to ten at night and I suspected more people would be downtown at a bar than at the lake. Alastair was quiet as we walked side by side toward the water.

"Is this where you were in that photo? The one from last summer?"

"We were on the opposite side of the lake huddled under some trees. This over here is the amphitheater," I pointed to my right. "And down a bit to the left are the infamous swan boats."

Alastair looked at me curiously. "Swan boats?"

"Yep. Come with me. I'll show you." I led him to a small dock surrounded by white boats shaped like giant swans. "See? People can rent them during the day and paddle around the lake."

"Interesting."

"Oh come on, it's fun. You stuffy Brits need a little something like this to loosen up." I jabbed him in the side.

"Stuffy Brits? I see."

Taking my hand in his, we strolled lazily along the water's edge. The park looked mysterious, but still inviting in the dark. Stopping under a large cluster of palm trees, he turned to me.

"I go back to England tomorrow night."

Hearing that hurt more than I thought it would.

"Why not Glasgow?"

"There's a board meeting in London on Thursday to make the final decision on who will take over from my grandfather."

"Any good candidates?"

"Me."

"Really? That's great." I was genuinely excited for him. He stared blankly out at the lake. *Fantastic. More stoic, hard-to-read Alastair.*

A rustling near the trees made both of us look toward the source of the sound. Not seeing anything, I sat on a nearby bench.

"Have a seat," I said, patting the metal.

He obliged, still wearing an unreadable expression.

"There's going to be a garden party at my family's estate after the announcement for CEO is made public. You should come with me."

My throat dried up.

"To England?"

"Yes."

"For the party?"

He raised an eyebrow. "Yes."

"When is it?"

"Next weekend."

"Next…this is really short notice," I stammered. "I can't just take time off like that."

"You don't have to give me an answer this second." He twisted strands of my hair around his finger. "Think about it."

My brain was so overloaded I thought it was going to ooze out of my ears. Everything was still happening at warp speed. Yes, I liked him. A lot. And yes, I might have spurred things on a bit too much this past weekend. Before I let anything else happen, I had to get answers to several questions that had been burning a hole in my memory.

"Can I ask you something?"

"Sure," he answered, not moving.

"Who were you on the phone with at the hotel the other day?"

"No one of consequence." His response was clipped. The look in his eyes urged me to move on from this line of questioning. Too bad I wasn't deterred by a chilly glance.

"Was it the same thing you had to take care of that night at the cocktail party?"

His stare was glacial. I held my ground, not moving a muscle.

"Yes," he said through clenched teeth.

Ah ha. Now we're getting somewhere.

I got bolder.

"The nightmare you had…" I paused, struck by the sheer terror behind his eyes. "Who don't you want to leave?"

Every last ounce of Alastair's fair skin drained of color. He turned an ashy gray.

"It doesn't matter. It was just a dream."

I tried a different angle.

"What did you mean by it was your fault?"

A visible tremor streaked through his statuesque facade.

"Nothing."

I was at the end of my rope with all his vague responses. "For crying out loud, Alastair. Just tell me."

Furious green eyes punctured a hole in my skull, unhinging me. The intensity burned straight to my soul.

"Leave it alone, Lia," he bit out acidly.

The malevolence that seeped out of him was brutal. I'd never seen anyone so angry, not even Nathan. I desperately needed to get away from him, from those eyes, from that anger. The only thing I could do was muster up tears. Lots of them. They burned my cheeks, streaking down my neck like clear rivers of lava. I wanted to run, but couldn't relay the message to my legs fast enough.

Alastair choked out a breath, reaching for me. I cowered away, repulsed.

"Please, I'm sorry," he whispered, slumping his shoulders. The suit seemed to swallow him whole. His body withered against the bench, defeated. "Please look at me."

I stood up, unsteady and shaking. "I have to go."

My legs were moving, but I wasn't controlling them. They carried me to the street. Tears blurred my vision, making it difficult to find a taxi. I did see the SUV idling at the curb. I froze, turning my back in an effort to hide in plain sight from Paxton. Squeezing the tears out of my eyes, I swallowed hard and ran away from the SUV, the park, everything. I only stopped when I reached an intersection. Leaning against a light post, I gasped for breath.

What I am doing? Running aimlessly through the city? That's good, Lia. That's intelligent.

Wiping my eyes, I stood up straight and kept walking until I managed to hail a cab. The first thing I did when I got home was fill the tub with hot water and bubbles. My body ached. I undressed and stepped in the water, lowering myself into the warm oasis. Sore muscles and tired limbs welcomed the silky heat as I leaned back. For a brief second, I forgot about Alastair and his fucked up secrets, whatever they were.

Steam rose off the water, fogging the mirror. I imagined that was what my brain looked like; a foggy, clouded mess that needed wiping. Sinking lower, the bubbles knitted together over my breasts and shoulders. Only my head remained above water, but just barely.

* * *

"I need to see you. Are you home?"

I gripped the phone in my hand, cursing myself for answering it. "Yeah. I'm about to go to bed."

"Ten minutes. All I need is ten minutes," Alastair negotiated.

"It's late. I don't think—"

"Please, Lia."

"Fine."

Twenty minutes later, he was sitting in my living room, failing to mask his nerves. Just the sight of him sent me into a tizzy. He'd changed into sweatpants and a fleece shirt, looking more like a dejected puppy than a powerful businessman. The only spark of control I saw was in his eyes. They were hard as stone.

"I wish you hadn't run off like that. I don't want you wandering the city alone late at night," he scowled.

"Wrong way to start this conversation," I scolded, standing with my arms crossed.

Keeping his eyes glued to me, he started to say something, then stopped. I remained statuesque, glaring at him.

"What is this, a battle of wills?" he inquired, rising to his feet. "I didn't come here to exchange heated stares with you all night."

"Then leave."

Rubbing his chest, he paced the room.

"I shouldn't have answered you so harshly at the park. For that, I sincerely apologize. What you asked is something…it's complicated. Please understand."

"That's all you had to say in the first place," I snapped.

"I know, I'm…I don't usually have someone sleeping next to me when I have that nightmare. You were…you *are* the first girl I've brought to my house and shared my bed with for the night."

"What?"

He half-smiled. "It's one of the conditions I have along with the no-dating thing. No sleeping over."

I massaged my temples. It did nothing to soothe the tremendous pounding in my head.

"Lia, look at me," he pleaded, holding my hands. "I meant it when I told you that you're different from everyone who's been a part of my life. I don't know what it is about you. I've wracked my brain, I've replayed our time together...I can't..." He threw his head back, exhaling loudly.

"You make me feel things I've spent the majority of my life avoiding. I have a system," he asserted, pacing the room again. "Then you showed up in your pretty dress and tripped on the bloody carpet. Not to mention when you stumbled on the sidewalk and used my car as a way to right yourself."

I gasped. "You were in the car?"

"Yes. You looked right at me when you peered through the window. You must not have seen me thanks to the tint."

"Unbelievable."

He locked his fingers through mine, trying hard to retain control of his emotions.

"I don't want to leave tomorrow with you upset or angry at me. I was a right prat for treating you that way," he stated simply.

"Obviously," I said. "Don't let it happen again."

Smiling, he put my hands on his hips, then snaked his arms around my waist. "Does this mean you forgive me?"

"Not quite."

He lifted my hand, kissing each fingertip. Every touch of his lips sent a bolt of lightning down my spine. "This thing we have...I want it to be exclusive."

Exclusive...?

"Amelia." His husky whisper made the hairs on my arms stand up.

"Are you ready for all this? I mean, it's more than just sharing dessert or having amazing sex on my couch."

Alastair raised an eyebrow and nuzzled my neck. "Amazing sex, huh?" He pressed his lips along my collarbone, slowly moving his hands over my hips. "Yes, I'm ready." His breath was humid and warm.

"Are you? It could get messy."

"Stop talking, love," he ordered, kissing me quiet.

"Wait." I pulled back. "Stop kissing me. Alastair…Stop."

He looked at me in amazement.

"You use your powers of seduction too much. I can't think."

"I like being close to you," he murmured, running his fingers down my neck. "I like touching you and feeling you against me."

He was too potent. Combine that with the soft glow radiating from his eyes and I was nothing but a pile of goo in his arms.

Bowing my head, I squeezed his shoulders in frustration.

"Lia, before your brain spins off its axis can we come to a mutual agreement on something?"

Looking up, I nodded.

"Good. We both have hang ups about dating. I've already managed to royally screw this up. I don't plan on doing that again. Can we just agree not to doom this whole thing before it even starts?"

"You were angry with me for asking a question. I'm not putting up with that nonsense."

Taking a few steps back, he scrubbed his face with his hands before running them though his hair. "I'm not used to anyone asking me those things. It doesn't excuse the way I reacted, but…"

Any traces of his impenetrable exterior vanished. He was a raw nerve, standing exposed in my living room.

"I like the way I feel when I'm with you. Can that be enough for now?"

"What are you so afraid of, Alastair?"

Moving closer, he cradled my jaw. Our eyes locked. I couldn't look away if I'd wanted. The overwhelming desire that filled his eyes was powerful. Nobody had ever looked at me this way. Enveloping me in a hug, he sighed. I buried my face in his shirt, inhaling his scent.

"Come to England," he whispered. "I want to see you again."

Feelings I never experienced before erupted, lighting up my

soul. The euphoria lasted a brief second, as paralyzing fear sunk in, making my heart race. *I'll disappoint him.* My insecurities would hijack any chance I had at making this work.

"Let go, love," he said, his words dripping in my ear like honey. "You're feisty, bold, sexy and strong-willed. I like that about you. I want you always to be that confident with me."

Ignoring the fluttering in my throat, I raised an eyebrow. "That's a bit ironic."

"What is?"

"You telling me to let go and all that. How can you expect me to do it if you're not willing to do the same?"

"I never said I wasn't willing," he answered. "You may not like what you learn."

I expected him to shrink back into his shell, but he didn't. He remained exposed, gazing at me with quiet intensity. Overwhelmed by the events of the weekend and tonight, I made a brash decision without a second thought. It was the first time I'd done that in over two years.

CHAPTER SIXTEEN

Time, the abstract wonder that it was, taunted me with its clever little mind games. One minute it crawled, the next it sprinted. The only time I applauded it was at the airport when I said goodbye to Alastair. It came to a dead stop.

My bossy, enigmatic Englishman kept me trapped in his embrace for an eternity. When he finally let go, he gave me one gentle order: to alert him if Nathan stirred up any problems. Not wanting to bother him with that nonsense, I nodded to appease his request, but had no real intention of following through. He had his own pressures to deal with; he didn't need mine.

I finished out the work week on a mediocre note. On Saturday, all hell broke loose.

"This is crazy," Stephanie lambasted me as she paced through her living room. "You can't go to London."

"I'm sorry, did I ask your permission?"

"Be smart. Take a step back and really think about this."

"I've thought about it. I'm going." I folded my arms, glaring at her. "He offered to fly you out, too. Darren will be there."

Stephanie muttered something under her breath. Her harsh reaction to my decision was unexpected and unwelcome.

"I have a bad feeling about it."

"It's a garden party, not a rave," I refuted. "Why is this such a problem?"

"You really want to know?" she asked, focusing a laser stare at my head.

"Yeah."

"Since the night you passed out drunk, you haven't told me one thing about what's going on with him. Nothing. This isn't like you. I get that you clam up about the other one, but please don't keep me in the dark about Alastair. I don't want to see you fall into the same traps."

"What the hell does that mean?"

She sighed. "You said it yourself in Scotland. This is how it started with Nathan. You fell hard for him and look what happened. You were so lost in your desperation to please him that you ignored his shitty side. You made excuses for him. I saw how he treated you. You weren't his girlfriend, you were his trophy."

I shook with rage, clenching my teeth so fiercely it set off jackhammers in my head.

"I am not that weak, Stephanie," I yelled. "You have no idea what being with him was like. He knew everything I did. Everything. What was I supposed to do? He's the senator's son. It's not like I could make a clean break."

"But you did make a clean break," she countered. "What really happened?"

I swallowed back my anger. How had this turned into a fight about Nathan? Why was he still controlling my goddam life?

"I'm done with this conversation," I said, grabbing my keys to leave.

"That's it, Lia. Avoid the problem. Start dating another controlling man. That will solve everything."

Her words stung me, stopping me in mid-stride.

"This was supposed to be a fun surprise for you," I said, shaking. "Why are you doing this?"

"Don't you dare turn this on me. Of course I'd love to go and see Darren. That's not the problem. Alastair isn't even the problem.

It's you, Lia. You're shutting me out. You have been since January."

Dropping my keys to the floor, I cracked. All the hyper emotional craziness I'd been through the past few weeks finally took their toll. I couldn't hold the tsunami behind my weakened barrier anymore. Stephanie's eyes overflowed as she watched me crumble in the middle of her living room.

I make him *feel? Look what he's done to me.*

"You're right," I sniffled. "You're right."

She ran over and yanked me into a bear hug.

"Don't lose yourself again," she pleaded. "I can't take seeing you go through that with another guy." She broke our embrace, holding me by the arms. "When I first met you, I was so impressed by how self-assured you were with everything. Especially with your career. I couldn't be bothered with all those needy, high maintenance personalities. You're like a breath of fresh air. You don't put up with anyone's shit, mostly mine."

I laughed, although it sounded more like a seal calling out in distress.

"All those great things about you are the reasons why Nathan wanted you. I always assumed he was threatened by your strong personality and that's why he used charm and seduction to wear you down. You're human, Lia. You have a weakness for sultry guys who like to assert themselves. I'm not surprised. I'd never peg you to end up with a wishy-washy dude who yessed you to death."

"Ugh, I've become the wishy-washy one," I lamented, wiping my eyes.

"No, you haven't. You just have a huge soft spot for really hot guys who have control issues."

"Have I thanked you recently for being my friend and kicking my ass when it's needed?"

She snorted. "Don't thank me. Just, you know, put yourself first this time. Summon that brazen chick I met on City Walk who tore a new hole in some guy's ass because he thought grabbing your boob was the cool way to hit on a girl."

"I forgot about that guy." I wrinkled my nose. "What a douche."

"Ah, there she is," Stephanie squealed and hugged me again. "Come on. Grab a water or something and tell me all about that hot fucking kiss in the photo."

* * *

MONDAY

To: Alastair Holden <aholden@holdenworldmedia.co.uk>
From: Amelia Meyers <ameyers@wmzb.net>
Subject: Press Release

I'm sitting at my desk, staring at a press release about some guy who is the new CEO of Holden World Media. Do you know him? He sounds persnickety.

Lia x

To: Amelia Meyers <ameyers@wmzb.net>
From: Alastair Holden <aholden@holdenworldmedia.co.uk>
Subject: Hmm

He's actually rather posh. I hear he drives a sexy little car and has a thing for American girls who trip over carpets.

Yours,

Alastair x

To: Alastair Holden <aholden@holdenworldmedia.co.uk >
From: Amelia Meyers <ameyers@wmzb.net>
Subject: Re: Hmm

Is that so? Sounds like he thinks quite highly of himself. How was your weekend?

Lia x

To: Amelia Meyers <ameyers@wmzb.net>
From: Alastair Holden <aholden@holdenworldmedia.co.uk>
Subject: Mundane

It was boring. Filled with meetings and boardrooms and old men in ties. I've only just arrived back in Glasgow this morning. Want to come over for dessert?

Yours,

Alastair x

To: Alastair Holden <aholden@holdenworldmedia.co.uk >
From: Amelia Meyers <ameyers@wmzb.net>
Subject: Tempting

I am hungry…

To: Amelia Meyers <ameyers@wmzb.net>
From: Alastair Holden <aholden@holdenworldmedia.co.uk>
Subject:

They don't feed you at work? Or do they, and you've been banned as a result of your voracious appetite?

To: Alastair Holden <aholden@holdenworldmedia.co.uk>
From: Amelia Meyers <ameyers@wmzb.net>
Subject: Smart-Ass

This must be that British humor I keep hearing so much about.

That's enough out of you. I have to concentrate on my show. Isn't it late over there? Or are you up taking over the world one media outlet at a time?

Lia x

To: Amelia Meyers <ameyers@wmzb.net>
From: Alastair Holden <aholden@holdenworldmedia.co.uk>
Subject: Saucy

I'm fairly certain you meant to say **humour**.
I'm not interested in taking over the whole world. Just yours.

Alastair x

To: Alastair Holden <aholden@holdenworldmedia.co.uk>
From: Amelia Meyers <ameyers@wmzb.net>
Subject: Not So Fast

Sticking an extra 'u' in the word only makes it look funny. It doesn't make *you* funny.

I won't be conquered that easily. Stop emailing me. I need to finish these scripts. Talk to you tomorrow.

Lia x

To: Amelia Meyers <ameyers@wmzb.net>
From: Alastair Holden <aholden@holdenworldmedia.co.uk>
Subject: Good Night

Don't work too hard. Please message me when you get home so I know you've arrived safely.

Yours,

Alastair x

TUESDAY

To: Amelia Meyers <ameyers@wmzb.net>
From: Alastair Holden <aholden@holdenworldmedia.co.uk>
Subject: Morning

I'm assuming since I never heard from you last night that you fell asleep at work. Good morning, Amelia Grace.

Yours,

Alastair x

To: Alastair Holden <aholden@holdenworldmedia.co.uk>
From: Amelia Meyers <ameyers@wmzb.net>
Subject: Comfy

For your information, I'm snuggled in my bed. I'd never sleep on that hard desk. No need to worry. Good morning, Alastair Reid.

Lia x

Sent by my DROID

To: Amelia Meyers <ameyers@wmzb.net>
From: Alastair Holden <aholden@holdenworldmedia.co.uk>
Subject: Jealous

You've just made it very difficult for me to concentrate on this very important conference call. All I can picture is you curled up under the blankets.

Yours,

Alastair xx

To: Alastair Holden <aholden@holdenworldmedia.co.uk>
From: Amelia Meyers <ameyers@wmzb.net>
Subject: Don't Blame Me

Focus, please. I'm off to run a few errands. I'll talk to you later.

Lia x

Sent by my DROID

To: Amelia Meyers <ameyers@wmzb.net>
From: Alastair Holden <aholden@holdenworldmedia.co.uk>
Subject: I Can't See You

I'm watching your live news stream online. Feel free to pop in front of the camera and wave hello.

Yours,

Alastair x

To: Alastair Holden <aholden@holdenworldmedia.co.uk>
From: Amelia Meyers <ameyers@wmzb.net>
Subject: Not A Good Show

Did you happen to catch the colorful language our meteorologist used in his toss back to the desk? Wait. Shouldn't you be watching YOUR station? What you're doing is against CEO protocol.

Lia x

To: Amelia Meyers <ameyers@wmzb.net>
From: Alastair Holden <aholden@holdenworldmedia.co.uk>
Subject: Protocol Expert

Well, Amelia Grace, you of all people should know that keeping a close eye on the competition is rather important. After observing your station's blatant disregard for language on live television (frowned upon by your FCC), I will be more than happy to instruct my employees not to follow down that path of destruction.

ARH xx

To: Alastair Holden <aholden@holdenworldmedia.co.uk>
From: Amelia Meyers <ameyers@wmzb.net>
Subject: Muppet

To: Amelia Meyers <ameyers@wmzb.net>
From: Alastair Holden <aholden@holdenworldmedia.co.uk>
Subject: Cheeky

I see your use of British slang is stuck on words you've already used. Need a lesson?

To: Alastair Holden <aholden@holdenworldmedia.co.uk>
From: Amelia Meyers <ameyers@wmzb.net>
Subject: No Lesson Required

Don't get your knickers in a twist. I know more than you think.

Lia x

To: Amelia Meyers <ameyers@wmzb.net>
From: Alastair Holden <aholden@holdenworldmedia.co.uk>
Subject: Disappointed

Knickers? The girl who knows fun British slang doesn't know that guys don't wear knickers?

To: Alastair Holden <aholden@holdenworldmedia.co.uk>
From: Amelia Meyers <ameyers@wmzb.net>
Subject: Relax

Don't be such a big girl's blouse.

Lia x

WEDNESDAY

To: Alastair Holden <aholden@holdenworldmedia.co.uk>
From: Amelia Meyers <ameyers@wmzb.net>
Subject: Hi

Hey. I was just having some lunch at my desk and wanted to check in with you. I hope you're not offended by the big girl's blouse comment. (Sorry) Also, I was just wondering what time we need to be at the airport tomorrow. You haven't told me when the plane takes off.

Lia x

To: Amelia Meyers <ameyers@wmzb.net>
From: Simone Turcotte <sturcotte@holdenworldmedia.co.uk>
Subject: FW: Flight Info - Meyers/Tempe - Orlando

Hello Amelia,

Mr. Holden asked me to forward you the flight information for Thursday evening. He's been tied up in meetings all day and sends his apologies for not doing this himself.

If you have any questions, please don't hesitate to ask.

Cheers,

Simone Turcotte

Executive Assistant to Alastair Holden
Holden World Media

——Forwarded Message——
To: Holden, Alastair <aholden@holdenworldmedia.co.uk>
From: Grimes, Kevin <grimesk@eliteavi.co.uk>
Subject: Flight Info - Meyers/Tempe - Orlando

Depart (MCO) 02.JUNE.11
20:25
Arrive (LHR) 03.JUNE.11
11:50

Depart (LHR) 07.JUNE.11
14:10
Arrive (MCO) 07.JUNE.11
18:35

PASSENGER: Meyers, Amelia G.
D.O.B. 15.SEPT.1983
PASSPORT: USA

PASSENGER: Tempe, Stephanie A.
D.O.B. 10.AUGUST.1981
PASSPORT: USA

I'll be flying to Orlando Wednesday. You can reach me by mobile if the itinerary changes.

Kevin

CHAPTER SEVENTEEN

"Mom is going to be so jealous that you got to see the wedding pictures before her." Dayna scrolled through hundreds of proofs on her computer. "Too bad, right?" She laughed and threw an arm around my shoulders.

"I think this one is my favorite." I pointed to a photo of us in the courtyard. It was candid; not posed. Dayna had her hands on her hips, laughing. I was holding both bouquets and smiling at her. The background was dominated by the castle.

"Aw. That's a cute one. I'll email it to you if you'd like. You can print it out and have it framed."

Andrew walked into the room carrying his iPad.

"She's already roped you into looking at wedding pictures? C'mon Day, she only got here this morning. Don't scare her away just yet." He sat on the chair opposite us. "Have you noticed there are three times as many pictures of her as there are of me? It's like I was a gatecrasher at my own wedding."

"Oh Andy. Please." Dayna brushed off his teasing with a wave.

"So, Lia. What time is this dashing date of yours stopping by to pick you up?" Andrew asked, crossing his legs at his ankles.

"He said eight-thirty. So, soon, I guess."

"Is my big sister nervous? This is so unlike you. You must really like him."

"I'm not nervous."

"Lies, all lies," Stephanie remarked as she bounded into the room. "You're pink in the face, you non-blusher, you."

"That's enough out of you," I grinned. "When's Darren getting here?"

"He just texted me. He's out front."

"What?" Dayna looked hurt. "Why didn't he ring the bell to come in?"

"He's hungry," Stephanie answered. "He sends his hellos and apologizes for being antisocial. Have fun with Alastair, Lia. See you guys later."

She waved, scurrying out the door.

Turning to me, my baby sister pursed her lips in mock disbelief. "I still can't believe you managed to snag one of the world's most eligible bachelors without even realizing who he was. I wish you'd said something at the wedding."

"There wasn't anything to say at the time. He was just some random guy I'd met."

"Alastair Holden is not just some random guy," she retorted. "Do you know how many girls would kill to be in your shoes right now?"

"Easy, Dayna," Andrew gently interjected.

I smiled at him, thankful for his ability to reel her in when she got overexcited about things.

The doorbell rang. Andrew popped up off the chair to answer it. Seconds later, I heard Alastair's distinct, smooth voice.

The chattering got closer as the two men walked into the living room. Alastair searched the room, honing in on me immediately. He was impeccably dressed, as usual, in faded jeans and a dark green button down shirt. The color accentuated his vivid eyes.

Dayna stood up and walked over to him with an outstretched hand.

"It's nice to finally meet you Alastair. My sister has told me so much about you."

"All good things, I hope." His animated grin was infectious. "It's lovely to meet you as well. How are things at the magazine?"

Dayna was momentarily stunned, but quickly recovered. "Pretty good. I have several new restaurants to write about in the next issue. Andy and I will be spending a lot of time eating over the coming weeks."

"Not that anyone's complaining." Andrew laughed and rubbed his stomach. "Best thing I ever did was ask a food writer to marry me."

"Thanks, babe."

I stayed by the couch, watching him interact with my sister and Andrew. His guard was up. His whole demeanor was impenetrable.

"Care to join us, Amelia?" he asked, catching my eye. He stared right through me as I walked toward them.

"Where are you guys off to?" Dayna asked, noticing Alastair lace his fingers with mine.

"Haven't decided yet," he said, squeezing my hand.

"Well, we don't want to keep you guys from your night out. Do you have the spare key, Lia?"

"I do, Dayna. Thanks. I won't be out late."

"It was nice meeting you, Alastair. We should all go to dinner before Lia has to fly back to Orlando. Maybe on Monday night?"

"That sounds great. Nice meeting you both." He led me out the front door and down to the car. His sporty Mercedes was parked against the curb.

"You drove here from Glasgow?"

"I did."

"Hmm." I slid onto the plush leather seat. Alastair got in and lightly squeezed my thigh. The warmth of his touch seeped through my jeans.

"Did you have a good flight?"

"It was alright. A little bumpy." Familiar piano music filled the car. "Is this what you listened to on your drive down?"

"Part of the way, yes. Do you recognize it?"

"I do. You were playing it at your house. John Field, right?" I smiled.

"Good memory. This piece is called *Nocturne Number Five*."

We drove past Westminster Abby, over a bridge across the Thames and headed toward the Jubilee Gardens. I saw the London Eye illuminated against the night sky. Alastair found a place to park at the Park Plaza County Hall and grinned at me.

"Fancy floating above the city with me?"

"Floating?"

"Yes. Floating. Come on." He got out of the car and opened the passenger door; all the while an amused grin remained plastered to his face. We walked a relatively short distance toward the London Eye.

"Are we going on that?" I asked, gazing up at the gigantic wheel.

"We are. Hence the floating."

"Your snark is duly noted, Holden."

"Feisty as always, Meyers."

Inside the welcome center, he led me to the Priority Desk. The girl working behind the counter nearly fell over sideways when she saw him approach.

"Good evening, Mr. Holden," she stammered. "I have your reservation here."

I watched in amused silence as she tried to maintain a professional expression. She placed a bottle of champagne, along with two glasses, on the counter.

"The champagne is yours to keep, so don't feel as though you have to finish it while on the Eye. Here are your glasses and your tickets. I'll let the priority boarding gate know you've arrived. Thank you and have a lovely time."

"Would you mind carrying the glasses, Lia? Try not to drop them."

I followed him outside and up the metal walkway toward the priority boarding area. A young man waved us into an open capsule.

Alastair walked in first, placing the champagne on the wooden, oval bench in the center of the capsule. I went in after him and put the glasses down. The sliding doors closed with a small swoosh.

"It's just us?" I looked around wide-eyed.

"Of course it's just us." He popped the cork and poured champagne. "For you."

He glanced at the capsules in front of and behind us. I did the same. They were empty.

"Come stand by the window with me," he requested.

Joining him, I watched the ground become smaller and smaller as the capsule lifted higher.

"Have you been on during nighttime before?"

"No. Just during the day." I looked at the twinkling city lights. "It's so pretty."

"You're so pretty."

"Cheesy," I muttered, rolling my eyes.

"I heard that." He squeezed my waist. "A toast," he grinned, raising his glass.

"To what?"

"To your being here with me. And to proper date number two." He lightly tapped his glass against mine. We sipped in silence.

"I didn't know you were keeping track."

"Well," he said, taking my glass and placing it on the bench with his, "I am."

I had a difficult time tearing my eyes away from his. A warm sensation spread through my body when he wrapped his arms around me.

"I'm glad you're here," he whispered.

"Me too."

The window was at my back faster than I said those two words. Panicking for a second, I pressed my hands against his chest.

"Sorry," he breathed. "You just look so…"

Slanting his head, he kissed me. It was gentle at first, then grew more intense. His quiet moans drove me insane. I knotted my fingers behind his neck, holding him in place. Parting my legs with his knee, the full weight of his body melted into mine.

For a second, I thought I was actually floating. My feet weren't touching the floor. He'd hooked my legs around his waist, cupping my behind in a firm grasp. I did not care one iota that I was plastered against a pretty sizable window in the middle of London. This long, deep lustful kiss we were locked in vaporized any sense of modesty I normally employed.

Trapping my lower lip between his teeth, he bit it lightly. I slumped against the window and groaned.

"Jesus, Alastair."

"My Lia." Keeping me caged against the window, he focused his stare. It was wild and hot. *And possessive*. I stiffened against the glass.

A strange expression crossed his features. His eyes cooled down as his gaze softened. Fearing I'd made him think he was scaring me, I pressed my lips to his neck. His breathing became labored while I moved my tongue up his neck before nipping at his earlobe. A growl rose from the back of his throat. His mouth found mine again and we were locked in another passionate kiss.

Not even the promise of a clear, perfect view of London could lure me away from the pressure and warmth of his lips. He placed his hands on the glass, on either side of my head.

"Touch me, Lia," he rasped. "I like when you put your hands on me."

Resting his elbows on my shoulders, Alastair pressed his body into me even more.

I yanked the tails of his shirt out of his jeans, running my nails up his back. Groaning, he kissed me harder, swirling his tongue around mine. At this point, I didn't care that we were in a glass capsule hundreds of feet above the ground. I was all sensation and I wanted him.

Breathing hard, he pulled away, lowering my legs to the floor. Not wanting to break this moment, I hooked my fingers through the belt loops on his jeans and held him against me. He closed his eyes and moaned softly.

"We're missing the view, love."

"Not really."

"But I want you to see it. You can stare at my boring face for the next few days." He grinned and peeled his body away. "Come on."

Vibrating with want, I half-heartedly pushed myself off the window. I took Alastair's outstretched hand and let him lead me to the opposite side of the capsule.

"Stand in front of me."

I did. He banded his arms around me, resting his chin on my shoulder.

"There, to the left, are Big Ben and Parliament."

The buildings glowed a soft gold that reflected off the river. I'd seen them at night before, but not from such a high vantage point.

"Wow. They look so lovely."

Alastair buried his nose in my hair. I looked farther out into the distance at the various buildings and homes. All of them were lit up and practically twinkling.

"There's so much of London I want to share with you. So much of England. Can you stay longer than four days?"

"I wish. I have a little something called a job to get back to at some point."

"Can you convince them to give you the rest of the month off?"

"You're cute," I laughed. "I can't do that. I've already taken so much time off this year between the wedding and now. I'm probably going to be working straight through to the New Year at this rate."

"Hmm." He turned me so I faced him. His crisp button down shirt was a tad rumpled, as was his hair. "We have another fifteen minutes left. Would you like more champagne?"

"Only if you can will it over here. I'm not letting you go."

"I like the way you think, Meyers." He brushed his lips against mine briefly. "My aunt and uncle are looking forward to meeting you. My aunt especially. She's been asking me tons of questions about you."

"Oh, God. Really?"

"Don't worry. I didn't divulge too much information."

"Why am I not surprised?"

"Cheeky. Come on. Champagne." He strode over to the bench and offered me a glass. I enjoyed a fairly sizable sip.

He turned and looked out the window. "If you peek out that way, you can still see Tower Bridge."

I looked in the direction Alastair was pointing. There, in the distance, stood Tower Bridge, glowing brightly as it stretched across the river.

"I may only go on this at night. These views are amazing."

"Glad you like it." He fidgeted a bit with his glass. An odd expression crossed his face briefly. I wasn't able to decipher it, as usual. I decided to nip any potential mood swings in the bud.

"Were you serious about wanting to show me around England?"

"Very. Why? Do you have something in mind?"

"Well, this will probably sound super touristy, but I've always wanted to see Stonehenge. Is it far from where your family lives?"

"Not too far. Maybe an hour or so by car. Would you like to go there?"

"Yes, please. Unless you'd rather not drive that far."

"I think I can handle a drive to Stonehenge." He grinned. "We'll go on Sunday. Sound good?"

"Sounds fantastic."

Standing close to him, I asked, "Feel like watching the rest of the skyline with me?"

"Most definitely."

Snuggling against his chest, I watched the ground draw closer and closer. The rhythm of Alastair's heartbeat sped up. Closing my eyes, I listened to it, knowing it was my touch that made him react this way.

I ran my hand lightly down the front of his shirt, stopping at the waistband of his jeans.

"Are you teasing me?"

I grinned. "No."

"No?"

He spun me around, holding both hands behind my back. His flashing green stare was filled with raw desire. He leaned in, but didn't kiss me. Instead, he let go of my hands and tickled me furiously. The playful, flirtatious look on his face was priceless. He was positively beaming.

Just when I thought I couldn't take any more, he stopped. A brilliant smile was plastered to his face.

The doors to the capsule swooshed open.

"Looks like our ride is over. Time to get you back to your sister's."

I smiled, knowing I had the whole weekend to spend with him. Butterflies rustled in my stomach. I had to remember to keep a cool head while I was here. The way he entwined his fingers through mine made me melt. He placed a light kiss on my knuckles. We walked along the banks of the river for a while, not saying anything to each other. It was a peaceful, relaxing stroll.

When we arrived at his car, he opened the door for me.

I studied his profile in the light and shadows of the passing street lamps as we drove back to Gypsy Hill.

"You're staring."

"Does it make you nervous?"

"No," he smiled.

Alastair eased the car down the street leading to Dayna and Andrew's place. A little tug of sadness pulled at me.

"Here you go. Back in one piece."

He offered his hand. I clasped it, letting him help me out of the car and guide me down the walkway.

"I had a great time tonight. Thank you."

"It was my pleasure." He stepped closer. "I'm looking forward to tomorrow. I'll pick you up around eleven. Sound good?"

"Sure."

"Eleven it is then. Sleep well, Amelia." He ran his thumb along my jaw and neck. "I'll see you in a few short hours."

Tilting my head up, I welcomed his kiss. He parted my lips with his tongue and melted into me. I was so close to the door, I leaned against it, pulling him with me.

"I should go."

"I don't want to you to leave," I whispered against his lips.

He grinned. "You'll see me soon enough. Get some rest. We have a busy weekend ahead of us."

"Good night, Alastair."

"Good night, love."

A lazy grin played at my lips as I watched him walk back to his car. He moved with such fluid control, it was mesmerizing. After he drove off, I went inside and found my sister typing furiously at the kitchen table.

"Hey. How was your date?"

"It was good."

"He's really nice, Lia. Andy and I both liked him." She stopped typing. "The way his eyes light up when he looks at you is incredible."

I smiled so widely it almost split my face in two. "He took me on the London Eye. We had champagne and looked at the city lights." The words gushed out of me like a teenager with a crush.

"I'm not just saying this to blow sunshine up your ass or anything, but he really does adore you. And from the look on your face, the feeling is mutual."

I stared at Dayna, swallowing hard.

"He's a big step up from you-know-who."

She started typing again, glancing at me from over the screen.

"You know," she continued, "he was on the society pages at Christmas. Some big charity holiday party or something. The only reason I remember it is because the restaurant that catered the event is a favorite of mine. In case you're wondering, he was dateless."

My curiosity perked up. "Is he in the papers often?"

Dayna laughed.

"Not a whole heck of a lot. Only when he's at official company social functions. Even then he avoids the cameras. At least that's what the articles say. He's generally described as stand-offish and private. If you ask me, it only adds to his allure. The girls in the office think he's so mysterious and handsome. All they talk about is wanting to meet him."

"I'm not surprised."

"Oh my God, Lia. It's sickening to listen to them. Wait until they find out you're dating him."

"Maybe you should hold off on announcing it to the office."

"Are you nuts? And miss out on watching those crazy bitches freak?"

I panicked. "Dayna, I'm serious."

"Okay, okay. I won't say anything." She searched my face. "Are you excited about the party tomorrow? It's supposed to be the social event of the summer."

"Thanks. That makes me way less nervous."

"You'll be fine. His aunt and uncle will love you. So will his grandfather. Just turn on the Meyers charm and you'll have them all under your spell."

"We shall see. Is Stephanie back yet?"

"Yeah. She got back about twenty minutes ago and went right to bed."

"I should do the same. Thanks for letting us stay here."

I stood up, pushing in my chair. Dayna got up and gave me a hug.

"Anytime. Our house is always open to you."

"You staying up for a bit?"

"Yeah. I want to finish this article. Polish it up. See you in the morning."

"Good night."

I tiptoed into the guest bedroom to change. Stephanie was fast asleep. The green notification light was blinking on my phone.

11:38pm Thank you again for a lovely evening. Sleep well. x
I curled up under the blankets and fell asleep with a big, stupid grin on my face.

CHAPTER EIGHTEEN

The car slowed, turned right and stopped at an iron gate. Stone markers on either side boasted the name Holden. Alastair leaned out the window and entered a code into the security keypad. Peering out the window, I saw nothing but a small, tree-lined road.

"Ready?" He flashed me a hundred-watt smile and drove through the gates.

Oak trees arched their branches overhead, providing a lush green canopy. The leaves were dusted in gold from the mid afternoon sunshine.

Out of nowhere, a massive gray stone mansion rose out of the grass, dwarfing me, the car, and anything else in its way. The road, which I quickly realized was the driveway, snaked around to the front of the imposing structure, curving into a circle. Sections of the stone front were covered in ivy near the windows.

It's not a house, it's Harvard.

"It's just a building," Alastair reassured me. "It won't bite you."
"I know," I glowered. "I just wasn't expecting it to be so, you know, big."

Chuckling, he squeezed my knee. "Let's go, Meyers."

Shaking off my ridiculous nerves, I stepped onto the gravel, smoothing down my blue cotton dress.

It was quiet. The air smelled like fresh cut grass and flowers.

White clouds pulled across the sky like massive pieces of cotton. A gentle breeze sent goose bumps running over my exposed shoulders. Looking to my left, I noticed a lone tree, its branches stretching toward the sky. *I wonder if that's where he was sitting in that photo.*

"Come with me." Alastair's warm breath tickled my ear.

I looked up at him, struck by his confident smile and relaxed demeanor. If I didn't know any better, I'd have thought he felt right at home here. But I did know better. His eyes betrayed him. It was subtle, but I saw flashes of dread.

"Sure."

He took my hand, leading me to the front door. It had the same iron as the gate covering a pane of thick glass. Seconds after Alastair rang the bell, I heard muffled footsteps approaching. The door swung open and a tall, attractive woman smiled warmly at us.

"Alastair. You're here." She engulfed him in a hug, pulled back, and looked at him. "You look wonderful. And you must be Amelia. I've heard so much about you."

She hugged me a bit too tightly for someone I'd just met.

"I'm Katherine, Alastair's aunt. Please, come in." She led us through the entryway, through another set of doors and finally into the marble foyer.

Katherine Holden's elegance blended right in with our surroundings. She fingered a piece of her short, light, blonde hair before addressing us.

"How was the trip down?"

I followed a couple steps behind them, soaking in every inch of the place. She led us into a spacious sitting room. Even with all the luxurious furniture and priceless paintings, it was lived in and welcoming. I couldn't help but compare it to the sterile, museum-like quality of Alastair's house.

Sitting in the far corner of the room was a baby grand piano. The wall behind it boasted window after window after window.

Tinny sounding voices lured me back to reality. My hand

warmed at Alastair's gentle squeeze.

"Why don't you two get yourselves settled? Alastair, your uncle and grandfather are in the study if you'd like to say hello. Your old room upstairs is ready and waiting for you. Do you need help with your luggage?"

"No, thanks. I can manage."

"Alright, darling." Katherine turned toward me. "You are every bit as lovely as my nephew said you'd be. Please make yourself at home and don't hesitate to ask if you need anything. I'll see you both later at the party." She smiled and walked out of the room.

"I'll go grab the bags from the car. Wait here." Alastair walked toward the front door.

As soon as he left, I explored the room. Bypassing all the ornate decorations, I stopped near an end table holding various framed photos. I recognized his aunt in a few of them, along with his parents. There weren't many pictures of him as a boy, which disappointed me. Moving on, I noticed a beautifully framed photograph hung above the fireplace.

"Do you like it?"

Alastair's voice scared the bejesus out of me. I spun around.

"Sorry, didn't mean to sneak up on you."

"Do you walk on air or something? I didn't even hear you come in the room."

"You were rather lost in the photo," he grinned. "Come on. Let's go upstairs."

He lugged the suitcases to the main staircase. I followed him, strolling down a long landing before stopping at the last door.

"Did you ever get lost in this place when you were a kid?"

"Not really." He pushed the door open. "After you."

I walked in, struck by the massive floor to ceiling windows that dominated an entire wall. Looking out, I was greeted by a breathtaking view of rolling green hills. A reflection pool cut through a portion of the backyard. I could also see the party tent and various staff making final preparations.

"Are you sure it's okay for Darren and Stephanie to stay here tonight? My sister offered for us to stay at her house again if it's a problem."

"Of course they're welcome to stay. We obviously have the space."

I turned, confused by the distant tone in his voice. He stood in the middle of the room, watching me. I could tell by the look on his face something wasn't right. Sympathy pains rumbled through my stomach.

He sat on the edge of his four-poster bed, keeping a steady gaze locked on me. Surrounded by everything that reminded him of his childhood, he chose to focus on what I was doing. My heart wept for him.

"Big fan of the color gray?" I asked, motioning to the carpet and bed linens.

"I suppose," he shrugged. "It's non-threatening. Neutral. I don't know."

"Does it make you uncomfortable that I'm in here?"

"No. Quite the opposite."

Hearing that rustled a few sparks in my stomach.

"So, it feels good to be home then?" I asked, sitting next to him.

"This was never home for me. It never will be."

A cold, hard layer snapped into place over his already rigid exterior. He tensed when I rested my hand on his arm.

"Sorry. I didn't mean to upset you."

"It's not your fault," he sighed. "It's this place. I try not to come here unless it's absolutely necessary."

Pulling me into his side, he rested his chin on my head.

"Let's go to the study so you can meet my uncle and grandfather."

We walked down the main staircase, passing through the sitting room. Alastair paused at a large set of wooden doors, tapping on them.

A booming voice told us to enter. Moving cautiously across the hardwood floor, I noticed it was scuffed and well worn. Rich, dark wood-paneled walls surrounded the room. Two men sat stoically in front of a fireplace.

The one who appeared to be in his mid-fifties stood. Smoothing down his tie as he walked, he was next to Alastair in a couple of long strides.

"Good to see you, Alastair." His voice was deep and rich, with a slight rasp. He regarded his nephew with a cool gaze before embracing him in a wooden hug. Extending his hand to me, he introduced himself as Jason Holden.

"It's a pleasure to meet you, Amelia." His sapphire eyes were guarded.

"You as well, Mr. Holden."

"Yes. It is quite an honor to finally meet you, Miss Meyers. My grandson speaks very highly of you." Deep-set gray eyes darted over my face as Samuel Holden walked toward me with authority. His presence commanded attention. I held my ground, meeting his probing stare.

"You are far lovelier than the photos led me to believe."

Air exploded out of my mouth in a ragged gasp. I clutched my stomach, desperate to untie the knot that squeezed and tortured my body. I couldn't breathe. *What photos?* My head spun at a sickening speed, blurring the room.

"If you'll both excuse us," Alastair growled, securing his arm around my waist. I melted into his side, shell-shocked. I didn't know how I made it upstairs. A thick fog coated my vision. Closing my eyes helped, but didn't make the horrible twisting in my stomach go away.

"Lia, look at me," he commanded quietly, cupping my cheeks. I cracked my lids open to discover I was sitting on the bed. "That's my girl. I need you to relax, love. Can you do that for me?"

"Relax?" I lashed out. "Are you fucking kidding me? What is going on?"

I was being stalked again. How? My panic transformed into a deep-seated anger that burned from the inside out.

"I'll tell you. I need you to promise me that you'll calm down," he said evenly, pulling our foreheads together. "Please."

His soothing tone extinguished some of the flames licking at my skin. I wanted to run. My legs tingled with the urge to escape. The only thing stopping me was the look in his eyes. Behind the soothing tone was a man paralyzed by fear.

He dragged in a shaky breath. "I have…I have a rather testy ex. For the most part, she leaves me alone. But every now and again she does something crazy. This time she's hired a private investigator to follow me around."

My mind raced.

"How long has this been going on?"

"It started about a week or so before we met."

Ignoring my anger and disbelief, I tried to start putting a few pieces together.

"Those phone calls that you got," I mentioned, "Is this what they were about?"

He nodded, brushing the pad of his thumb over my lips.

"Why didn't you tell me?"

"I really didn't think it was something you needed to be bothered with."

"But I'm in the photos," I said, my voice rising.

"I know. I'm sorry. I was trying to protect you."

"How many are there? And don't lie to me."

Leveling a hard stare at me, he scowled. "The night we met. The football match. The cocktail party."

Fighting off the coiling panic, I swallowed. "So, since the beginning…"

"Yes."

"Nothing from Orlando? What about the kiss seen round the city?"

"No, that one was all tabloid fodder," he smirked. "I'm not the only one with paparazzi issues."

"Whatever." I waved my hand. "Don't change the subject. How

does your grandfather know about all this?"

"We monitor her email."

"Oh," I paused. "What? Why?"

His face turned ashy. "It's a really, really long story. What's important is we found out what she was doing and put a stop to it."

"Is she dangerous?"

"No. She's just very bored and very rich."

Not sure what to make of all that, I flopped back on the bed and stared at the ceiling. This weekend was shaping up to be a doozy. The mattress dipped when Alastair laid back next to me. Flashes of the past few weeks zipped through my memory. Incredibly, I laughed.

"What's so funny?"

"I don't know." I rolled over to face him. "I think I'm just really looking forward to a fun night with you, Steph, and Darren. We deserve it, don't you think?"

"I agree," he said, turning to look at me. "You continue to amaze me, Amelia Meyers."

"Why?"

"I know how much stalking and all that freaks you out. I'm sorry you got dragged into my mess. I'm also sorry for my grandfather's lack of tact."

"It's not my favorite thing, but I know how much it sucks. I can't fault you for not wanting to tell me. Although, it does strengthen my secret theory that you are, in fact, Batman."

"What?" He looked at me like I'd just told him two and two equaled six. "You're bloody barmy, you know that right?"

"But I got you to smile, so barmy or not, I win."

A lascivious grin curled his mouth. "Not so fast."

Moving with the speed and agility of a cheetah, he pinned me down and started tickling me. My squeals echoed through the bedroom, rising high into the vaulted ceiling. I laughed so hard I thought I might burst. It would be worth it though, because his eyes were free again. Shining and unguarded, they danced with elation.

When he finally stopped, I stared at him, breathless. Leaning down so our noses touched, he whispered, "You have that look again."

"So do you," I said, running my hand through his hair.

Confused, he cocked his head to the side. "What do you mean?"

"You look happy."

For a second I thought he was going to kiss me. Then, his expression shattered. My heart deflated watching the light and joyfulness seep from his eyes, replaced by stone. I waited, letting him find his balance. When he did, I was rewarded with a long, slow, passionate kiss. It was different from all the others he'd given me. This one was mind melting.

"I have a confession," he murmured on my lips.

"What?"

"You're the first girl I've kissed in this room."

Smiling like a loon, I ruffled his hair. "I better be."

"Someone," he squeezed my waist, "has a smart mouth."

"Would you expect anything less?" I laughed.

"I suppose not," he said, sitting up. "What color dress are you wearing tonight?"

"Burgundy. Why?"

"What color shoes?"

"Silver." I sat up, watching him walk to his suitcase. "Do you want to wear my outfit this evening?"

"Cheeky," he grinned slyly, pulling out a neatly wrapped box. "This is for you."

He'd bought me a present? My stomach and heart switched places. I took the box, staring at it in disbelief. The wrapping paper was shiny and silver, professionally folded and smoothed out over the box. Unwrapping it slowly, I kept an eye on the guy with the dark red hair hovering next to me.

As soon as the paper fell to the floor I gasped. The name Christian Louboutin stared at me, etched into an oversized shoe box. Opening it, I saw the red soles through the tissue paper. A pair of five inch platform heels covered in clear Swarovski crystals glittered inside.

"Oh my God."

"You looked so amazing wearing the red ones at the gala. I saw these and thought they were perfect for you. Do you like them?"

"They're gorgeous," I breathed out in awe.

"Will they look good with your dress?"

I couldn't tear my eyes away from the sparkling heels.

"Yes. Yes, they will," I said dreamily, a smile crossing my lips. "Thank you."

"You're welcome."

Glancing up at him, I saw shades of happiness flicker behind his eyes again. I secretly hoped it would stay there.

CHAPTER NINETEEN

Hundreds of guests mingled under the massive party tent set up in the backyard. Mini white lights were wrapped around tree branches and lantern lights sat strategically along walking paths so guests could find their way around easily. I heard Stephanie squeal in delight from the dance floor. She was bent backwards in a dramatic dip courtesy of Darren. The small group of people who had gathered to watch them dance applauded with gusto.

I watched as Alastair charmed several partygoers. He looked so dashing in his charcoal suit. Glancing up, he caught my eye. Grinning, he tilted his head and motioned for me to join him.

"Here we go," I muttered. "More introductions."

"Doctor and Mrs. Wilson, I'd like you to meet my date, Amelia Meyers."

Smiling more at the fact that he called me his date than actually meeting these people, I shook their hands. We engaged in polite chatter before escaping to a quiet corner near the reflection pool.

"You're beautiful," he whispered as we stood in the moonlight by the water. He slid his hand along my hip, dipping his fingers dangerously close to the impressive slit that exposed my thigh.

"You're a big hit with everyone. They all want to know about the mysterious Amelia."

"Mysterious?" I scoffed. "If they only knew how truly boring

I really am."

"You are far from boring. You are intriguing. Exquisite." He kissed me. "Smart. Sexy."

I stroked his tie, grinning. "You have quite a way with words."

He moistened his lips, fixing a dark stare on me. "You like my tie?"

"Yes." I looked up at him coquettishly. "I have a thing for sexy guys in suits."

"Do you?"

"Mmhmm. I like to wear their ties, and nothing else."

The stunned silence amused me. I bit the inside of my lip to keep from laughing. A provocative smile spread along his mouth.

"Don't make promises you can't keep."

Cupping my chin, he stared with such longing I almost stumbled backwards. A persistent dull ache grew in my stomach. I hooked my arms around his waist, pulling him closer. The heels had given me some added height, but not enough to be eye to eye. I'd have to settle for eye to mouth.

"Keep looking at me like that and our time at this party will be cut short."

The dangerous tone in his voice sent a pleasurable shiver through my lower abdomen.

"Is that a promise?"

Raising an eyebrow, he slanted his head. My lids fluttered closed as I anticipated the warmth of his lips on mine.

"Alastair Holden. It's been a long time." A breathy voice cushioned by a light English accent floated through the night air. It knocked me out of the seductive haze I'd been enjoying. Alastair cringed.

Standing a few feet away from us was a strikingly beautiful raven-haired woman. She glided closer, offering a manicured hand to him. He shook it politely.

"Hello, Emma. You're looking lovely this evening."

I took some satisfaction in hearing no warmth in his tone. He was all business.

"Always so proper," she laughed. "I suppose it's fitting now that you're CEO. Congratulations." She rested a hand on his arm, hooding her violet eyes. I wanted to claw them out of her cherubic face.

"Emma, have you met my girlfriend? Amelia Meyers, this is Emma Whelan."

It was a good thing he had a firm grip around my waist otherwise I would have fallen ass over elbow into the reflection pool. *When did I graduate from date to girlfriend?*

She plastered on a sugary smile and shook my hand.

"Nice to meet you, Amelia."

Perfectly white teeth remained frozen in a plastic smile. I didn't miss a beat and smiled with just as much saccharine. Tension crackled above our heads.

"Lovely to meet you as well, Emma."

Her smile faltered for a moment. "You're American? How fantastic. Where are you from exactly?"

"Connecticut, but I live in Florida now."

"And how did you two meet?"

Her shrewd eyes sized me up. Alastair laced his fingers through mine.

"We met in Glasgow several weeks ago," he answered. "She was in the area for her sister's wedding."

Emma's burning amethyst stare met Alastair's warning emerald gaze.

"That's lovely." Her beguiling smile cut through the night. "If you'll excuse me, I'm going to make my way to the tent for dinner." Her hips swayed seductively as she walked away.

Alastair let out a slow breath.

"I think she liked me," I joked.

"She has her moments."

"How do you know her?"

"Our families go way back," he answered, smoothly deflecting any follow up questions. "Hungry, Meyers?"

"Always, Holden, always."

Arriving back at the party tent, we took our places at the table with Katherine, Jason, and Samuel. Alastair also arranged for Darren and Stephanie to sit with us so I wouldn't be too overwhelmed by the Holden clan.

"Oh my gosh, Lia," my best friend gushed.

"Oh my gosh, Stephanie," I mimicked.

"I have news."

She stared at me, her ice blue eyes glittering.

"Well are you going to tell me or stare at me all night?"

"I have an interview with Finley Marketing and Advertising," she beamed. We both squeaked in delight, trying not to draw too much attention from the rest of the table.

"That's fantastic news, Stephanie," Alastair said. "It's a great company."

"Thank you. I guess this means if I get hired I'll be doing the graphic design work for you."

"Possibly," he grinned. "Unless MacCourty puts you on something he deems more exciting."

"Aye, he has a point," Darren volunteered. "Wouldn't want to bore her to death with broadband internet."

I relaxed into the chair, glad to see them all getting along. The wait staff arrived with dinner. We all quieted down to eat and then listen to several speeches before Alastair was introduced. Even though he was shrouded by his protective shield, he looked right at home in front of the large crowd. Hundreds of eyes focused on my handsome, newly minted media mogul.

He embraced the spotlight, his magnetic charm commanding attention. It was impossible for anyone to tear their eyes away. I was so proud of him.

Once he finished, several well-dressed gentlemen surrounded him and engaged him in a rather spirited discussion. The band started playing again.

"Come on, Lia. Let's dance," Darren offered his hand and smiled. I accepted and trotted off with him. Darren was a phenomenal dancer. Even though I could just about keep up, I never lost my footing and was spun, dipped, and twirled around the dance floor. The raucous applause at the end of the song shocked me. Breathless, I looked around at the smiling faces that had gathered to watch us.

"That was brilliant," Darren exclaimed, pulling me into a hug. Another song started, much slower than the last. A bit wobbly, I made my way off the dance floor and almost walked into someone.

"Sorry," I said, putting my hand on his back.

"No problem," he answered, turning to me.

I stared into a pair of familiar hazel eyes.

"You're Brent, right?"

"Good memory. Nice to see you again, Lia."

"Yeah, you too." I smiled.

"Care to dance? Granted, I'm not as skilled as your friend there."

"Oh, I don't think—"

"I realize I acted like an arse that night at the cocktail party. My apologies. Let me make it up to you. I promise I won't step on your toes."

Skeptical, I scrutinized his expression. Seeing nothing but a genuine offer, I accepted. Back out on the dance floor, he pulled me into a gentle, but firm, embrace. He smelled pretty good, too. Not as great as Alastair, but he had a fresh, clean scent, like he'd just stepped out of the shower. Grinning, he did a little spin move.

"Not bad." I laughed.

"I've been practicing all week."

Relaxing into his embrace, it hit me that this was first time in a long while that I've been able to enjoy an innocent moment with a guy and not be afraid of any repercussions.

"What is it you do in Glasgow, Brent?"

"Real estate. Rather boring stuff, but it keeps me busy. I own a few properties in the city and have plans to open a new ultra lounge. Actually, that's coming up soon. Two weeks from now."

"Wow. That sounds exciting. Good luck."

"Thanks," he said, turning us so I faced the band. "Listen, this may not be my place to say, but be careful with him."

I stiffened. "You're right. It's not your place."

"He uses women, Lia. He treats them like objects and when he's done, he throws them away."

"I know all this," I seethed. "Not that it's any of your business—"

"He fucked my sister for years and when she fell in love with him, he told her to bugger off. She hasn't been the same since."

My lungs collapsed on themselves leaving no room for oxygen.

"You don't know him like I do, Lia. He's cold. He has no regard for anyone's feelings."

We weren't dancing anymore. People swayed and moved around us while I remained caught in a prickly bubble. I didn't want to process anything Brent said. Backing away, I uttered a weak goodbye and blindly made my way back to the table. I grabbed two champagne flutes off one of the trays a server was carrying, knocking each one back. Relieved to see the table empty, I sat down heavily.

Rubbing my temples, I scanned the crowd for Alastair. He'd disappeared. So had Darren and Stephanie.

A light floral scent appeared out of nowhere.

"Hello, Amelia."

Ugh, not now.

I looked up to see Emma leaning against the chair.

"Do you mind if I join you?"

"Not at all," I answered in my most sugary sweet voice.

She sat, politely folding her hands in her lap. "How did you do it?"

"You're going to have to be a little more specific," I said, annoyed.

She half-smiled. "How did you get him to call you his girlfriend? I've known Alastair since we were teenagers. We have…history." A cunning smile crossed her overly glossed lips. "In fact, it was just a few weeks ago that I was in his bed."

I wanted to vomit.

"I'm the closest thing to a girlfriend he's had," she bragged, leaning in. "Not Olivia, not you, not that clingy bitch Sarah. He comes back to me. Always."

The dark recesses of my mind spread its poison fast and furious. I wanted to scream at her, but I was paralyzed by dread and insecurity. The champagne swirled in my stomach like a witch's brew.

"I don't know what you're trying to do," I responded, much stronger than I expected, "but he's with me. If you had any class whatsoever, you'd go back to the hole you crawled out of now."

She laughed. "He used his charm with you, didn't he? It's rather infectious. No wonder so many women think they'll be the ones to change him or break down his defenses. You'll never get him to love you back."

"So why do you bother with him, then?" I bit out. "He'll never love you either."

"He's a great shag, as you no doubt already know. And he's attentive. I don't need his love, just his body."

An intense ringing in my ears echoed through my head. I sat still as a statue, not able to breathe or move.

"Emma. A word. Now," Alastair snarled from behind me.

"Of course," she said, her eyes frosting over. "It's been a pleasure, Amelia."

Alastair held her by the elbow and guided her away from the table. Still in a daze, I watched their heated conversation. He looked furious. Every bone in my body ached.

When the discussion ended, Emma walked away brusquely, but not before shooting me a smug grin. Alastair lowered himself to one knee in front of me, holding my hand.

"Talk to me," he insisted.

Wetting my lips, I met his gaze. He was completely shielded. There wasn't a trace of emotion on his face or in his eyes.

"I think maybe it's time I found Steph and Darren and went back to my sister's."

Air pushed out of his lungs rapidly. "Okay. Before you do, will you walk with me? Please?"

"I don't—"

"It'll just take a moment."

Locking his fingers through mine, he pulled me up from the chair. We stole away to the opposite end of the reflection pool, away from everything. A cool breeze coasted over my bare shoulders, making me shiver.

"She was out of line."

"But she didn't tell me anything that wasn't true, did she?"

"No," he answered, a marked coolness to his tone. It reminded me of something.

"That night at the cocktail party, when you took off to take care of something. It wasn't about any photographs, was it? It was Emma. She was there."

He paled under the moon's silver glow. "Yes," he said in a strained whisper.

"Why didn't you just tell me that you already had a date that night? It's no—"

"I told her not to show up. The night I asked you, after I left the hotel, I called her and told her not to show up. I didn't know she was there until she walked into the lounge. She'd already checked into our room—." He stopped short, regret seeping out of his pores at the slip of the tongue.

"Your room?" I asked, shaking.

"I didn't mean it like that. I don't bring women to my house and she has a…Why does it matter anyway," he groused.

"Because up until half an hour ago I didn't know you still socialized with your former fuck buddies," I attacked. "Especially ones who think you belong to them."

He winced, backing away from me. I kept laying it on thick.

"This is the messy part you said you were ready for, Holden.

These are the ups and downs in a relationship. I'm not some pawn for you to label as a girlfriend just to make another woman jealous. I'm. Not. Interested. I can deal with your hang-ups about dating. They're workable. But I will not be the ace in your pocket to show when it's convenient."

I only stopped because I needed to breathe. I was so wound up I wouldn't have been surprised if sparks shot off my head. Alastair stared in disbelief, then without warning, lunged at me, kissing me so feverishly I lost my balance and fell to the ground. Arms, legs, lips, and tongues tangled in an unruly mess on the cool grass. It would have been comical if I hadn't been so aroused. This was not a gentle kiss. This was crushing. Lip-bruising. I didn't want it to stop.

"You make me lose control, Lia," he panted. "But it feels so good with you."

Our mouths collided together. My mind was a scrambled mess floating somewhere in oblivion. I clawed at his back when his hips started grinding into mine. Pulling on his hair to yank our lips apart, I gasped.

"There are hundreds of people in that tent. Do you want to give them a show on your first official day as CEO?"

The untamed gleam in his eyes dulled briefly. "Fair point. I'm taking you inside." A sexy grin spread across his mouth. "Then, I'm taking you."

CHAPTER TWENTY

My dress hit the floor a second after we got into his bedroom. Moonlight spilled in from the windows bathing the room in a soft silvery glow. The serenity of the light clashed with our desperate movements.

Tossing his jacket and tie to the side, Alastair unbuttoned his shirt and shrugged it off. I froze in place. His physique was glorious. Toned, cut muscles defined his chest, arms and stomach. I took a breath before lowering my eyes to his hips. The way his pants were hanging, I could just about see the enticing v-shape of his lower abdomen.

I practically mauled him, unbuttoning his pants to shove them down. An inescapable urge to run my fingers through the reddish-brown smattering of chest hair took over. It tickled my nose as I kissed and nipped his skin. He exhaled slowly, trembling a bit. I lightly ran my fingernails down his stomach. He unclasped my bra, freeing my aching breasts. Cupping them, his tongue circled one nipple, then the other.

Kissing me with ravenous desire, he pushed me against the wall.

"Tell me what you want," he ordered. The hot stiffness of his erection pressed into me. I reached down and felt him through his boxer briefs.

"This. You."

He finished undressing himself and me with great finesse. Pinning me to the wall again, he flattened his chest to mine. His lean, athletic body felt so good against my softer, curvaceous build.

"You are stunning, Amelia. Absolutely stunning."

His hooded, calculating stare gave me a rush. I parted my lips, ready for whatever came next.

"This look," he whispered, running his knuckles down my cheek. "What are you going to do about it?"

Eyes burning with lust, he wrapped my left leg around his hip. "We'll start here," he declared, pushing himself into me. The sudden fullness and pressure made me cry out. He slid into me possessively, staking his ownership over my body with authority. His thrusts were fluid and deliberate. The only sounds echoing through the room were his groans and the soft thudding of my back against the wall.

All I could do was grab his hair. I locked onto his feral eyes, astonished that he was being so wild and untamed with me. Keeping our bodies connected, he pulled me from the wall and sank onto the bed. His heat and heaviness blanketed me. I was immobile.

In one swift motion, he pulled out, kissing and licking my breasts, my stomach and my inner thighs. A delicious mess of ecstasy and desire clouded my brain in the best way possible. The smooth skin of his cheek brushed against mine.

"My Lia," he murmured, guiding himself back inside me inch by delectable inch. My toes curled as he pushed in deeper. I sank my nails into his back, reveling in every flex and twitch of his muscles. Unleashing a guttural moan, he thrust harder and faster, panting heavily into my neck. I grabbed at every available inch of flesh on his back, finally wrapping my fingers around his perfect ass, pulling him into me.

This was far more carnal and raw than what we had done in my living room. He was claiming me, possessing me. I went limp beneath him moments before blazing heat seared through my body.

I surrendered to each sensation, burning, clenching and tensing as I shook with anticipation.

"Look at me," he ordered, teasing my body with slower, methodical thrusts. I could barely open my eyes. When I did, I saw all of his energy and attention centered on me. Our connection at this moment was so much more than physical. He let himself go with me, just as I did with him.

Surrendering to him, body and soul, I lost myself to the increased rhythm of his movements as he ravaged me on the bed.

The world around me ceased to exist. I was weightless, floating. My body convulsed in an explosive wave as a mind-blowing orgasm surged through me. I shouted incoherently, quivering from head to toe. Awareness flooded back as Alastair abruptly stopped his feverish pumping, sliding in and out with deliberate, measured intensity. He cried out my name, swelling inside me, before collapsing in a panting heap on me.

We remained entwined with each other until our breathing slowed and temperatures cooled.

"I can't move," I marveled.

Alastair rolled onto his side, studying me with an astute eye. "Good."

His lazy, crooked grin accelerated my already frantic heartbeat.

"Glad you approve."

He curled his body into my side, draping his arm across my stomach. "Get used to it."

"You want me immobile and useless?" I teased.

"Not quite," he smirked, tracing the curve of my breast. "My goal is to keep this look on your face permanently."

"I could say the same about you."

His post-coital reverie stuttered, then smoothed out, accompanied by a warm glow behind his eyes.

"So this falls under the 'amazing sex' category, then?"

"It was alright," I shrugged, trying to hide a smile.

"Wow," he chuckled. "Do I at least get another chance to redeem myself?"

Laughing, I straddled him and kissed along his neck. "You can have as many chances as it takes, Holden."

Fisting his hand in my hair, he pulled it gently until I met his white-hot stare. "Do you have any idea how gorgeous you look right now?"

I swallowed hard and shook my head.

"You're an angel," he whispered, cradling the back of my neck. "My angel. My Lia."

* * *

I ran my fingers along the cold piano keys. For the time being, I was alone in the sitting room. Peeking out the window, I could see the last guests waving goodnight. We'd missed the remainder of the party after going another round in the bedroom. I was more than happy to put on some comfy clothes and relax. A satisfied ache hummed along my hips and thighs. Taking one last look out the window, I saw Darren and Stephanie sitting by the reflection pool, chatting.

"Do you play?"

I whirled around at the sound of Alastair's voice. "Again with the sneaking."

"Sorry." He grinned sheepishly. "So, do you play?"

"Um, not technically. I've never taken lessons or anything, but I can sort of play by ear."

"How so?"

"May I?"

Alastair nodded and motioned for me to sit. Closing my eyes, I thought for a moment. A disjointed melody echoed in my memory. Focusing harder, the melody sharpened, becoming clearer. I remembered it being soft and soothing then becoming a little louder, but not too intense. The notes were gentle. Placing my fingers on the keys, I started playing the opening to John

Field's *Nocturne Number Five*. It wasn't perfect by a long shot, but it was decent. I played about thirty seconds of it, stopped and opened my eyes.

Alastair stared in wonder.

"How do you do that? It's incredible."

"Not sure, really. I've always been able to just pick out a tune and duplicate it. If I hear something enough times part of the melody sticks with me. Sadly, I can't read music so that's as far as my alleged talent goes."

A clattering of shoes and laughter echoed from the main hall. Darren and Stephanie burst into the sitting room.

"Uh oh, Lia's at the piano," Darren teased. "Up for another round of My Bonnie Lies Over the Ocean?"

Clapping my hand to my forehead, I laughed. "I totally forgot about that. Where were we that night?"

"City Walk," Stephanie answered. "It was Two For Tuesday and you had triple that amount."

Alastair straddled the piano bench, hugging me into this chest. "Two For Tuesday? Is that what it sounds like, Meyers?"

"Exactly," Darren and Stephanie responded in unison.

"Thanks guys. You're all aces."

"About tomorrow," Stephanie started, plopping on the couch, "um, would you be severely pissed off if I went back to Glasgow with Darren to get ready for my interview?"

"When is it?"

"Monday morning. When Cassie found out I was over here, she asked if I could come in for it."

"You don't have your portfolio or anything with you," I cautioned.

"She knows. She just wants me to get in there and meet a few people."

"Okay," I shrugged. "Go for it."

"What are you two doing tomorrow?" Darren asked.

"We're going to Stonehenge," I answered.

"Plus something else that only I know the answer to," Alastair said with a smug grin.

"Good luck keeping it from her," Stephanie laughed. "Lia's a pain in the ass when she wants answers."

"So I've learned. She is quite the curious kitten, isn't she?"

A ridiculous grin almost split my face in half. Darren and Stephanie exchanged glances. I flushed from the nuanced way he stroked my back and arms. *Much too potent*.

"Okay, well, you two go on then. Thanks for the invite, mate and for letting us stay here."

I stood up to hug Darren goodnight.

"If your girl gets this job, you best be coming out to visit," he grinned.

Stephanie tackled me. Sometimes her hugs were a bit too dramatic. "Of course she will. But let's not get ahead of ourselves. Right? Right."

We all said our goodnights and retired to our respective bedrooms.

* * *

The cool, hard wall calmed my flaming skin. I wrapped my arms around his neck, waiting to welcome the exquisite fullness. Grasping his thick, unruly hair, I pulled his head back to gaze deep in his eyes. Dark, liquid emerald irises met mine. He was so beautiful, so perfect. And then, he wasn't. Chocolate-red hair faded to dirty blond. Verdant eyes darkened to a threatening sapphire. I was trapped, held hostage. He shouted and raged at me. I couldn't squeeze my eyes shut to block out his fury. The plaster cracked and shattered next to my head. Dust billowed and circled around me.

Shivering, I opened my eyes. Silky strands of moonlight pooled on the carpet. I tried to keep from gasping, forcing the air to move in measured bursts through my lungs. The gentle sounds of slumber floated from the mattress. Propping my head up so as not to wake him, I watched Alastair for several minutes. His face was the one I wanted to see in my dreams.

Climbing out of bed with great care, I grabbed my cell phone. The bright green notification light was flashing. Locking myself in the bathroom, I checked it. Twenty-five unread texts. *It's starting again.* Clutching the sink, I choked back a sob. I refused to let him ruin this.

* * *

The circular formation of ancient stones stood silently in the middle of a field. Faded gray rocks imprinted upon lush green grass. Mist hovered above the ground, adding to the mystical aura of the surroundings. I couldn't help but walk with reverence, absorbing every last detail on the stones. Some were covered in moss, others were shattered on the ground. Light gray clouds mixed with blue sky, casting a peaceful gloom over Stonehenge.

"You're very quiet," Alastair mused, standing behind me with his arms around my waist.

"I'm just taking in the view. I had no idea it was so mystical. And it's smaller than I thought." A little twinge of jealousy pinged in my heart while gazing at the stone's self-assured stance in the world.

"Thinking about me?" He nipped at my earlobe.

No, I'm trying to figure out how to deal with those two dozen text messages.

"Maybe."

"I saw my aunt this morning while you were showering. I think she likes you."

"You think," I inquired.

"I know," he whispered.

"Really? We haven't said more than five words to each other."

"She has a knack for reading people. Says you have a genuine way about you. No pretenses. I say she's spot on in her assessment."

Curious to see his expression, I turned to face him. The soft breeze that had been blowing through the field caught a piece of my hair, delicately twisting it until it landed under my chin. He reached for the strand and tucked it behind my ear. His goofy grin was too precious.

"Have you seen enough of the Henge? I have somewhere else I want to take you."

"I think I've seen all there is to see here. By all means, take me away." Smiling, I linked arms with him as we walked back to the car.

"So where are we going?" I asked once we were on the road.

Alastair rolled his eyes and laughed. "Took you long enough to ask. Sadly for you, my answer hasn't changed. I'm not telling."

"Will I like it?"

"Yes."

"Have you been before?"

"Yes. I'm still not telling you."

A triumphant smile spread across his face. I pouted, grabbing his thigh and squeezing. He jumped.

"Causing an accident will only delay the arrival, Amelia." His tone grew serious. "Patience. Is. A. Virtue."

"Sorry."

"It's alright. Wouldn't want to crash my sexy little car now, would I?"

He switched the radio on and scrolled through his iPod via the fancy buttons on the steering wheel. James Morrison's *You Give Me Something* filled the car. Settling into the plush leather seat, I lost myself in the music watching the muted green scenery fly by. I still had several unresolved questions from what had transpired last night. *Who's Olivia?* Plus, the whole annoyance from back home. For the time being, I decided just to enjoy a drama-free day with him.

"We've arrived," Alastair announced as he parked the car.

"Oh my gosh. Are we at Ascot?" I squeaked, getting out of the car. A massive stadium-like building with a curved design and steely glass exterior sat next to a grass racetrack. I noticed a horse lazily galloping along.

Much to my delight, Alastair laughed at my giddiness. Leading me through the Grandstand entrance, we walked hand in hand along the edge of the track.

"Wow. This is amazing," I gushed. "I didn't know you could just walk out here like this."

"Well, technically you're not supposed to when a practice is in session. But I may have pulled a few strings."

His shy smile tugged at my heart. I stopped walking and hugged him, whispering my thanks.

"You're welcome."

I squeezed him tighter.

"Your hugs are a thing of beauty but please don't cause me to pass out."

"Sorry." I released him. "Don't know my own strength sometimes."

"No harm done. This was a nice surprise then? Worth all the secret keeping?"

"Absolutely."

"Good. I like making you happy and surprising you. Your whole face lights up. It's like watching a rose bloom."

The atmosphere shifted between us. Not in a lusty, pulse pounding way, but in an everything-is-falling-into-place way. His sensual gaze and warm touch were mesmerizing.

"I wasn't expecting this to happen. You. Me." He paused, running his knuckles down my cheek. A kaleidoscope of emotions was etched upon his face. "I'm completely enchanted by you."

Time stopped. The world stopped. The only thing that mattered was this moment. An incredible warmth flowed through me, spreading from my stomach to the tips of my fingers and toes. Unable to speak, I blinked rapidly. *Christ, I must look like a lunatic.*

"Seems I have you at sixes and sevens."

"Enchanted you? How?"

Shrinking a bit into his shell, Alastair swallowed. "I've spent so much time running from who I am, I never considered the possibility I'd run into someone along the way."

"Why would you ever want to run from who you are?"

Retreating further, he looked down. I cupped his chin, tilting his face up. "Tell me."

Luminous green eyes darkened as sadness, anger and fear twisted through them. His expression hardened and the muscles in his jaw twitched.

"No."

"Alastair. Please," I persisted in a gentle tone. "You can tell me."

"No," he barked. "I'm not ready yet. Please don't ask me again." He walked several feet away, clenching and unclenching his hands into fists.

"My eyes deceive me. Is that little Alastair Holden?"

The unknown voice cut through my despair over his reaction. A kindly, elderly man smiled as he approached us. Alastair looked at him curiously.

"You wouldn't remember me; it's been too long." He walked over with his hand outstretched. "Ian Stone."

Recognition spread across his face as he shook hands with Ian. "I do remember you. You took care of that gigantic thoroughbred. How are you?"

"Yes, yes. Elusive Lightning I think his name was. I'm well, very well. How are you? How's your grandfather?"

I stood silently, watching them chat and reminisce. I was struck by how at ease Alastair always seemed when he spoke with people he either barely knew or was meeting for the first time. When he turned on the charm, it sparkled.

Sadness filled my heart. His words from before still echoed. I'd hoped we'd reached a point where he could trust me with his secrets. Patience was never one of my strong suits and it was certainly being tested these days.

"I noticed you were walking with a lovely young woman," Ian

paused, turning to me. "Ah, there she is. Come here, love."

Tucking my hands in my pockets, I walked over, hoping a smile brightened my face.

"I'm assuming this pretty lady is your girlfriend, Alastair."

Ian looked at him expectantly, waiting to be introduced. I held my breath.

"This is Amelia Meyers." He stood next to me, placing his hand on my lower back. "Ian takes care of the horses here."

Exhaling at a snail's pace, I tried to keep a relaxed smile in place. *Last night I was his girlfriend, today I'm just Amelia.*

"A beautiful name for a beautiful girl. Pleasure to meet you. Care to take a tour of the stalls and see some horses? Training has pretty much ended for the day."

"Would you like that, Lia?"

A tornado of emotions swirled through me as I nodded in agreement. He didn't confirm or deny the girlfriend comment, but I was supposed to embark on a tour of the stables with unbridled enthusiasm. *Oh, of course he's holding my hand.* Pushing down any burgeoning insecurities, I chose to focus on the present and not worry about the invariables.

Ian rambled on and on about all the horses who'd ever stayed there. The sweet smell of hay and pungent odor of the animals coated the air.

One horse had his head hanging out of the stall. His large, soulful eyes sized us up. Muscles rippled down its legs and through its impressive chestnut colored body. His coat was more like velvet on steel, than skin on muscle. He was tall, he was lean and he was powerful. I gazed into his friendly eyes.

The horse nodded its head up and down, almost as a greeting.

"Look at that. He wants you to pet him. Go on," Ian motioned for me to approach the animal.

"Hold out your hand, palm up," Alastair instructed.

Not wanting to scold him for his well-intentioned assistance, I just grinned and moved closer to the horse. This wasn't the first time I'd been around these magnificent beasts.

Holding out my hand, palm up, I waited for the horse to sniff me. Its hot breath blew against my palm. The warm, suede-like muzzle brushed over my skin, tickling me. Running my fingers under its throat, I scratched him.

"Someone is well versed in the equine world. You've really got a way with him," Ian leaned against the stall, handing me an apple. "Here. It's his favorite snack."

"Thanks." The beautiful creature immediately gobbled it up, nudging me for more. The force of his affection almost sent me flying.

Ian laughed and clapped Alastair on his shoulder. "That's it. He's got a friend for life now. You'll have to bring her back here often or else he'll think she's abandoned him."

Patting the horse's neck, I turned to Ian. "What's his name?"

"Steel Rhapsody. He's a rare one, a force to be reckoned with on the track."

"He's beautiful."

"Glad you like him." Ian turned to Alastair. "It's good to see you again. It's been far too long since you've been round these parts. I remember when you were just a boy, running through here with Grace. Don't be a stranger."

Hearing someone mention his sister's name out loud was a shock. I hadn't heard anybody utter his parents' or sister's names since I'd been here. Being mindful not to stare, I kept petting the horse while gauging Alastair's reaction. His features were frozen solid. No emotion, positive or negative, gave itself away.

"It was an absolute pleasure meeting you, Amelia." Ian approached me with a half-hearted smile. He must have known he'd struck a nerve. *Poor guy.* "I do hope to see you again soon."

Waving goodbye to us, he shuffled toward the opposite end of the stable. Alastair still hadn't moved.

"Feel like walking around a bit more or would you like to get home?"

"We can go back to the house." He pushed out the words, exhaling harshly.

I'd lost him again behind that damn impenetrable shield.

CHAPTER TWENTY-ONE

The house was empty and eerily quiet. Jason and Katherine had left a note saying they'd gone out to dinner with friends. I didn't mind the alone time, but I wished Alastair's mood wasn't so dark. He'd been silent the whole drive back.

We walked upstairs, not saying a word to each other. Almost at my breaking point, I excused myself to use the bathroom. Once I was locked behind the door, I sat on the edge of the tub. Caked mud from the stables fell off my shoes in zigzagged clumps. I took the filthy things off and wiped the floor. What was it about his sister that upset him so much? He'd even had a negative reaction the night I asked what her name was.

I'd never lost anyone close to me, so I could only imagine how painful his childhood had been. Surely his aunt and uncle had sought out professional help for him? A six-year-old boy couldn't possibly escape a major loss without some emotional scars. Sighing, I tapped my nails on the porcelain.

A soft knock at the door interrupted my thoughts.

"Lia?"

Opening the door, I saw a worried looked engraved on his face.

"Are you alright? You've been in there a long time."

"I have? Sorry. I was just, um," I turned and glanced at the tub, the toilet, anything that could give me a spark of inspiration. I turned back, defeated. "I was just thinking."

A faint smile ghosted across his lips. "There's shepherd's pie in the kitchen if you're hungry."

"Really? I love shepherd's pie."

"Brilliant." He offered his hand. "Let's go."

I held his hand tightly as we made our way downstairs. A large casserole dish sat on the island in the middle of the kitchen. Alastair had already taken the liberty of setting out two plates with utensils. I never usually admired kitchens, but this one was rather beautiful. It was open and airy, with all the walnut cabinets banded in stripes of dark grain in warm, sepia-gray tones.

"Make yourself comfortable," Alastair pointed to bar stools at the island. I waited while he grabbed a bottle of wine. When he put it down in front of me, my eyes widened. It wasn't wine. It was champagne.

"Are we celebrating something?" I stared at him.

Silent as stone, he popped the cork and filled the glasses. His expression was unreadable. A sense of impending doom spread though me. By the time he served the food and sat down, I'd lost my appetite.

"You're not hungry?" he asked without looking in my direction.

"I am. It looks great," I lied, pushing the food around with my fork. I took a tiny bite, sending my knotted stomach on a rampage. It didn't want to be nourished, it wanted to be left alone.

Echoes of the grandfather clock chiming in the new hour filled the house. I forced myself to eat several more bites and drink most of the champagne. *One mustn't waste a glass of Veuve Clicquot.*

Resting the fork on the plate, I folded my arms. This was ridiculous. His mood was so uninviting. Even his body language was off-putting.

"Is there a problem?" I asked.

Not looking away from the food, he answered, "No."

I wanted to grab his rigid shoulders and shake the life out of him.

"Well, I'm done. I'm going to take a bubble bath."

Alastair stood up, collected the plates" and then looked at me. His eyes were dark. "Will you be long?"

"I don't know. The usual bubble bath time, I guess."

"Don't be long," he ordered.

"Hey," I said, my voice rising. "Watch your tone with me. I'll take as long as I want. What does it matter to you anyway? You haven't said more than ten words to me in the past hour."

Getting off the stool, I planted my feet on the floor and engaged him in a challenging stare. His stunned silence didn't last long. A wall of terror surrounded me when I saw him come around the island. Two realities merged together into one horrific scenario. He was coming at me. I was going to be trapped again. Not sure what I was seeing or what was going to happen, I backed away fast, slamming into the wall. Panic strangled my heart. Squeezing my eyes shut, I could still see him looming in front of me.

Bracing for what I knew would happen next, I lowered my head, praying for it to be over fast.

"Lia."

My whispered name wafted through the tunnel of my mind, beckoning me. Every muscle in my body mimicked steel. I was unable to move.

"Lia. Open your eyes."

The soothing, calm cadence of the request broke through my fear. Still not certain as to what I'd see, I cracked open my eyelids. Blinking, I stared at the floor, seeing nothing but my own feet. Nothing else was in front of me, nobody was holding me against the wall. Lifting my head, I saw Alastair, pale with shock, standing by the island. He took a step forward.

"Don't come any closer," I begged, tears flowing down my cheeks in rivers.

My plea stopped him dead in his tracks.

"I'm not going to hurt you, love," he reassured me, holding up his hands.

Trembling from head to toe, I let his words bathe and comfort me. I knew he wouldn't hurt me. I knew it with every piece of my being.

"Alastair," I whimpered, slumping against the wall. With great caution, he walked toward me. When he was close enough, I collapsed in his arms. Securing me in his embrace, he held me, letting me cry into his shoulder.

"Sweetheart, I've got you. I've got you," he repeated, stroking my back. "You're safe with me."

Hearing his declaration launched another wave of tears. I hugged him so tightly I was afraid I'd crush his ribs. He didn't seem to mind. I stayed latched onto him forever; I didn't know how long and I didn't care.

"Let's go to another room," he suggested. "Somewhere cozy and quiet. Alright?"

Lifting my head, I met his gaze. His eyes were huge, filled with worry. I melted into his side, letting him lead me through the house. We passed a formal dining room and what appeared to be a library. At the end of a short hallway, he pushed open a large door. Inside was a dimly lit room. It was inviting and warm and had a plush wraparound couch nestled against the walls. I relaxed almost instantly. The comforting hues of creams, golds" and olive greens wrapped around me like a blanket.

"This was the playroom when my sister and I were little," he explained, settling onto the couch with me. "There used to be a toy box there. We'd play in here for hours and hours. It's my favorite room in the house."

He wiped my tears with his thumb.

"I can't bear to see you cry, Lia."

Welling up for the millionth time, I curled up next to him, resting my head on his chest.

"May I ask you something?" he proposed, kissing the top of my head.

I nodded against him.

"You don't have to answer if you don't feel comfortable doing so, but will you tell me what happened with Nathan?"

I didn't want to. If I had my way, I'd bury every memory I had of him. But to be fair, I had to answer.

Wiping my eyes, I sat up. "It started out fine. He was charming and fun and exciting. I mean, his dad's a senator, so I got to experience some great things. After about a year or so, I noticed a change."

Glancing at Alastair, I saw I had a fiercely attentive audience.

"I consider myself a friendly person. We'd be at public functions or big, fancy dinners and I'd talk to whoever struck up a conversation with me. One time, some guy started talking to me. He was harmless, but Nathan..." I paused. "I never told you his name, did I?"

"No."

"How do you know it?"

"That night at your flat, when Stephanie called, you said you had an incident with Nathan. I sort of figured it out."

His impish grin made me smile.

"Right. Anyway. Um, to make a long story short, he'd get upset when I talked to other guys. It didn't matter who it was; he didn't like it. Then he started leaving gifts on my car when I was out with my friends."

"Gifts?"

I nodded. "Roses, little notes, things like that. It was cute at first, but then things would show up on my car when I hadn't told him where I was going. He would text me incessantly wanting to know where I was, who I was with, stuff like that. I brushed it off for as long as I could, thinking maybe he's doing all this because his dad is so high profile. But I got tired of it and wanted out."

I blew out a shaky breath. This was harder than I thought.

"Take your time," he said, rubbing my arm.

"It wasn't just the stalking or the jealousy. He would, um, if I didn't want to have sex or whatever, he would tell me that I was nothing but a tease and that no guy would want me. He said I wasn't worthy of a real man and that he could have any woman he wanted." I squared my jaw. "He called me a pity fuck once."

The couch dipped as Alastair shifted his weight.

"You continued seeing him after he said that," he seethed.

"Do you want me to continue?"

Alastair ran both hands through his hair, looked at me, and nodded.

"I had a pregnancy scare. I'm on birth control but at the time I was in the middle of switching the kind I used. I always made sure we were careful, but nothing is one hundred percent." I laced my fingers together. *This is too hard.*

Sensing my trepidation, he ran his knuckles over my cheek.

"When I told him, he got angry. He said I did it on purpose and wanted nothing to do with it or me," I paused, gulping. "We were standing in his kitchen. I was by the table and…and he came at me. It all happened so fast. He had me pinned against the wall. He was yelling and swearing. I tried to get away but he grabbed my arm and pushed me back against the wall. Then he—" I stopped short, afraid I'd break down.

"Hey," Alastair said softly, cupping my chin. "Look at me."

What little emotional strength I had left was supported by his unwavering gaze.

"He was so angry," I continued.

"What happened?"

"He punched the wall next to my head." My voice shook. "His hand went right through it."

"I should have torn his head off that night," Alastair snarled.

"Everything sort of moved in slow motion after that. He let go of me and started yelling that his hand was broken. I grabbed my bag and ran out. I don't remember getting into my car or driving away. The next thing I knew I was home." I shrugged and slumped into the cushion. Blood pounded in my ears.

"Was the gala the first time you'd seen him since that happened?"

"Yep."

"Have you heard from him since then?"

Averting my eyes, I shook my head.

"Don't keep things from me, Lia."

Swallowing back a salty lump, I squeezed my hands together.

"He texted me a few times. That's it."

"What did he say?"

"Nothing. Stupid stuff. It's not a big deal."

"I'd feel better if you changed your mobile number." He clenched his jaw.

"I'm not doing that."

"You need to."

The commanding tone he used pissed me off. *Seriously? After what I just finished telling him?*

"You need to cool it with the orders," I snapped. "They're just text messages. I can handle it."

"I can't keep you safe if he has a way to harass you."

Raking my fingers through my hair, I leaned into the cushions. "I'm not in mortal danger. Stop being so dramatic."

Letting out a short burst of air, he relented. "Fine. But if he so much as touches you—"

I pressed my finger to his mouth, cutting him off. I was tired. I was emotionally drained. I didn't want to hear it.

"Leave it alone for now, please. I appreciate your concern. Scale it back a little. I'm sitting in a cavernous house in the English countryside. He can't get me here."

I still had my finger on his mouth but could see the wheels turning in his brain. Puckering his lips, he kissed it.

"You're stubborn, Meyers."

"I know. It's part of my charm."

"Hmm." Tenting his fingers in front of his mouth, he grinned. "Go upstairs and change into your little pajamas, then meet me back here."

"Why?" I arched an eyebrow.

"Just do it," he insisted, standing up.

Ten minutes later, I was back in his childhood playroom, lounging on the couch in my PJs. Bored, I decided to explore a bit. There was a bookcase next to the media center. I checked out all the different titles. They were mostly reference books. One shelf was dedicated to photo albums. Dozens of them. The temptation to snatch a few off there and look through them was strong.

"There you are."

I turned and saw Alastair standing at the door with his hands behind his back. A calculating grin was on his lips.

"Sit," he ordered, angling his head toward the couch. Doing as I was told, I narrowed my eyes at him.

"You're very bossy all of a sudden."

"Think so?" He grinned and knelt down in front of me. "Right foot please."

"Why?"

"No questions, kitten. Just give me your foot."

Holding onto my calf, he produced one of the crystal-encrusted heels he'd given me from behind his back. I stifled a laugh as he slipped it on my foot, thinking this was a weird Cinderella-esque moment. He wrapped his fingers around my left calf, lifted my leg and put the other shoe on my foot.

As pretty as they were, they looked silly sticking out the bottom of my pajama pants. *Someone has a thing for high heels.*

"Don't move. I mean it." He wagged a finger and walked to the media cabinet. I'd grown quite fond of his choice in sleepwear. Those cotton bottoms hugged his butt nicely.

"Enjoying the view?" he asked with a crooked smile. "Go stand by the windows. Please."

Mock saluting him, I stood nearest the windows in the corner of the room so I was surrounded by glass. Peering up, I marveled at the onyx sky dotted with stars.

Soft piano music filled the room.

"Ella Fitzgerald?" I asked, turning to see Alastair next to me. He nodded, sliding his hands around my waist.

"We still haven't had a proper dance," he said, pulling me close.

"The one at the fair doesn't count?"

"Not technically. It was rather abrupt. No talking during this song. Listen to the words."

Swaying his hips to the music, he moved me with him. I melted into his embrace much more readily this time, although I was a little nervous I'd step on his feet with these heels. Snuggling against him, I smiled. The guy who didn't 'do' relationships was a romantic at heart, and probably didn't even realize it. Running my nails up his neck and through his hair, I let the lyrics to *You Leave Me Breathless* swirl through my heart.

As Ella's satiny voice crooned out to an unseen lover to give their lips to her, I tilted my head up. Alastair pulled our foreheads together. The same fire that burned through my belly when we danced at the fair ignited.

"I do feel safe with you," I whispered.

Slanting his head, he sealed our mouths together. This would never get old for me; the sparks, the glorious mess my mind transformed into with every movement of his lips. He had me; body and soul.

"Upstairs. Now," he moaned.

My clicking heels echoed through the massive expanse of the house as I walked with purpose across the marble floor and up the main staircase. We collapsed in a tangled heap on the bed, tearing each other's clothes off. I didn't even care how many pairs of underwear he ripped off me. I loved the way he made my mind scramble with just a touch. I loved the way he kissed every inch of me like I was a goddess. I loved the way he sounded when I kissed him and worshipped his body.

Listening to his labored breathing as we waited for our bodies to cool down, I accepted the realization that I was lost in his haze and didn't want to be found.

CHAPTER TWENTY-TWO

"Good morning, Amelia."

I turned to see where the breezy, English accent was coming from. Katherine was standing by the entrance of the sitting room, smiling.

"Good morning," I replied.

"It's a beautiful photo, isn't it?" she asked, standing next to me. I nodded.

"Alastair took it about five or six years ago when he was in Rome. He'd been walking around on his own and saw that little flower poking out from a pile of dirt near a renovation area by the Colosseum." She smiled. "He'll never admit it but my nephew has a soft spot for fragile beauty. Something about how unexpected and delicate it is draws him to it I suspect."

"I never pegged him to have a soft spot for anything," I said out loud without thinking.

"He does," she smiled. "He's making breakfast now. Come join me in the sunroom while you're waiting."

I followed Katherine past the main staircase and through the kitchen.

"No peeking, Meyers." Alastair grinned from the stove.

"Cheesy omelets again, Holden?" I teased.

His aunt waved me through a set of French doors. The sunroom was warm and cheery, even though the skies were gray and bleak. Baskets of hanging verbena and sweet peas hung from some of the windows, filling the room with a sweet, floral scent.

The view outside was unreal. It was pastoral. Mile after mile of rolling hills, green grass and trees reaching for the sky. If it wasn't for the imposing mansion I could have sworn I was in a small, secluded cottage. *Like the one in Scotland.*

"Would you like some tea?"

Katherine's voice broke into my reverie.

"Oh, sure. Thank you."

"Here. Have a seat. Breakfast will still be several minutes. My nephew is a perfectionist, in case you hadn't noticed."

There was a platter of scones sitting on the table, along with a bowl of fresh fruit.

"Help yourself to whatever you'd like, Amelia. I have to admit, the scones are rather delicious."

"Please, call me Lia."

I smiled, reaching for a scone. It was still warm to the touch. I broke it in half, spreading clotted cream and jam on each piece.

"You prepared that like you've lived over here for ages," Katherine beamed.

"I've spent some time in London. When my sister moved there four years ago, I was volunteered to fly over and help her get settled in. Not that I minded. London is an amazing city."

"Alastair was still living in London at the time. Shame you two didn't bump into each other then." She tried to hide a sad smile with her teacup. My chest constricted. "But you know what they say, the timing is everything."

Questions jumped and bounced against the walls of my brain. This was my chance to ask just about anything. If anyone knew Alastair inside and out, it would be his aunt.

"He's very taken with you, Lia."

I almost choked on the scone. Katherine smiled apologetically.

"I don't mean to embarrass you. But it's true."

"He's very special to me."

Oh my God. I said that out loud.

"I know he is. I can tell by the way you look at him. He's lucky to have found you."

Our conversation was interrupted by the person we were discussing. Alastair walked into the room carrying a tray filled with food. The forced quiet was noticeable.

"You were talking about me weren't you?" He arched an eyebrow at me.

"Oh Alastair, stop teasing her." Katherine stood up and glanced at the tray before leaving. "Looks delicious. I'll let you two enjoy breakfast alone. Nice chatting with you, Lia."

He placed the tray carefully on a small table next to the window.

"Alright," he rubbed his hands together. "We have scrambled eggs, pancakes, sausages and toast. Sound good?"

The aroma of freshly prepared food filled the room. At the mercy of my stomach, I scurried over to the table.

"This looks amazing. And here I thought hangover food was the only thing you knew how to make."

"Does that smart mouth of yours ever stop?"

"No," I said, loading up a dish. "Get used to it."

We ate in comfortable silence for several minutes. He was a good cook, I had to admit.

"What are we doing today?"

Grinning mischievously, he answered, "Flying to Glasgow."

"Really? Why?"

"Stephanie is already there and it'll be easier if you're both in the same city when you fly home tomorrow."

All the food congealed in my stomach. "I don't want to go home."

Apparently my brain was on hiatus again, giving my mouth full range to do as it pleased. My words sucked the relaxing aura right out of the atmosphere. There wasn't any response from Alastair. Not a flinch, not a sigh, nothing. I didn't know what to think about that.

After we finished breakfast, he went to his grandfather's study to gather some files and sit in on a conference call. While relaxing in the bedroom, I decided to call Stephanie and wish her luck. Of course, I got her voicemail, so I left a long, cheerful message telling her that I'd see her later in the afternoon. Thankfully there weren't any additional texts from Nathan. I deleted all his messages from the other night.

About two hours later, Alastair appeared in the room looking stressed.

"Everything alright?" I asked, packing the last of my clothes.

"Yeah," he answered, distracted.

"You sure?"

A knock sounded at the door.

"Shit," he muttered, opening it. I saw his aunt, pale with worry.

"We're going to the hospital now." Walking into the room, she addressed me. "Sorry to leave like this, Lia. Alastair's grandfather has fallen ill."

Anxiety cast an uneasy pall in the room. Alastair was stony-faced.

"Is it serious?" I asked, trying to even out my nerves. Zero emotion emitted from him. He didn't even flinch when I put my arm around his waist.

"We're not sure," she admitted. "He left by ambulance half an hour ago. They have him in critical care as a precaution."

Ambulance? I didn't even hear the sirens. This house was a soundproof fortress.

"You both stay here." Katherine hugged and kissed Alastair. "We'll let you know as soon as we hear anything."

Hugging me, she whispered, "Keep an eye on him for me. He needs you."

She'd just placed a heavy burden on my shoulders. I was still navigating through the cracks and holes of his exterior. I'd had some success, but not enough to be comfortable thinking he'd use me as a crutch in times of uncertainty. I feared the exact opposite.

"Is there anything I can do?" I squeezed his arm, trying to catch his eye.

"No."

He appeared to be more agitated and tense than upset over this. It was hard to get an exact read on his demeanor. I selfishly longed to have just one uninterrupted day without any drama. It was almost as though fate was taunting me.

"If you want to go home a day early, I don't blame you."

His dull, lifeless tone tore a hole through my chest.

"Home? I thought we were going—"

"Plans have changed," he glowered. "I've arranged a flight for Stephanie from Glasgow, explaining what happened here."

"You what? She hasn't called me."

"I talked to Darren and told him you were already on your way back to Orlando."

Anger flamed from the pit of my stomach, fueled by disbelief. I didn't know who this pod person standing in front of me was, but I wanted him gone.

"Why would you say that?"

"Because you're leaving."

"No, I am not," I shouted. "You can't just tell me to go. Not when something like this has happened. I want to be here for you."

"Your wide-eyed approach to everything is something to behold," he laughed bitterly. "Not all situations can be solved with a warm hug or an encouraging smile."

His eyes were lifeless, dark pools. There wasn't even a glimmer of the man I'd danced with by the windows last night.

"I'm not trying to solve anything with a hug or a smile. I'm supporting you. That's what people do for one another."

"I don't need your support. I don't need anything or anyone," he said without an ounce of warmth or regret. "I've managed this long getting by on my own."

The room imploded with desolation. I froze in place, surrounded by the fallout of his harsh words.

"You're joking, right? You have a family that adores you. You—" I was cut off by his laser stare. It was tortured and angry.

"I have no family. They were taken from me in the most violent, horrible way you can imagine. I have no one."

"What about me?" I shook, tears brimming.

"You?" Dropping his stare to the floor, he inhaled slowly. Hairline fractures threatened to crumble his shell. I waited, hoping he'd soften so we could stop this frigid exchange. The silence suffocated me. Desperation and fear grabbed hold of my logic.

"I care about you, Alastair," I blurted out.

He snapped his head up, staring at me. There was something much more dangerous in his eyes now. Confusion and pain twisted his features. Turning his back on me, he walked to the windows.

The gesture hit me with the force of a freight train. Sinking onto the edge of the bed, I was consumed by the full weight of his fractured soul. All his charm, all his wit, everything that made him the person I adored really was just a flimsy exterior.

I'd fallen for it hook, line and sinker.

Weak.

This was the real Alastair Holden.

"Do you really want me to leave?" I challenged him one last time.

Nothing. No movement. Not a sound. Just an immobile silhouette by the window. I was done banging my head against the impenetrable shield. Upset as I was, I knew enough to stop torturing myself over something that would inevitably destroy the last shred of dignity I had left. I wasn't naïve enough to believe I could change him.

Yanking my suitcase off the bed, it hit the floor with a thud. I wasn't sure how I'd get to the airport, I just wanted to get out of this house.

"I'll drive you." A small voice skated across the room, stopping my heart.

"No, you won't. I'll take a taxi."

"You don't know which one to call."

"Then call one for me," I exploded. "Just do it so I can get the hell away from you and this house."

I rolled the suitcase into the hall and stormed toward the main staircase. Fury and adrenaline gave me enough strength to carry it down one-handed. I waltzed outside and stood on the driveway. A few minutes later I heard footsteps behind me.

"It'll be here shortly."

The deadness in his voice turned my stomach. I refused to look at him. The only thing that mattered was controlling the impending tidal wave of emotion.

"Kevin is already waiting for you at—"

"I'm not going on your plane. I'll fly stand-by if I have to."

"Lia, don't do that. You'll be sitting at Heathrow for hours."

A bit of his commanding tone colored the statement.

"I'll be fine."

"I don't want—"

"What you want is not a option," I yelled, spinning around to face him. "Go back inside, Alastair. You said you didn't need anyone and you do just fine on your own. Well," I gestured to the door, "you can't get any more alone than this."

I thought I saw him tremble, but figured it was just my delusional mind. Tires crunching on the gravel driveway provided much needed relief. The cab driver got out and placed my suitcase in the trunk. Weakened for a brief second, I turned to look over my shoulder. Alastair was still standing at the edge of the grass. This time, he was visibly shaking.

I wanted to run to him. I wanted to throttle the emotions out of him. Swallowing a sob, I climbed in the car. The last thing I saw as the cab pulled away was his face crumbling into despair. Curling up on the seat, I cried all the way to the airport.

CHAPTER TWENTY-THREE

Suitcases, backpacks and other assorted baggage circled methodically on the conveyor belt. A red light spun as an alarm sounded announcing more luggage arrivals. I stared blankly at the column jutting up from the baggage claim area.

"I see your bag."

Stephanie's voice barely registered on my radar.

"Come on, let's get you home."

Somebody else was probably controlling my legs from a distant universe with a crazy remote contraption. As far as I knew, I was just a floating head, detached from my body. I had zero awareness of time. No sooner had I sat in the car, I was being told we'd arrived. Whatever that meant.

"Why don't you go lie down. You look exhausted, Lia."

Stephanie busied herself closing the blinds. I stood in my living room, surrounded by familiar, comforting objects, feeling desolate. I wanted to shower. I'd been wearing the same clothes forever. I wanted to sleep, but couldn't quiet my mind. Everything was foggy and disjointed. I didn't know what I wanted.

"Can I get you anything? Are you hungry? Would you like something to drink?" Stephanie's soft voice cut through some of the murkiness.

"No. I'm not hungry," I paused. "You can go home. You're

probably still tired from your flight. Thank you for picking me up." I didn't recognize the sound of my own voice. It was listless and unexpressive.

"I'm staying with you. It's not up for discussion. You just spent the past sixteen hours hopping on and off planes to get home. You're miserable. And whether you believe it or not, being alone is the worst thing for you right now."

She bristled at my eye roll.

"I don't know what happened between you two, but your message scared the daylights out of me. I've never heard you like that before. I'll stay out of your way but I'm not going home."

I rubbed my eyes, not caring if I smudged whatever mascara was left.

"I'm going to shower," I droned, going into the bathroom.

Peeling off my clothes, I kicked them into the bedroom. I turned the nozzle all the way to scalding. Hot water streamed over me, washing away only what was on the surface of my skin. When I couldn't take the heat any longer, I got out and wrapped myself in a fluffy robe. Wiping away the steam from the mirror, I caught a glimpse of the most horrific dark circles known to man. Not caring, I pulled my wet hair into a low bun and went back to the living room.

"Feel a little better after your shower?"

I glared at Stephanie. *What a stupid question.* She shrank into the cushions after seeing the look on my face.

My cell phone beeped. Anticipation swept through me. It could mean a number of things, all of which I wanted to avoid. It beeped again.

"Does it need charging?"

She reached for it, tapping the screen.

"Yeah, it's dead. I'll plug it in for you."

I sat on the couch, still not fully grasping what was happening. "Maybe it'll help if you talk about it," Stephanie suggested gently.

I tensed, not wanting to unleash this torrent of despair. If I pushed it down far enough, maybe it would shrivel and die in the pit of my stomach.

"Don't do this to yourself, Lia. Let it out. I promise to listen. I won't comment or anything."

Exhaustion messed with my emotions more than anything. I ground my teeth, trying to overcome this hurdle. Tears squeezed out from my eyes, betraying my resolve. I blurted out everything in a stream of consciousness.

True to her word, she didn't say anything. She listened without judgment or bias. When I finished, I hugged my knees to my chest and sobbed.

* * *

Hours later, I woke up sweating. I'd gone to bed still wearing the robe and it was burning my skin. Ripping it off, I put on a t-shirt. The quiet room clashed with my frantic thoughts. Unable to rest, I went into the living room. Stephanie was asleep on the couch. I crept through the room and grabbed my phone.

Returning to the bedroom, I crawled under the blankets. The notification light blinked in all its green glory. A crushing sense of loss crippled me. The phone slipped out of my fingers and landed on the blankets with a soft thud. Rubbing the pain in my chest, I hoped it would relocate somewhere more manageable, like my little toe. Damn thing was stubborn and wouldn't budge.

Reaching for the phone, I woke it up to look at the home screen. My fingers trembled as I slid open the message bar.

To: Amelia Meyers <ameyers@wmzb.net>
From: Alastair Holden <aholden@holdenworldmedia.co.uk>
Subject:

I just want to make sure you've arrived home safely. Please let me know.

Alastair

I tossed the phone onto the nightstand. *Why does he care?* Angry tears bullied their way down my cheeks, landing in hot pools on the pillow. He told me to leave. He said he didn't want me there. An inferno of grief and emptiness spread through my body. When sleep finally wrestled the last bit of strength out of me, I dreamed of falling leaves.

Morning. Or maybe it was afternoon. Did it really matter? The bright sunlight hurt my eyes. Burying my head under the pillows was a novel idea, but it became uncomfortable after a while. Throwing the blankets off, I stared at the ceiling.

Hangovers had nothing on the discomfort that plagued my body. I was sore, I had a headache, and, oh yeah, a gaping hole in my chest. All the major players were present and accounted for. Glancing at the time I saw it was noon.

The one salvation in all of this was the fact that I didn't have to go back to work until tomorrow. Dealing with the high-octane personalities of the newsroom was something I needed to psych myself up for. The phone rang. I stared at the screen with moderate disinterest. *Christ. My mother.*

"Hi, Mom."

"Lia. Are you alright?" Her worried voice cascaded through the phone. "What happened?"

"I'm fine. I just woke up."

"Your sister is driving me crazy. Have you talked to her yet? She's been calling me non-stop."

"No. I haven't talked to her," I answered, monotone and annoyed. "Tell her I'm fine. I made it home."

My mother's voice softened. "Lia, honey, we're worried about you. Dayna was beside herself when she called us. What happened?"

"I don't want to talk about it. I'm home. That's all that matters."

"Maybe you jumped into a new relationship too soon after Nathan."

I fought an urge to vomit.

"Is there anything else you needed to talk to me about? I'm home. I'm fine. There's nothing more to say."

"I've been at this a lot longer than you have, Amelia." Her tone sharpened. "Don't let this consume you. Misunderstandings happen. It's what you do in the aftermath that defines the relationship."

I squeezed the phone. "I appreciate what you're trying to do, but right now I just want to be left alone."

"You'll figure this out. The heart is very vocal in these matters. Listen to it. Don't be afraid of what it tells you."

"Thanks, Mom. I'll talk to you later."

"I love you, Lia."

"You, too."

I hung up and shuffled into the bathroom. Broken, worn out and exhausted, I splashed cold water on my face and brushed my teeth. Hunger pangs tentatively made their presence known.

Stephanie was sitting on the couch flipping through an issue of Cosmopolitan. She brightened when I appeared.

"Good morning. Or should I say afternoon. Did you sleep alright?"

Biting my tongue against a sarcastic remark, I responded, "As well as can be expected."

"You look a lot better than you did last night."

I shot her an incredulous look.

"Well, I mean you look somewhat rested." Stephanie fidgeted with the magazine. "There's coffee if you want some."

"Thanks."

"I heard you on the phone. Did your mom call?"

"Yeah."

"I'm glad you finally got to talk to her. She called me when I was on my way to the airport to get you. She's pretty worried. Dayna is, too. You should probably call her next."

"Not right now. Maybe later."

Stephanie tried a different approach. "I was thinking, if you're up to it, we could go catch a movie today. There's a lot of new stuff out."

I prepared a cup of coffee and sat on the couch with her. Staying in bed all day, curled into a ball under the blankets was much more appealing than showering, getting dressed and being out in public.

"You know what, I don't want to see a movie. If it's all the same to you, I'd rather stay in. Sorry."

"Okay. Just thought I'd throw that out there in case you were up for it." Stephanie sat awkwardly. "So, are you okay?"

I snapped my head up and stared coldly across the room at the wall. "I'm fantastic. Never better."

"I'm sorry, Lia."

The hole in my chest expanded. Immense emptiness spread through the space where my heart should be.

"I can't do this. I can't. It hurts and I miss him."

Never-ending waves of tears and sobs seized me. I surrendered to the insurmountable pain and let it completely take over. It squeezed my chest until I thought I would break. When the tears finally slowed, I sat up and let out a big, shaky sigh.

"God. Look at me. I'm a mess."

"So am I, so am I."

I looked at Stephanie. Her eyes were red and she was wiping her nose. "We make a great pair though."

"It's like we're starring in our own Lifetime movie. All we need is the sweeping musical score to enhance the mood."

"Yeah, and the ridiculous title. She Cried, I Cried. Rogue Tears. Hysterical Sadness." Stephanie laughed uncontrollably. I tried to join in, but was only able to muster a few small giggles.

"Thanks for being here, Steph. I'm not the most pleasant person to be around."

"It's all part of the experience, my friend."

The experience. Right. This was an experience I would gladly skip. After wiping away what I hoped would be the last of the tears for at least ten minutes, I grabbed the remote and turned on the television. Stephanie stood up.

"Mind if I hop in the shower?"

"Not at all. Towels are in the closet."

Settling into the couch, I flipped through the channels. Talk shows, soap operas, and of course, the aforementioned Lifetime movies were all that was on. The next best thing was the news. I stopped at CNN to watch the big stories of the day. Politicians bickering, flooding in the Midwest and fires in California topped the headlines.

For a jaded news producer, that was a typical day. As the reporters and talking heads droned on and on about various hot topics, my thoughts wandered.

A flashy graphic caught my attention. There was some big, important news update and it warranted bold graphics and stern music.

"We have an update from London now, where media tycoon Samuel Holden has just been discharged from the hospital. The eighty-five year old collapsed at his home on Monday. Doctors say he suffered from exhaustion and dehydration. Holden left the hospital this morning and is said to be in good spirits."

I stared at the footage, enraptured. Indeed, there was Samuel waving to the cameras and walking toward a waiting vehicle. Behind him were Jason and Paxton. Then, there was Alastair. He was slightly hidden behind his uncle but the cameraman made a point of zooming in on his face. The reporter talked about how he'd just been named CEO and was the heir to the media empire.

He appeared tense and pale. His eyes looked tired as he tried to avoid to media glare. My heart lodged in my throat, beating hard and fast. He had his hands shoved in his pockets and walked slowly to the front passenger door.

"Anything interesting happening on the news?" Stephanie walked back into the living room. She looked at my face, then looked at the television. "Oh my God."

The footage looped back to show Samuel exiting the hospital again.

"I had no idea this was such a big story here," I admitted sheepishly. "I should have known. He looks so worn out."

"Maybe you shouldn't watch this."

"Why not? Chances are I'll have to write about it at work. May as well desensitize myself to it."

"Do Sydney and all the rest of them know he's the one you've been seeing?"

"Yeah. That, uh, picture and stuff."

"Right," she said, nodding.

The talking heads were very animated as they spoke of the Holden family. Much of their chatter was about Alastair and his new role within the company. The video played over and over as they talked endlessly.

The more I watched it, the more I could pick out subtle things about his expression. His mouth was turned down. His eyes were expressionless and dull. It hurt to see him like that. Mercifully, they finally moved on to another story. I flipped to one of the movie channels. Some nondescript action-adventure flick was already in progress.

"Hey, Steph? Do you know where my carry-on bag is?"

"I put it next to the kitchen table. Do you need something?"

"No. I was just going to unpack a little." Grabbing the bag, I went in the bedroom. I figured it was easier to unpack toiletries than clothes. Stephanie poked her head in the room.

"Do you want a sandwich or anything? I'm going to make a Chik-Fil-A run."

"No, thanks."

"Okay. I'll be back soon."

I unzipped the bag, removing a few styling products. Something tumbled onto the mattress. Without looking, I picked it up. It was small and hard. Confused, I looked down and almost passed out. I was holding a blue box with a white ribbon. I dropped it like it was on fire. It landed on the floor next to the bed. Clutching my chest, I knelt down. *A Tiffany box?*

I stared at it.

And stared.

"It's not going to open itself," I muttered.

Picking it up with shaky hands, I untied the ribbon and removed the lid. Inside was a white suede box. I took that out and sucked in a breath. I wasn't ready for what was in there. When did he put this in my bag? We'd been inseparable most of the time. The night we danced in his childhood playroom, maybe? He'd obviously been in my suitcase to get the shoes. *Why not just give it to me?*

Sitting on the floor speculating about this box wasn't going to get it opened any faster. Closing my eyes, I opened it.

CHAPTER TWENTY-FOUR

Wake up.
Shower.
Go to work.
Hide in a bathroom stall and cry.
Go home.
Barely sleep.
Repeat.
Repeat.
Repeat.

That was my list of things to do each day over the next week. By Friday, I was getting weird looks from my co-workers. Clearly, my attempts at acting normally at work failed. I threw myself into show preparations each day. Nothing too exciting was happening, so I had to settle on stories about car crashes, drug busts and one birth-in-the-breakdown-lane.

"Hey, Lia."

I hung my head, dreading whatever it was Jeanie wanted.

"Yeah?"

"Do you have any time in the show for a nat-sound piece on that new attraction opening this weekend? You know, the one based on that action-adventure movie with all the pyro?"

Oh good, an easy request. One that she could do on her own by LOOKING AT THE RUNDOWN.

"We're a little tight, but if it's short, like a minute or so, I can sneak it in after weather"

"Perfect. Thanks."

I half-smiled, watching her do the slouched-typing-talking thing again. *At least she's consistent.*

"Are you looking forward to Violet's birthday party tomorrow?" Sydney poked her head around the monitor.

"Absolutely. I hope she's ready for all the cupcakes I made."

"Violet and her dad are ready. Her brother just wants to throw her in the pool as a present. Boys," she shook her head, laughing.

"I'm going to get some water. Want anything?" I asked, standing.

"Nope. Thanks though."

Going for water was my secret code to myself for sobbing in the bathroom. This time, I did just want water. Raucous laughter floated down the hallway as I made my way back to the newsroom. I returned just in time to see Wesley fall flat on his face trying to catch a frisbee.

Laughter erupted and echoed through the room. Jeanie's scolding put a permanent end to the fun.

"That's enough. You guys are going to break something."

Everyone groaned and went back to their pre-show tasks. I spent the remainder of my shift avoiding my inbox. I had a new message from Alastair waiting for me every night at the same time. My index finger got quite a workout hitting the delete button. The clock ticked down slowly. It was excruciating.

"You're anxious to get out of here." Tyler sidled up and perched himself on the edge of the desk. "What's got you so twitchy?"

"Just looking forward to the weekend."

"How is it that you've managed to score weekends off and I have to work every other Saturday? I'm always stuck in this prison."

"I have my ways. Besides, you're the best assignment editor we have. Why let perfection have a day off?"

"Your logic is flattering and infuriating," he grinned. "Have a good weekend, Lia."

I walked out into the stifling June night. My goal was to only cry for half of the drive home. Much to my surprise, I didn't shed one tear.

Little victories.

* * *

"Lia! Lia! Lia!" Sydney's daughter ran down the walk toward me at full speed. She wrapped her small body around my legs. "Are those my cupcakes?"

"Yes, Violet. These are all yours." I laughed, tightening my grip on the plastic container.

"Violet, would you please let Lia go so she can walk into the house?" Sydney waved from the front door.

"Okay, mommy." She abandoned my legs and grasped my hand. "Come on. We can put those on the table with all my presents."

"I swear she's seven going on twenty." Sydney shook her head. "Everyone's out back by the pool. Feel free to—"

Violet shrieked. "Let's go to the pool."

Her dark brown hair bobbed up and down with each excited bounce.

"Maybe a little later," I said.

Sydney gave her daughter a stern look. "Lia will join you outside in a few minutes. Go play with your friends."

The little girl obeyed and ran out the back door.

"She adores you. I've never seen anything like it."

"I have a way with kids and animals. Go figure." I put the cupcakes on the table. Laughter and splashing from outside floated in through the screen door. "Do you need help with anything?"

"Nope. It's all under control. Go enjoy the party. Ray is out there grilling burgers. Make sure you let him know what you want."

Through the gaggle of seven-year-olds running amok, I spotted

Tyler and Wesley lounging at one of the tables.

"Well, look who's here." Tyler looked up through lowered sunglasses.

"Ah, Lia. Smile for the camera." Wesley aimed the lens at me. Mustering up a decent fake smile, I kicked out my hip and posed.

"Is this going on your blog, Wes?"

"No. These are just for Syd and Ray. It would be a bit weird if I posted photos online of little kids swimming."

"True," I laughed. "Then I'd have to put you as my lead story and things would get awkward."

"Save it for November. Great sweeps piece," Tyler drawled.

"Enough, you two. I'm going to do a whole summer photo blog this year. The biggest thing will be the fireworks next month."

"Will you be around for that, Lia?" Tyler asked. "Or will you be jet-setting somewhere with your new boyfriend?"

I cringed internally.

"I'll be here. If only to annoy you."

"What was it like being at that big party? Did you meet a ton of people?"

I could barely meet Wesley's inquisitive gaze.

"It was fun," I answered, watching the kids splash and play. I put up the good fight and hung around for most of the party. It was nice being out in the warm sunshine, even if it meant dodging questions about Alastair. Once Ray started spouting off about the Miami Marlins, I was in the clear. Baseball talk trumped boy talk.

I helped Sydney clean up before retreating to a quiet table by the pool house. Something glinted off the sunlight in the distance. I peered toward the neighbor's yard, but didn't see anything. Small hairs rose on the back of my neck as uneasiness settled around me. Laughter from the pool and the general happiness of the surroundings conflicted wildly with my instincts. I looked around the yard again, but still didn't see anything. Dismissing it as paranoia, I went back to the patio.

The guys were still talking about baseball.

This is my ticket to leave.

"I'm going to head out guys."

"What? No." Ray feigned a hurt look. "We were just getting to the meat and potatoes of the Marlins' issues."

"As exciting as that sounds, I think I'll pass," I replied dryly.

Ray leaned across the table. "One of these days Lia, I'm going to convert you and make you like sports. And then, you'll be just as miserable as the rest of us."

"Ray, if you can accomplish that, my dad will probably enshrine you in some hall of fame."

* * *

I stared at the bouquet sitting in front of my door. Oriental lilies and white roses were nestled amongst white seasonal blooms and lush green foliage. It was stunning. Picking it up, I went inside and placed it on the kitchen table. Opening the envelope, I removed a small card.

I'm sorry. I haven't stopped thinking about you.

Ignoring him this time was much harder. The emails were one thing. I could hit a button and they'd disappear. This was different. This required some degree of thought. I laughed bitterly. *Now I'm going to cave because he sent me flowers? Please.*

* * *

I ran along the shoreline on Sunday morning as though I was being chased. The sun was just peeking above the horizon, casting a magnificent display of colors in deep oranges and reds. Golden beach sand glistened beneath my feet. I ran faster. I wanted to catch the sun and rise with it, above all this. I wanted to escape my sadness.

The muscles in my legs burned and strained. Gritting my teeth, I pushed harder. Air wheezed in and out of my overworked lungs.

The sun was a blazing half-circle on the water, turning the golden sand to copper. Tears streamed out of my eyes as I pushed myself to the limit. If I could just run fast enough, I'd be free.

Fire torched my lungs. I still didn't stop. *I wouldn't stop.* My legs gave out before I did, folding under me, forcing me to the ground. Defeated, I stayed on my hands and knees as the tide nipped at my skin. I wasn't crying. I didn't have any tears left. Sitting back on my heels, I watched the sun complete its triumphant climb. My quest to catch it had to wait for another day.

There wasn't any rush to get back to the car, so I strolled along, watching the early beach-goers claim the perfect spot in the sand. I was jealous of their stress-free movements, their easy banter and joyful laughs. I'd parked in a lot reserved for residents who had access to a private entrance to the beach. It was one of the few things I'd kept from Nathan. He knew how much I loved to run and arranged for me to have the pass.

I stopped short. The lot was empty except for my car and a gray Mercedes SUV.

"Lots of people drive those," I whispered.

The closer I got, the more I was convinced I'd overreacted. I was maybe ten yards from my car when the driver's door opened. My whole body went cold. I knew it was him before he stepped away from the car. The early morning sun set his chocolate-red hair ablaze. His face was pale and drawn, but his eyes were luminous.

I was so shocked, I didn't know whether to laugh or cry.

"Lia."

The richness of his voice carried on the ocean breeze, massaging my senses. He was here, in front of me. *I certainly can't delete this.*

Tilting his head, he looked at me curiously.

"Are you—"

"How did you know I was here?" I demanded. "This is a private lot."

Not flinching, he squared his jaw. "I followed you."

Although I was standing outside, everything closed in around me. Leaning forward, I put my hands on my thighs to steady myself. Dizziness blurred my vision. Righting myself, I walked to my car and sat on the hood. The sun hadn't been up long enough to heat the metal, but it was warm on my butt and legs.

"Why are you here?"

Now that I was sitting on the car, he moved to stand in front of me.

"Why didn't you answer any of my emails?" He furrowed his brow, staring at me darkly.

I had an answer ready; I just couldn't find the words. He walked closer until his legs touched the bumper.

"I needed to know you were alright. Why didn't you answer me?"

Heat radiated through me the second Alastair placed his hands on my thighs. I was trapped in the undertow of my feelings for him. The more vigorously I fought them, the faster they overpowered me.

"You said you didn't...I thought you didn't need me."

Cradling my face in his hands, he answered, "I still need to know you're safe."

I whimpered, squeezing my eyes shut. His touch was too powerful.

"You flew all this way to find out if I was safe?"

"Look at me," he whispered. "Please."

I opened my eyes. Two beautiful, clear, unshielded emerald irises met mine. He still had a gentle hold on my face, caressing me with his thumbs.

"Do you really think that's the only reason I flew here?"

"I don't know what to think." Tears flowed freely down my cheeks. "One minute I'm your angel, the next I'm cast aside like an unwanted dish rag."

"You're not unwanted," he countered.

"Oh no? I spent sixteen hours flying home stand-by because you didn't want me," I glowered. "After everything we shared, it wasn't enough."

"I can't change what happened."

"Why are you doing this?" I yelled, pushing him away. "Why do you make me feel these things for you, then destroy me? What have I ever done to deserve being treated this way?"

I was so enveloped within my own turmoil, I barely noticed his. A nightmarish roar shattered the peaceful lull of the waves crashing.

CHAPTER TWENTY-FIVE

He stood with his back to me, hands planted on the hood of the SUV. I watched his body quiver and heave. I'd never heard a sound like that come from a person. It was filled with something far greater than pain. Wiping my eyes, I got off my car and went to him. Not knowing what to do or say, I stood to his left. The expression on his face tore a hole through my soul.

Turning to face me, he made no effort to hide his emotions.

"Why is it so different with you?" he choked.

"I don't know."

"This wasn't supposed to happen. You weren't supposed to mean this much."

He was in front of me before I had a chance to react, holding my head in his hands again. Stripped completely of his outer shell, he stood before me; vulnerable and exposed.

"Say something," he implored.

"I don't—"

"Tell me I haven't ruined this." He pressed his forehead to mine. "Tell me I haven't fucked up the one good thing that's happened in my life."

The sun burned a little brighter, bearing down on us. Its heat was uncomfortable. I couldn't answer him. I couldn't tell him what he wanted to hear.

"I don't know, Alastair."

"Fair enough." He brushed his thumb across my lips. "I'm just so relieved you're okay. Not hearing from you drove me mad."

"I'm far from okay," I responded, annoyed.

"Come back to the hotel with me?"

"Now? I'm gross from my run. I want to take a shower and change."

"You can clean up in the suite. Please. Come with me."

"Is this a good idea?"

Pulling me into a hug, he nuzzled my neck. "I hope so."

"Okay," I breathed.

He studied my face.

"Really?"

"Don't give me the option to change my mind, Holden."

"Alright. Do you want to go together? Or should we meet there?" He stood close, lightly running his hand down my arm.

"Together. We can come back and get my car later, right?"

"Of course."

Climbing into his car, I hoped I wasn't making a mistake. It was about a half hour drive back to his hotel. I felt so grimy and icky from my run. I couldn't wait to hop in the shower.

I watched the flat green scenery zip past as we drove down the highway. Palm trees stood at attention as we approached the more populated, tourist-filled area near International Drive. Crowds of tourists clutching cameras and maps all hurried off to find something exciting to do. I could see the tall glass and steel hotel glittering in the morning sun.

A weird déjà vu crept through me as we walked through the lobby and waited for an elevator. I kept my arms folded in an effort to remain protected in my little bubble.

"I'll wait for you out here while you shower," he said when we both walked into the suite.

He kept fidgeting with the car keys. I'd never seen him so antsy. I took them from him and put them on one of the end tables.

He sat on the arm of the couch, rubbing his eyes with the heels of his hands.

"I treated you horribly at the house. Those things I said…" he trailed off. "I have no excuse. I'll spend the rest of my days apologizing if I have to."

"You don't have to be so dramatic," I muttered.

"Ask me anything. Whatever you want to know, I'll tell you."

Exasperated and still grimy from my run, I threw my head back in frustration. "Right now, I want to get out of these disgusting clothes. I have sand everywhere."

"Okay."

His small crooked smile melted some of the apprehension from his face. Before he could say anything else, I turned on my heel and went to the master bathroom. Letting the hot water drench me, I wondered how much more of this emotional roller coaster I could stand. Was I really willing to sift through the caverns of his past and help him heal? I scratched the shampoo into my scalp, harshly rubbing it through my tangled wet hair. There was something buried deep inside him that caused him to flip a switch and push me away.

One thing I knew for sure was that he wasn't a bad person. I'd seen too many instances of gentleness to think he was really rotten to the core. He was damaged, not unsalvageable. I let the water run over my head, washing away the suds. I didn't want to delude myself into thinking I'd change him or save him. That was a fool's game I wasn't willing to play.

Stepping out of the shower, I wrapped myself in the white hotel robe and towel dried my long, thick hair as best I could. *Guess I'll be spending the day in a robe.* Walking into the master bedroom, I saw Alastair sitting on the bed. He smiled at me.

"They're probably going to be a little big, but you can wear these until I take you back to your flat."

On the bed next to him lay a gray fleece shirt and black boxer shorts.

"Oh. Thanks."

We stared at one another for a minute. This whole morning had been so surreal I thought maybe it was all a dream.

"Right, then. I'll let you get dressed. Are you hungry? I can order breakfast if you'd like."

"You don't have to do that," I answered, ignoring the loud growls in my belly.

"It's not good to exercise on an empty stomach," he admonished gently.

Hearing that little bit of bossiness made me smile. He'd been such a wreck all morning it was good to see some of his dominant personality reappear.

"Okay, but don't order the entire menu. Eggs and pancakes are fine."

Standing up, he lifted an eyebrow. "Eggs and pancakes? As you wish."

By the time I finished dressing and blow-drying my hair, the food had arrived. It looked really good. Aside from that first day back when the thought of food was undesirable, my appetite hadn't suffered along with the rest of me. I loaded a plate with scrambled eggs and two pancakes.

We ate in silence, sizing one another up from across the table. He looked pleased that I was eating. *Silly boy. Just because I'm upset doesn't mean I'm not hungry.*

Scanning the living room, I noticed several bags from various clothing stores.

"How long have you been here?"

"Not long. I got here yesterday."

"Did a little shopping already?" I pointed to the bags.

"Yeah, I suppose," he sighed. "I flew here with no luggage. I needed a few things."

I stopped mid-chew. *No luggage? He flew across the Atlantic with nothing?*

Seeming to hear my thoughts, he answered, "I just wanted to get here. So long as I had my passport, everything else was secondary."

I finished the mouthful of food and had some juice. Now wasn't the time to get caught up in the romantic notion that he was so distraught he hopped on a plane with just the clothes on his back to get to me. I wasn't that delusional. It did hit me that the clothes he'd let me borrow didn't smell of his cologne. Looking down, I noticed something round and shiny on the boxer shorts. I peeled off a clear sticker with a capital M on it.

"Guess I'm the first one to wear these," I said, adhering the sticker to my finger and holding it up.

"Missed that one," he smiled, standing up.

Assuming he was going to use the bathroom, I started when instead, he grabbed my hand and pulled me out of the chair.

"I'm sorry," he said, hugging me tightly.

Melting into his embrace, I hugged him back with just as much force. His heart pounded so quickly, it vibrated against me. I think he needed this more than I did. I think he needed to know I wasn't abhorred by him and what happened at the estate. I let him hug me as long as he wanted. Pushing out a shaky sigh, he stepped back and studied my face.

"You're beautiful with no make-up."

Throwing him a skeptical glance, I huffed, "Nice line."

"I mean it," he responded, unabashed. "So delicate and strong. If we make it through this, I still hope to photograph you one day."

"Do you want to make it through this?"

"Yes." He cupped my cheeks, fixing a heated stare on me. "I want this. I want you."

"Then why did you push me away? Why did you make me feel like that?" I lost some of the grasp I had on my emotions. I didn't want to break apart in front of him, especially when he had so much to explain.

Guiding me to the couch, he waited for me get settled on the cushion before sitting and facing me.

"It was my fault," he muttered. "I caused the accident."

"What?"

"I killed my family," he said slowly, clenching his jaw.

"No you didn't. You said someone fell asleep at the wheel and—"

"Yes, I did," he interrupted, anger flaring in his eyes. "I was pestering Grace. My parents told me to stop but I didn't. I thought it would be funny to unbuckle her seatbelt. She started yelling that I was annoying her, so my mum turned around and my dad looked at me through the rearview mirror. They never saw the other car cross over the line."

His eyes glazed over.

"At the hospital, when the doctors were talking to my aunt and uncle, I heard them say that if," he swallowed hard, "if Grace had been wearing a seatbelt, she would have lived. It's my fault she died."

Speechless. I was absolutely speechless. Rationally, I knew a six-year-old boy didn't cause a fatal accident. The rawness of his guilt left me breathless.

"Alastair," I said calmly, stroking his hair. "None of it was your fault. The oth—."

"Do not say that," he yelled violently. His entire body shook.

The remnants of his outburst and their underlying pain hung in the air while the ebb and flow of time, movement, and breathing stopped. This scar was deep.

"You've been holding on to this guilt for too many years. You have to forgive yourself."

"Forgive myself?" He choked out the words. "I killed my family. I'm no better than any other criminal locked up in prison."

"You're not a criminal. You were a little boy teasing his sister in a car. Do you know how many times Dayna and I fought in the car on road trips? I thought hearing my mom say '*do you want your father to pull this car over?*' was a standard vacation announcement."

He blinked.

"There was an accident, Alastair. Someone else caused it."

"You don't understand," he insisted. "They were distracted. They didn't see the other car. My father could have swerved to avoid it if he had. They're dead because of me." Pain and guilt ravaged his body. I was powerless to stop the onslaught of emotion pouring out of him. He had kept it locked away for years and years.

"I should have died with them."

It took a second for me to realize the agonizing moan that echoed through the room was mine.

"You don't mean that," I whispered.

"I do," he answered, looking at the floor.

This was too much for me to handle. My body vibrated with a frantic need. I just didn't know what it was or how to deal with it. I didn't want him to say those things about himself. I didn't want him to feel this guilt anymore. I couldn't help him. I sat, debilitated by my own failure to make this all go away for him.

Then, I got angry.

"Look at me," I ordered, straddling his lap. He took a second, then did as he was told.

"Say that again," I demanded.

"Why?"

"Look me in the eye and tell me again how you wished you'd died in that crash," I shouted. He stared at me, not moving. I watched the tears gather around his eyes like a growing storm. They never fell. They just glistened.

He shook his head, placing his hands on my waist.

"I dream about Grace. It's always the same. We're children, playing in the yard. Everything's fine and then I start teasing her. She gets upset and leaves. But as she's walking away, she promises she'll stay the next time if I stop bothering her. I yell and cry to get her to stay, but she never does."

He brushed his thumb across my lips.

"The night you were with me, I thought I'd finally caught her. I was holding onto her. It felt so real. When I woke up and saw you cowering at the edge of the bed, I knew I'd been holding onto you. I never apologized for that."

"It's okay."

"I'm sorry I said those awful things to you when my grandfather got sick."

I swallowed back a thick, sandpapery lump. "You were hurting. It's the only way you knew how to react."

"Not with…I don't want to be that way. Not with you."

Slumping his shoulders, he bowed his head. It destroyed me to see him so upset.

"It wasn't just your words," I said gently. "When you turned your back on me, it felt like you threw a bag of bricks at my chest."

He frowned. "I'm sorry."

"Stop apologizing," I tilted his chin up, "Just don't do it again."

A small grin curved his lips.

"I knew the minute I saw you, that you were different from the others."

"Why? Because I don't know how to walk in heels when I'm overtired?"

I jumped at his gentle squeeze. "No. What you're doing right here. You keep me on my toes. You have no pretenses. You're not afraid to call me out on things. It's…remember the night we met, when you looked through the car window but didn't see me?"

I nodded.

"You did, Lia. These beautiful amber eyes saw through me without realizing what they'd done. Catching you at the bar and having you stare directly into my soul again only intensified what I already knew."

"And what was that?"

"I wanted you," he said, lowering his tone. "I didn't know how it was going to happen, I just knew it had to."

"Well," I sighed. "That explains your intense seduction techniques."

"Intense?"

"Yeah. You came after me like a dog in heat. Stephanie even

picked up on it."

He smirked. "Did she?"

"Hey." I poked him in the chest. "Focus on the matter at hand."

"You're the matter at hand," he murmured, brushing his lips on my cheek. "I shouldn't have pushed you out and told you I didn't need you. The truth is…"

His eyes clouded over.

No, no, no. He's so close.

I remained as calm as possible, waiting for him to find his balance again. Even if he did stop now, I'd be satisfied with everything he'd shared already. There was so much to process. Resting my forehead on his, we sat in a quiet embrace. I closed my eyes, running my fingers through his hair. The serenity of this moment washed over me, making me realize just how much I cared for him. We were both broken by different sets of misfortune, but we'd managed to find our way to one another.

The aggressive, controlling guy I'd met in Glasgow was still there. He'd always be there. He just needed to find his own way through all the years of pain and suppressed emotion. If he wanted me to, I'd be with him every step of the way, but that wasn't for me to decide.

Banding his arms around my waist, he pulled me closer. I snuggled against him, content we'd survived the biggest hurdle thrown our way so far. It wouldn't be perfect. It certainly wouldn't be easy but I was willing to try.

CHAPTER TWENTY-SIX

"What's wrong?"

I ignored Alastair's question and kept staring at the black sports car parked in front of my unit.

"Do you know that car?"

He pulled into an open spot and cut the engine.

"Who is that?"

Shit.

Nobody was sitting in it. Icy water coursed through my veins.

How did he get in here?

"Oh my God," I grunted, jumping out of the car and bolting through the door.

"Nathan," I called out. "Nathan, where are you?"

His tall figure appeared from the doorway to my bedroom.

"Hello, Lia."

A blur of color flew by me as Alastair lunged at him. I grabbed hold of his shirt before he could make it across the room.

"How the fuck did you get in here?" he demanded.

"I have a key, *mate*," he gloated.

"No you don't," I seethed. "You stole it."

"Correction. I borrowed it from the leasing office after a romp in the mailroom with what's-her-name. She was very accommodating. Even put my name on the entry list."

"You son of a—"

"Easy, Lia. We don't want to say things we'll regret." His dark blue eyes seared through Alastair. "My girlfriend and I have things to discuss. Go wait outside."

"Get out," Alastair growled. "Or I'll put you out myself."

The material on his shirt stretched as he tried to move closer to Nathan. I tightened my grip on it. I wasn't about to have a fight break out in my living room.

Nathan laughed and folded his arms. "Always ready to scuffle, this one. Did he tell you how our last meeting ended, Lia?"

The strength drained from my body. I lost my hold on Alastair's shirt, stumbling backwards. He secured his arm around my waist, holding me up.

"Keeping secrets from my girl? That's not nice, Holden."

The walls closed in, crushing me. I saw how their last meeting ended, didn't I? I was there, in a heap on the floor.

"What are you talking about?" I asked.

"He has a quick right hook," he answered with a smug grin.

If I hadn't been using Alastair for support to stand, he would have shot across the room like a bullet. All his muscles tensed.

"Nathan, just go," I requested harshly.

"We still have to talk."

My vision blurred. Holding a hand to the side of my head, I glared in his direction. "No, we don't. You said all you had to say when your fist went through the wall. We're done."

"You never gave me a chance to explain," he lamented. "I'm not proud of what happened that day or at the Black and White Ball. You know how I get. I would never hurt you."

I stiffened.

Alastair tightened his hold on my waist. Baring his teeth, he ordered, "Get out. Now. While you still have legs to walk on."

"I thought you Brits were supposed to be polite. Or does that not apply to you?" He scowled. "I guess all the money in the world can't buy you manners."

"That's enough. Both of you. I'm not going to have you two ruin my apartment with some crazy fight. Nathan, leave. Now. If you want to tell me whatever it is you feel is so important, say it now. Otherwise, stop bothering me."

Nathan narrowed his eyes. "Have it your way, Lia. Don't say I didn't try."

Before walking out the door, he stopped and looked at me. He'd dropped the tough guy act and for a nanosecond, appeared to be the charming person I'd met a lifetime ago.

"Take care of yourself, Sparkle. No matter what, you were always my favorite girl."

He smiled. It was the first genuine one I'd seen on his face in months. I glared at him.

"Don't call me that."

His eyes hardened. "We'll talk soon."

It sounded more like a threat than a promise. He walked out, slamming the door. The bang echoed through the room. Neither one of us moved for several minutes after he left.

"I need to see if he touched anything," I muttered, walking into the bedroom. Nothing was out of place. The bed wasn't even rumpled. It didn't make me feel any better.

"You should change your locks first thing in the morning." Alastair said, standing in the doorway.

"Right," I replied, folding my arms. "You punched him?"

He flinched at my tone.

"When did it happen?" I tried to keep calm.

"It doesn't matter."

"When did it happen?" I repeated louder.

Expressionless and stoic, he leaned against the doorframe. "The Monday after he manhandled you at the hotel," he grumbled. "I wanted to have a little chat with him so we had an understanding when it came to you. He wasn't too receptive."

"The night you came here at two in the morning?"

Scowling, he nodded.

"How did you know where to find him?"

"It doesn't matter," he answered smoothly.

"Jesus," I muttered. "Were you planning on telling me about this clandestine meeting?"

"No."

I paced the room. "Why is it that every time we make any headway, I get knocked back twenty feet by something?"

"I didn't want to upset you about this. He seems to think you belong to him. You don't. I made it clear you're not available."

"So, you two discussed me like I was a piece of property up for grabs?" I asked, raising my eyebrows.

His piercing stare scorched me. I held it without flinching.

"No, Amelia, we didn't. I told him not to go near you again. Obviously, quick right hook or not, he didn't listen."

"Please don't put yourself in that position again. I don't want to hear that you're starting fights. He's not worth it."

I sat on the bed, cradling my head in my hands. The thought of him being hurt didn't sit well with me. The mattress dipped as Alastair lowered himself to my right. He draped his arm across my shoulders and tucked me into his side.

"You're worth it," he breathed. "A black eye or bruised jaw is nothing compared to your safety. I'd lay down my own life to ensure you were protected."

I burrowed into his chest, squeezing him.

"Don't say that."

He kissed the top of my head. "Too dramatic again?"

I jerked my head up, meeting his amused gaze.

"Alastair Reid Holden, that was not funny," I exclaimed.

He lifted a precarious brow. "Don't think anyone's called me by my full name in ages."

"Well, don't say asinine things and I won't have to resort to sounding like a harried grandmother."

"All kidding aside," he stroked my cheek, "you are worth it. I just hope you don't think of me in the same way as Nathan. We've both done horrible things to you. Treated you like less than the exquisite creature you are."

"Never compare yourself to him. I'd rather spend a hundred days without you, than one minute with him."

"My Lia," he whispered, kissing my forehead. "Get changed. I want to take you somewhere."

"Where?"

Nudging me with his elbow, he laughed. "I'm not telling."

After he left the room, I went into my closet and stared at the wall of clothes. I shuddered thinking about what might have happened if I'd come home alone and found Nathan here. I wanted to believe he wouldn't hurt me but his track record warned against falling into that trap. Grabbing some capris and an embellished lace scoop neck top, I got dressed. I folded Alastair's shirt and boxers and put them on a shelf. I doubted he'd want those back.

I rolled my shoulders to try and loosen them up a little. I'd fallen asleep on the couch at the hotel for a bit and woken up stiff.

"All set?" Alastair grinned up from the couch when I walked into the room.

"Yep."

"Give me a minute. I just have to use the loo."

A few minutes later he emerged with a confident grin on his face.

"What's got you so happy?" I inquired.

"Nothing in particular," he answered. "By the way, I'm glad you liked the flowers."

I looked at the bouquet sitting on the table.

"They're pretty. Thank you."

"You're pretty."

"Cheesy," I smirked, shoving him.

"I'm glad I haven't lost my touch. Let's go."

* * *

Alastair stood on the path leading into the Kraft Azalea Garden.

Scratching his head, he looked at me.

"This is, well, embarrassing. I'm not sure which way to go."

I laughed. "You're new at this romance thing, aren't you?"

"You think I'm romantic?"

"You have your moments." I grabbed his hand. "This way."

I led him down a path through the park. Enormous cypress trees created a natural canopy over our heads. The winding path ended at Lake Maitland. A large, curved columned monument faced the water.

"We can go sit by the water's edge if you like. Or, seeing as nobody's here, we can sit on the Exedra Monument."

Alastair gave me a funny look. "The what?"

"That big columned Athens-looking thing right there. Come on, Holden." I pulled him toward the monument. We sat on the smooth stone bench that was built into the structure.

"This is rather nice. Admittedly, I had no idea this monument was here. I was planning to park by the lake. Well done." He massaged the back of my neck and smiled. I relaxed against him, watching the sun start its descent.

I had an urge to catch it again, only this time I wanted to keep it above the horizon so this day wouldn't end. Never in my darkest, craziest moments did I expect he'd fly out here. I figured I'd fade from his memory and he'd move on to the next one.

The bright, friendly rays slowly disappeared. In their wake was a warm lavender and orange glow. As the last bit of sun was swallowed by the horizon, a calming dark blue spread across the sky. Stars twinkled and danced to life one by one.

"I wouldn't want to share this moment with anyone else but you, Lia."

He sounded nervous. *Impossible.* I lifted my head, meeting his bright eyes. I melted. That gaze was so pure.

"Dance with me?" he asked, standing up.

"Okay."

I took his outstretched hand and molded my body to his.

"Too cheesy for you?"

"No," I chuckled. "Not this time."

"I don't want to come across as a total swot. Or formulaic, for that matter."

Leaning my head back, I grinned up at him. "You're not a nerd. At least not that I've seen."

"Good." He hugged me close. "I may never leave Orlando."

The exact moment my legs turned to Jell-O was unclear. I was just thankful he had a firm hold around my waist.

"I've got you, love," he murmured. "I'll always be here to catch you."

"You'd stay here?"

"Of course," he said, shrugging slightly. "Would you like that?"

The ability to speak was lost on me.

"You can't just stay here. You have a company to run."

This was what I could come up with as a response? What an idiot.

"True. Have I mentioned we have offices in the States?"

"You do?"

"Yes. In order to buy television stations here, we had to have an American base. In the early eighties my dad and grandfather went through all the proper channels to secure some smaller stations in Pennsylvania and Ohio. They established the main offices in New York and became American citizens to satisfy the legal requirements. When I accepted the position of CFO after university, I also became an American citizen."

I staggered backwards. "What?"

He grinned. "I have dual citizenship so I'm still as British as they come," he affected an American accent, "but I also have a soft spot for you Yanks."

"And all this time I thought I was being wooed by an Englishman," I marveled. "For the record, don't ever fake that accent again. It sounds weird coming out of your mouth."

"As you wish, m'lady."

Footsteps approached from the path behind us. Turning, I saw the night guard walking our way.

"Evening," he said curtly. "The park closed at sunset. If you folks wouldn't mind, I'm going to have to ask you head back to your car now."

"Okay. Sorry," I blushed. We'd just been scolded like two teenagers caught making out in a parking lot. Holding Alastair's hand, I led him back to the car.

"Your place or mine?" he asked.

"Seriously, no more fake accent. I like all of your Englishness."

"Is that even a word?" he chuckled as we climbed into the SUV.

"Does it matter?"

"Fair enough." He squeezed my knee. "Where to?"

"I need my car."

"Right. The wind-up toy."

He put the SUV in gear and headed for the highway. We rode in silence for the majority of the drive. I stole glances at him every so often when the streetlights cast just the right glow through the windows. He appeared deep in thought, stroking his chin. I wondered what could be weighing so heavily on his mind. Kicking myself mentally, I shook my head. He'd pretty much spilled his guts to me today, opening up about things he probably never told anyone.

I think he's allowed a pensive moment without my wondering what's going on.

Pulling into the small private lot, I saw my car sitting all by itself. He parked next to it.

"Can we go down to the beach first?" he asked.

"It's closed."

"And your point is?"

"We'll probably get arrested."

"Who's being dramatic now?" he laughed. "Come on, Meyers. Live a little."

He got out and walked toward the beach. I followed suit, scurrying up next to him and grabbing his hand. Smiling to myself,

I knew nothing would happen if we went out here. I'd done it a zillion times before with Stephanie and some other friends for bonfires.

The waves crashed and pounded on the shore, making their powerful presence known. Alastair led me down to where the sand was still dry, but the waves reached dangerously close.

"See? It's just us," he said, lowering himself in the sand. I did the same, wishing we'd brought a blanket or something.

Salty sea air swirled around us. Alastair leaned back, propped up on his elbows. I stayed sitting with my legs crossed. I was glad we came here instead of going back to the hotel or my apartment.

"I have something for you."

He said it so softly I wasn't sure if I was supposed to hear it.

"What?"

He sat up, facing me so our knees touched.

"I left it in your carry-on bag when you were getting dressed one morning. I thought you'd find it right away. When you didn't, I planned to take it out of the bag and give it to you when we got back to Glasgow." He frowned. "Obviously, that never happened."

My heart raced. *The Tiffany box.*

"It fell out when I was unpacking. I didn't...It was a bit of a shock."

"Did you open it?"

His eyes shone in the moonlight. I touched his cheek, tracing my thumb along the corner of his mouth.

"Yes."

Lowering his head, he smiled. His breathing had become a little labored, but he was still unshielded.

"Did you like it?"

"I had my eyes closed. I couldn't look at it. It didn't feel right with you not giving it to me yourself."

Cocking his head to the side, he raised a brow.

"You opened it but didn't look?"

I shook my head. "I wanted to. I closed it a split second after opening the box. I put it on my nightstand and tried to forget about it."

"Don't you want to know what it is?"

My heart was now somewhere in my throat, vying for a spot in my mouth.

"Yes," I answered, low and breathy.

Reaching into his pocket, he brandished the white suede box. Holding it in the palm of his hand, he fixed the most sultry, gorgeous stare on me. I moistened my lips, garnering a slight smile from him.

"You're my reason for living now, Lia," he pushed the words out. "I need you. I want you. I…"

His expression faltered. Large sections of his protective shield locked into place. I carefully placed my hands on either side of his face, never breaking eye contact.

"One step at a time, Holden. When you're ready."

Remaining stoic, he nodded and handed the box to me.

"Open it," he ordered gently. "And don't close your eyes this time."

Swallowing hard, I did as I was told.

"Oh my gosh," I gasped.

Nestled inside was a delicate white-gold necklace. Hanging from it was a platinum 'A' in beautiful script, encrusted with small diamonds. They glittered in the bright moonlight. I ran my fingers along it.

"Do you like it?"

"It's beautiful, Alastair." I looked at him. "Thank you."

The shy little smile that I'd grown to adore curved his mouth. Sitting like this, under the moon, he looked serene.

"Let me put it on you," he offered, reaching for the necklace. Lifting my hair, I leaned forward so he could clasp it. The 'A' landed at the hollow of my neck.

We stared at one another. The softness of his skin on mine when he caressed along my shoulders gave me goose bumps.

Seeming to fight against some sort of internal protest, he steeled his expression.

"You take my breath away," he said quietly. "There is no one else for me. There is only you. My angel. My Lia."

I crushed my body against his, hugging him as though both our lives depended on it. Our hearts beat in unison with the pounding waves, strengthening and fortifying our bond. Burying my face into his neck, I whispered, "I love you."

His body tensed.

Oh please no.

Lifting my head, I looked everywhere but directly at him.

It's too soon. I shouldn't have said it.

Alastair squared his jaw. He placed a hand on either side of my face, forcing me to look at him. "Tell me again."

"Are you sure?"

Closing his eyes, he wet his lips. The longer he stayed quiet the more nervous I became.

"Yes," he finally answered. When he opened them they were clear and bright.

"I love you, Alastair Holden," I said with resolve. His eyes flickered in disbelief before a dazzling smile illuminated the beach. He looked up to the star-filled sky and ran a hand through his hair, ruffling it back and forth. I marveled at how such simple words broke through his rigid exterior. He tucked a strand of hair behind my ear and cupped my jaw. His eyes were glittering. I shuddered, gazing into them.

"You are the best thing that's happened to me. I've never felt more like myself than I do when I'm with you."

Knowing this was as close as I'd get to him saying those three words back to me, I smiled. I could wait an eternity until he said them because I knew he felt it. For me, for us, for this to work the way I hoped it would, that was all I needed.

"You have that look again," he said, raising an eyebrow.

"So do you," I replied. "What should we do about it?"

Locking a molten green stare on me, his lips curved into a sexy grin. When he kissed me, all the anguish from our separation disappeared forever. I was alive again. A hum vibrated through me, rousing every part of my body, bringing them to a heightened sense of awareness. Tangling my fingers in his hair, I kissed him back with all my heart. He held me fast against him. Without question, all the times he'd kissed me before paled in comparison.

Don't miss the next books in the series,

Unravel Me

Effortless